God's Unwanted Child

By

Reece LeResche

First paperback edition September 2019

Cover Art by Dylan Gray

ISBN 978-0-578-58499-7 (paperback)

https://reecedleresche.wixsite.com/godsunwantedc
hild

"God conceals from man the happiness of death…
so that he may endure."-Lucan

Chapter 1

Hello. My name is Joe Delaney, and I'm a dead man. Joe is actually my birth name. Most of my friends and family just call me Jack. It's hard to examine your life; it's even harder to try and relate it to someone you don't know. I'm hoping you can maintain some semblance of engagement throughout it. My story is told in delirium with reckless abandon from an apostate of the human race. I know it takes a lot to care about another man's life, but everyone has a story to tell... even me.

Looking back, I always lived with regrets. Sure, my life's philosophy was never to have regrets, yet I still retained a piece of humanity that kept me in perpetual regret. Doubtless, this never helped modulate my search for spirituality. A friend of mine once asked, "Jack, don't you want to go to Heaven? Wouldn't it be better to believe and make sure you're safe than not believe and go to the other place?" I'd roll my eyes and sneer, and he would rebuke my flippancy. Of course, it wasn't that I never believed in Heaven. To be honest, I always believed in life after death and in a magical place where we can hang our hats in eternal bliss. It's just, I never thought I'd end up there. I spent too much time cursing destiny and the ill-fated box it put me in. Time, tide, and tragedy wait for no man. Tragedy, especially, is in all of us. Comedy, however, is not. That is what makes tragic works of fiction so universal. Life will always start funny and end tragically.

I never saw myself as a depressed person. I still don't. I guess I always saw myself as a realist. Reality was just so invidious. Of course, with that being said, drinking has always been a constant variable in my life. At any rate, even though alcohol never helped, it was not the cause of my depression; it merely fueled it. Most of my life was, in short, filled with a combination of bliss and pain. Yin and Yang. Apollonian and Dionysian. Always a blast at parties but a real motherfucker depending on my mood. I mean, honestly, by the end of my story, you **WILL** hate me. At least by then, we will have something in common. Yet now, I realize, momentary pain is something to be suffered; eternal bliss is not. I used to love the transcendentalist philosophers in high school and college. And yet, as time reared its unforgiving head, I found the German philosophers of the same era more palatable.

    I'd like to start by telling you that if you could survive this long in life, congratulations. I commend you. If you don't find suicide appealing or attractive, I admire you. You are either truly valiant or pleasantly ignorant. Of course, I'm still wondering whether suicide is a genuinely courageous or cowardly act. The masses will tell you it is cowardly to not persist through the pain. While this may be true, mankind is also so afraid of death that evolution has placed trace amounts of DMT in our brains to alleviate the inevitable experience. I suppose, if I ever accepted who I really was, I would have killed myself long ago. In truth, there are only two types of people that commit suicide. The first are those that have lost all control of their mind, their reality, and a square footing in this world. They see nothingness as an adequate respite from the sensory offenses of life. The second ones are absolute madmen. They leave thinking the afterlife is better than here. The problem with suicide is that, when you finally do it, it's too late. It makes us happy to think of infinite jubilation here on Earth. Finality is far too frightening of a concept to any of us. Our species is afraid of the darkness that will make our memories all cease to be. If only we could hang on to them forever, we might feel whole. Instead, we live a wholesome, righteous life that we have been frugally saving up to exploit on Judgement Day. We curse fate and hail free will but never stop to think of either concepts' importance. As a human, there always has been a necessity to believe in fate on some level or another. Writers and artists of great ingenuity execrate it at great length while simultaneously crafting their masterpiece around it. Despite your age, we are all living on borrowed time.

I can't even remember the day it happened; the day my life would 'transcend'. Memories are sort of falling into this abysmal pit of dementia. I think it was a Saturday. We were definitely going to a friend of my Dad's retirement party. Yet most importantly, I remember being content with life for the first time in several years.

It all started with a text from my Dad.

"Meet me for a drink at the pub."

When your Father texts you that, you don't say no. But what struck me as odd was that Dad was asking to go to a bar before we went to a party. Any excuse to see my Dad was welcomed though; even if it meant I had to meet him at the 'Furious Shrimp'. The 'Furious Shrimp'... not my idea of a good time. Any port in a storm, I guess.

Where to begin...

The truth is, I plan on telling you everything. My memories will become a part of you, and you and I will share an eternal consciousness through them. For now, though, I want to recount the more fundamental moments that lead me to this point.

I won't tell you now where I work (or rather worked). I'll get to that later. I will say that I am in the lower-middle class, twenty-seven years old and single. I make about 35,000 dollars a year. I hang out with my friends as often as possible, and I do my job as diligently as possible.

Work has always been an essential detail in my life. I was never the guy to complain about a job. You see, I was raised with that "Protestant Guilt" and that makes it hard to do anything but work hard. That's me. The leal proletariat. The worker bee. I'm that guy you love or hate because I will always pick up an extra shift at work. The 'guilt' concept is all I know when it comes to working. From a young age, my Father always told me:

"Never take shit from anyone. If someone gets in your face, punch 'em the fuck out! I don't care if they were only talking shit! If you're arrested, tell the cops to fuck off and that you want a lawyer. But, if your boss tells you to do something, you do it. No questions asked."

Live like a free man...unless you are working. I remember every job I ever had and how perfect I was at it. Every kitchen manager and supervisor thought I was sent from Heaven. They had never seen anyone listen to orders so well. I'd get shitfaced while working the kitchen and no one would be the wiser or even care 'cause I got shit done. I would've made a fantastic soldier. My Old Man always wanted me to join the service... or at least the police force.

As for my Father; he is (sorry was) a manager at a local Harley Davidson. But let's back up and start from the sixties. Dad and his family were originally from the Midwest. He was born and raised in a little province near Downtown Detroit called Corktown. I guess that's where my ancestors came from long ago. They lived there for generations until he and my grandmother moved to LA when he was ten years old. By the time he was thirteen, they had to move to East LA on account of all of the shootings in South Central. Dad told me that every night, in 1968, he would hear gunshots right outside of his window. It was for the best that he moved out of Corktown anyway. Dad was protestant, and it was filled with Catholics. Who doesn't hate those pricks?

Dad became a carpenter after he graduated high school. He loved the work, but the pay just wasn't there. Appropriately, he landed a job with Corona. The same Corona beer that you like to put down every Cinco De Mayo while yelling "Look! I'm part Mexican!" or "Another American Beer Please! I'll take a Corona!" as they brew another vat of the stuff in Sweden somewhere.

You would be amazed at the stories I could tell you about the beer industry. Of course, most of them are probably apocryphal. Dad got right on the bandwagon as soon as Grupo Modelo started distributing in the United States in 1976. I should've followed in the family footsteps. He used to say how great of a job it was. He went town-to-town, distributing Corona and marketing it to liquor stores. Plus, all the beer he could drink. Nowadays, I'd have to pay someone for that job.

It wasn't long after that (I'd say the early 80s) that Dad started working for Coors Brewing

Company. Coors Light has always been our family's favorite inebriant. So many people in our family drank Coors that it had become a part of our ancestral heritage. My Uncle Sully would slur, "I want it on my headstone!" He would continue to rhyme his epitaph:

Here lies the brute named Sully
Who was never less than bully
When asked what to pour
He always said, Coors!
So they tossed his ass in a gully

It wasn't long after that he died of a massive coronary.

Dad taught me at a young age that the only good beer is Coors. No IPAs. No Craft Beer. Absolutely NO BUDWEISER. Because of this, I never had any Budweiser around the house. I always hated the taste anyway. Come to think of it, there's probably some psychological effect in play there...

Anyway, my youngest memories of my Dad were of him in the beer industry. It was in the early 90s, and he hit every bar in our little southwestern town to distribute. To this day, bars that I go to still know me as "Lil Jack" and "Jackie the Bijou". Unfortunately, I'm 'Jack Jr'. There's nothing like naming your son after you to give him his own identity. Hell, at least I get a discount when I'm out. Dad used to bring home cardboard cutouts of Elvira from her Halloween promos and even little Coors Light robot beer cans that could dance. It was the first erection I ever got. From Elvira...not the beer robots.

So, that's the long and short of it. We'll get more acquainted as my story transpires.

Chapter 2

It's a beautiful evening for May. The temperature is seventy-six degrees, it's slightly overcast, and I am meeting my Dad for a drink. I run through my head all of the possibilities of why Dad would want to have a clandestine meeting before the party.

- He lost his job
- He lost his retirement pension playing craps at the illegal gambling hall at Uncle Mickey's house
- He wants to give me money
- He is getting a divorce
- He is siring a child with some prostitute

None of those seem likely. Those excuses don't even sound like my Dad. However, I can't help but wonder… So when I pull out onto Gray Avenue to get on the freeway, I am curious. I don't know why, but for a moment I think of my mother. I won't bring her up though.

For the record, she is a saint. I know, I know…everyone says that about their mother. But honestly, if you knew Emily Delaney, you would be floored. It is astonishing the love she has for her children. My Father and mother got a divorce when I was very young. He got remarried shortly after that. Amid all that anguish, my mother never dated another man. She dedicated her entire life to her children. She is above this story though, and for that, I will be mentioning her as little as possible.

During my right hand turn on to merging traffic, I have one of those musing, philosophical moments. Well, not really "philosophical" but what

us common folk call "*Deep*". Every decision you
are ever going to make has a reaction. Cause and
effect. I know you know this on the surface level,
but you do not know it on a practical level. Choices
are eternity incarnate. You can rectify a choice, but
you can never change it. Does that action matter?
Probably not, but no matter what, it will always
spark a reaction down the road, whether big or
small. The lack of clairvoyance we as humans have
is nothing more than a catalyst to our basest desires.
And while life is about superimposing our will on
what is just and moral, we will never learn from our
mistakes.

While driving down the freeway, I play a
game in my head. "Guess what the motorist is
thinking." I take a peek at people I pass or who pass
me, and I wonder what their life was like today;
what they did that day. What have they seen? Are
they happy? Or are they altogether miserable? I
never find any middle ground here. Everything is
purely hyperbolic. This man just got a blowjob from
his secretary. This woman buried her son, who was
born with elephantiasis. This girl hit the lottery.
This guy is going to kill his entire family. I might be
right sometimes. However, as I stare off at the
motorists, I am reminded of one thing. We are all
humans, and the only thing we care about is
ourselves. Honestly, ask yourself when the last time
you cared about another was.

It isn't long before I have gotten to the
Furious Shrimp. The stupid, maniacal, crustaceous,
cartoon above the bar indicates I am at my
destination. Inside, my Old Man is already at the
bar eating an order of fried clams. I walk up and pat
him firmly on the back.

"There he is!" My Dad roars while hugging me firmly

"Dad," I respond, "Great to see you."

"Have some clams! They're great."

"Thanks." I look to the bartender promptly, "Coors light, please."

"So…why the meeting before the party?"

"Do I need a reason to see my son?"

"No." I mutter understandingly "I just thought something was up. I mean, we are meeting at a bar right outside of Pat's house. Couldn't we just hang there?"

"I thought it'd be nice to catch up before the hustle and bustle of the crowd."

If you were expecting a story about a son and his Father and their distance, then you were misled. My Father has always been there for me. As a matter of fact, my Dad is one of the only people I can count on regularly. He was the ideal Father in every way. I look up to Him. I am everything I am today because of Him. One time, when I was young, I saw my reflection while entering an elevator, and for a brief moment, I only saw my Father.

Okay, so He left my mom when I was seven and moved across town to start another family, but it isn't as bad as you think. He was never absent. He was at every sporting event. He called every day of the week. Even if He wasn't there, Dad meant it when He said He just wanted to see me. My Father loves (loved)…. (No…loves) me. To be honest, He couldn't ALWAYS be there. He was two hours away, and unless it was an emergency, any trouble I got into was dealt with by my mom. Often, mom never even told Dad. A big "Fuck You" to show Him she could raise me herself.

We talked for an hour and got a decent buzz on before taking separate trucks to the party. There, at my uncle Patty's, we walked through the door like we owned the place. I remember it like it was yesterday (maybe it was?). Pat greeted us and introduced us to his long, lost sister from Boston. I congratulated Pat's daughter Reilly on her high school graduation before pouring myself three fingers of Makers Mark. Dad never drank his whiskey with ice. I did. My friends and I used to say:

"One day, when we are older, we'll have developed the same habits as our Fathers."

The same habits of our Fathers:
· Drinking your whiskey neat
· Keeping a bottle of Chivas Regal in your desk at work
· Gutting your dip spit
· Not chasing your liquor

That was our inheritance.

Dad and I hung out by the bar most of the night. Everyone always looked at us. They wanted to be like us; a Father and son duo that exultantly demonstrated our social skills amongst the party goers.

My Uncle Pat was always fond of me on account of him having no sons. He had two daughters, and he loved them dearly, but he always wanted a son. My Father never told me this, but I could tell. He was so happy to get coffee or go fishing with us and always cheered me on just as much as Dad. He is a great guy. So, when Uncle Pat pulled me aside at the party to get more beer, I was happy to help him out. The second time, when Amanda (who I have known since I was a whelp) asked me to get some vodka, I obliged again. I brought my Old Man with me the second time. After that, Dad and I spent most of the evening hanging around the bar and laughing at the guests and their enervating attempts to mix a cocktail. Of course, looking back, we probably looked like a bunch of drunk assholes at this point. What we mistook for admiration were most likely glares of agitation.

Before long, it was eleven o'clock. Dad and I were as intoxicated as two barflies on dollar beer night. It was time to get home. Time to stop at the local liquor store and pick up beer for the rest of the night. I was being called home.

Just as I was leaving, Dad said, "Drive slow! Drive nice and slow. No need to get there fast Jackie!" But before long, after He almost took a spill down the stairs, He was asking me for a ride home as well. I obliged.

Chapter 3

Dad wanted to play some Bob Seger as we drove. I just happened to have his greatest hits in the car. *Night Moves* was the song that came on first after I hit the shuffle button. Don't ask me why, but I began to think of the first night I ever got drunk. In the haze of all of my alcohol fused memories, I thought of that night.

It was 2002 and I was about to start the seventh grade. My best friend, Quinn, was at my mom's house for a sleepover. Quinn was small and skinny but very wiry. He had dark black hair and, much like me, looked like a cruel little prick. We were the kind of searing little shits that you would take one look at and know their futures were going nowhere. It was our first time drinking and we were twelve years old. Quinn came over a lot but I never really went to his place. His parents were separated like mine and Quinn lived with his mother. His Father had custody of his sister. I had never met his Father or his sister for that matter.

We were products of our generation and decided to steal three bottles of champagne from my grandfather's liquor cabinet. I didn't know any better. Even if it was kept in a warm, poorly ventilated liquor cabinet for three years, alcohol was alcohol, right?

We went into the den at mom's house around midnight and started to drink the noxious contents of those warm bottles. They were warmer now since I couldn't hide them in the fridge and had to put them on top of the shed in the backyard while they baked in the Southwestern sun. I had picked up a VHS of Mudvayne live from 2001 at a local video store and we played that while we gulped down what we could. It didn't even take an hour before each of us was finished with the first two bottles. Quinn finished about a third of the last bottle before he opted out and I finished the rest. We smoked cigars I had stolen from my Father the weekend before. In our minds, this was the brass tacks of maturity; drinking, smoking, and most importantly, acting like you knew what you were doing.

Around 2 AM, we stumbled out to the couch to pass out. It wasn't even 3 AM before I was awakened by the less than pleasant sound of Quinn retching his guts out all over my mother's already trashed carpet. Of course, the mystery remains; was it the warm, most likely expired, champagne from three years ago, or was it inhaling cigar smoke like a cigarette? The part that makes me laugh now isn't Quinn losing his shit all over my mom's carpet but instead me yelling at him for waking me up. I wasn't trying to be an asshole, it's just that I had the most splitting headache I have ever had to date and on top of that, I had to deal with his vomit. Pizza, Oreos, and sparkling wine spackled the floor around us like a Jackson Pollock painting, and of course, my mother had to come out after all of that yelling. She was concerned at first and then disappointed. She had been married to my Father. She could smell the vomit. She knew what we were up to. Quinn and I stared at each other for a moment before she left and I passed out once more. I knew I would have to clean it up come the morning. Needless to say, I felt terrible. Not for stealing or drinking, but because of my mother's carpet.

They say the morning after your first-night drinking will deter you from ever drinking again. That was never the case with us. Quinn and I were inseparable ever since that night. Good 'ol Quinn...

no one in my life has dealt with my baggage better than he has. No one in my life has had the same baggage as he and I have.

Back to present-day, Dad and I are trying to find a good CD to play. Dad hands me a flask filled with…well, I'm not sure, but it has alcohol in it, so I drink while He picks a song. The warm hooch tears through my esophagus like Drano down a clogged toilet as I fight back a tear that I would be contrite to show my Father. The twang of a bass guitar on a familiar song pulls up and I nod my head at my Father in approval as "In Hell I'll Be in Good Company" by the Dead South comes on. Dad nods His head to the song and takes a swig of His medicine from the flask that I just passed back to Him. I can tell by the way He drunkenly sings the song and bobs His head that he loves being here with me. I know because it is exactly how I feel.

Before long we are rocking out to *Lydia* by Highly Suspect. I fucking love this song! Dad is rocking His head melodically back and forth and pulling on His flask again and again before handing it to me. As I take a pull from the stainless steel container, I do my best to lip sing the song. My brain warms up for a moment and my vision is becoming noticeably blurry.

I feel inside my pocket and make contact with the smooth, tiny container there. I get chills just feeling it, but I quickly remember that it is what has made me happy for the first time in years. I take another drink.

I look over at my Dad and smile at His enthusiasm towards the song. I'm just happy He enjoys it.

I concentrate on the road for a moment more before downing another sip of the rotgut in the flask.

Again to my pocket, to feel its flush exterior. It's funny how, when you're wasted, everything starts to become repetitive.

I can't help but think of her...

The first stoplight is behind me. We only have about four more to go. I might just stay at Dad's tonight. He has beer.

This song fucking speaks to me...

Almost at the house now; just two more lights to go after I get through this next one. Every drunken drive is a mission. You have to concentrate harder and harder on the road as you drive along. But rea-

And then....darkness...

Chapter 4

Without warning or care and in the midst of chaos, life will end. Life; the one thing we can equivocate on to no end that only death can rescind. A car crash isn't exactly how I always pictured myself going out. All those years driving under the influence and I never thought it would happen to me, but I finally bought the farm. However, before I attempt to equivocate on my own life, I'd like to stand on my *'ill-informed'* soapbox for just a minute and tell you what I really think.

First, the world, society, people, the human hive mentality (whatever you want to call it) believes that alcoholics are all the same. AA has touted that for years. This is where we get our narrow-minded way of thinking. And it isn't their fault for believing this. It is, as I stated before, our human hive mentality. AA (aka Alcoholics Anonymous) would have you believe that a thirty-seven-year-old man who drinks occasionally is an alcoholic. AA is a business like any other. The more people that AA gets indoctrinated the more people they have to donate and buy their books or whatever the fuck they're selling.

Now, let's be clear; there are alcoholics out there. I am not so short-sighted that I don't believe that or care about it. I've had plenty of friends and family lost to the bottle.

- Jessica Anderson, age 47, jaundice of the liver
- Matty Ford, age 17, car crash
- Dylan Walsh, age 21, stabbed to death in a bar argument
- Josh Koprivneck, age 25, alcohol poisoning

I've had experiences in life that make me especially privy to the dangers of alcohol. I have plenty of friends still alive that have that cruel burden of addiction. I love them. But how can I have an impact on them when I drink myself. Alcohol does that to you. Nothing matters. No one cares. Life is going to end. There is nothing you can do about it. You cannot help but feel that way under the influence. People will say, "You drink all the time…" and I will callously slur, "It makes dying easier…" This is the unfortunate psyche of most drunk people. I'm not talking about your typical frat boys at the bar. Those are the second wave drunks. They are just there for a good time. No. I'm talking about drinking yourself silly and sitting alone and contemplating whether life is worth living or not. That is your true 'moment of clarity'. Alcohol is a test of the will. Self-control meets self-destruction.

Of course, in spite of alcohol's benefits, the world adheres to the same aforementioned rules of AA. Here are a few more AA tenants to be aware of if you are concerned that you're an alcoholic:

- If you drink alone, you are an alcoholic
- If you get blackout drunk, you're an alcoholic
- If you don't drink for a week and then drink again, you're an alcoholic
- If you only drink on the weekends, you're an alcoholic
- If you have gotten into trouble while drinking, you're an alcoholic
- If you order a pizza but get too drunk and pass out before the delivery driver shows up, you're an alcoholic

- If you have a few drinks and are unsatisfied, you're an alcoholic
- If you drink your scotch neat, you're an alcoholic
- If you eat McDonald's after drinking, you're an alcoholic
- If you have thought about drinking beer, at precisely 10:34 PM, after the Kentucky Derby, and it is raining outside, you're an alcoholic
- If you have ever thought about drinking, you are an alcoholic

I hang on to the notion that I abuse alcohol; I don't need it. I'm just past the point of being addicted. Yes, yes, I *abuse* alcohol, but an alcoholic? No way. I'm too young to quit smoking and drinking. At least, I was too young…

There are differences between a man who wakes up every morning needing a beer to stop himself from shaking and seizing to death and a man who, after 12 years of drinking heavily, does not need to drink every day. If we went by the collective peoples' mindset of what an alcoholic is, then two-thirds of our population would be alcoholics. You cannot win — thou loosest labor.

Chapter 5

In my ascent, I can only fathom what lies beyond in the "Unknown" that so many fear. I'm past the point of fear. I imagine many would fear floating up to their imminent demise. But unlike those who scream as they descend from the sky in a crashing plane, I remain the sole passenger that knows it is too late and takes a breath, waiting for the end. I'm ready to tell you precisely what you are missing out on up here. I'm a dead man.

The crash killed us and there are two things on my mind:

1. Where is my Father?

2. What are they going to do with the contents in my pockets?

As I float up, I am immediately enclosed by a brightness that blinds me. I have no choice but to close my eyes.

I hated that death came so quickly, but the truth is, the way I lived my life, I was going to die soon anyway. Death is nothing more than a mordant cursor in the game of life. It's funny, being dead, you would think you would be greeted by St. Peter or maybe even Satan. I mean, one of those passages from the Bible has to be right… History tells us one thing, but the truth is, in fact, always so much duller.

In an instant, I find myself in a room with hundreds of other people. The place looks like a padded cell that is being remastered as a doctor's office inside an airplane hangar. Each one of us is dressed in a white hooded robe. When I look at myself to study my newly, gifted attire, I notice the sleeves end about halfway down my forearms. Each hood is gilded with a sort of white gold as well.

People are pooling through every manifested portal each moment. Some drop from the ceiling while others are suddenly shot out of the ground. I mean, let's face it, one hundred and twenty thousand people (roughly) die every day. That is five thousand an hour. That is eighty-three a minute, and almost two every second. I got a lot of time on my hands now that I'm dead.

People pass by me in waves, uttering languages I've never heard before. One man grabs me and says:

"S'il vous plait! Savez-vous ou se trouve ma famille?"

"S'il vous plait? That's French right?"

The man, distraught, releases his grip from my robe and continues down the hall.

Another woman passes by frantically before barely uttering:

"Andizi ukuba ndiphi…"

I didn't know that one.

There, in front of me, is the receptionist and her name tag simply reads "Shannon". She is beautiful aside from the scar across her jaw. The scar resembles a big purple gash that could easily be holding her face together. As I approach, she seems reticent to tell me just how fucked I really am. I do what I do best and try and think of something witty to say as I approach her, but by now, you probably know that isn't my forte.

Everyone behind me is motionless and either crying or touching the walls as if they were an overstimulated baby entering this world for the first time. Am I really the only one from this horde who dares speak to her? Everyone else is crying and confused and walking around like a bunch of

fucking idiots. Life and death aren't much different
I guess…

"Hey" I pause for a moment to cordially
reread her nametag and smile as I say her name
aloud "Shannon. Is there-"

"Oh! You're here. We are glad to have you a
post-mortem de nuage. How may I help you?"

"Post-Mortem de Nuage? Did you make that
up?" I say in a coy tone

I get only a blank, insouciant stare from
Shannon as I clear my throat.

"So…I just sign in or something I guess?"

"Well, not exactly…"

"Thanks for clearing that up. Let me
rephrase; Am I able to get into Heaven, or am I
crawling to Hell?"

"That is up to you."

A smile crosses her face as she raises her
eyebrow and purses her lips. I try to smile back, but
I'm still processing her response and reading the
plaques behind her. Though meant to be a
heartwarming welcome, the insignias had a far more
somber appeal to the dead than initially expected.

One read:

"Take a deep breath…You're HOME now."

And the other:

*"Today is the first day of the rest of your
eternity."*

"What do you mean? I thought we were
supposed to build up a reputation on earth and
repent, or die, or at least always be good…" I can
hear myself wondering and getting off-topic
"Heaven and Hell!"

"Oh yeah?" Shannon scoffs the words out
like a real bitch, "And where would you end up if

that were the case? Do you remember your time on earth?"

I give her a weary glare before answering in an increasingly perturbed tone.

"Only too well…"

"Yeah, because Christianity is the only religion on earth, right?"

"Well, no. I didn't mean that. But aren't all the concepts of the afterlife pretty much the same? What am I in for here? Olympus? Valhalla? Tartarus?"

"Which would you like? You can technically choose any of them," she takes a moment to laugh condescendingly "Of course, Olympus isn't real. It's a myth!"

I stand there, with my eyebrow raised, visibly nonplussed while Shannon sizes me up. I say nothing and wait on her.

"You get to choose, in death, which afterlife suits you."

There goes any sense of justice I had in the universe.

"Wait, so you're telling me I get to choose which afterlife I have regardless of what I did on earth?"

"That's right," Shannon says, taking out an emery board and filing her nails while rolling her eyes as if she has done this a billion times before

"Right, so Hitler gets to go to Heaven? Is that it?"

"Strike One, Delaney. Why is it that everyone always goes to Hitler?!" Shannon composes herself recognizing, with good reason, this is what most mortals epitomize as true evil "Yes, Hitler can choose, and Hitler can go where he wants, and no Hitler is not in Heaven. Look, what do you expect? There are over 4,000 religions in the world! We aren't going to pool people into some confusing afterlife they didn't intend to go to in their mortal life. And it isn't our job to punish or banish evil. Sure, some bad guys-"

"'SOME' bad guys?!" I interrupt Shannon and emphasize my first words "'SOME'?! There has to be more-"

She cuts me off once more.

"SOME bad guys fall through the cracks, but it doesn't matter now that you are here and you get to choose what suits you best does it?"

The irony of this entire situation has officially overwhelmed me.

"Look, the afterlife is like a-" Shannon stops for a moment to think of a good simile while she waves her emery board like a baton "Um, like a water slide. The Hindus go down it, and each time they get off, they get to come back up as a different person or animal. Christians fall into a pool of fire or pillows. Jews go head first. Muslims-"

"Alright, alright, I get it…"

I can tell by her condescending tone that she is fucking with me.

"Down this hall is every choice you will have." Shannon doesn't even look as she points with her emery board a bit behind her to a corridor entrance on her left before picking up a fashion magazine and thumbing through the pages "Enter the door of the afterlife you want to check out and there is a large ante-chamber that will lead you to a secretary that will show you what it is and if it is right for you. If you want that afterlife, walk through the second door. If not, walk back into the hallway. Just remember, when you choose your afterlife, it is permanent. Eternal, if you will."

Shannon laughs.

I give a mocking giggle back as I mutter "*Cheeky*" under my breath

"By the way, do you know where my Father is? I saw both of our dead bodies on the way up."

"He must've died a few minutes before you." She says seeming exasperated "He was already up here and wandered. I don't know. Look around…"

"Why don't these people in the waiting room just go already?"

"Choosing your afterlife is a big decision. You can't just do it on a whim. Plus, like you, most of them are waiting for their family members."

I guess people aren't as stupid as I thought.

"So, there is no Hell then?"

"Oh, there's a Hell…"

"Wait, why the fuck would anybody choose Hell?"

"Pfft- keep that language up and I'm sure you'll find out" she gives me a cursory glance before going back to her magazine, "Why don't you go and find out for yourself?"

I am cursed with the freedom of choice. Before I can completely turn around, Shannon beckons me once more.

"Oh! Don't forget to fill out a comment card! My boss always insists that I get them from anyone I helped"

"Sure." I laugh, "We have a pretty good repartee, you know?"

She bites her lip and twirls a pencil around her finger as I grab a card and a pen. After putting it in the bowl, she immediately grabs it. The empty bowl demonstrates to me just how bored she must be up here as she excitedly reads my comments. Her

enthusiasm turns sour, and she looks up with a
sneer.

"Thanks…" she says twirling back in her
chair and lifting a middle finger towards the air

I look down once more at my comment card
with a smile as I read:

*Love the décor and the ironic vision of
Death. The place could use some new magazines
though. The receptionist is easy on the eyes but a
real twat.*

Signed,
Heywood Yableauxme

Chapter 6

My initial impulse was to find my Father.
But what the hell? Why not see what all these
corridors have to offer?

I walk through the front entrance by the
waiting room and I am immediately met with a
seemingly infinite white hallway that has doors on
the right and left as far as the eye can see. The first
two, naturally, are Heaven and Hell. I double-check
with Shannon to make sure I am not making my
final choice and she says:

"What did I say the first time?!"

I return the sentiment of a middle finger
when she turns around. I'm not feeling too antsy
just yet and decide to go through Door Number 1. It
takes a moment though as the stubborn door is
nearly impossible to open. Once I finally get
through, there is nothing but white light. For
Christ's sake, it couldn't get more hackneyed than
this. The hospital feel of this place has my head
spinning. Again, the only way to describe it is like
the inside of a mental patient's padded cell with
diameters around 100 feet by 100 feet.

I was hoping to find God, but it was just
another receptionist that greeted me. She looked
EXACTLY like Shannon. Maybe her twin?

"Hi!"

Her vibrancy is nauseating, considering the
circumstances.

"Hello. I'm looking for-"

"Your father, right?!"

"Uh, yeah....are you omniscient?" I say with
an almost genuine interest

"No," she says lovingly, "Shannon told me!"

Once again, not the level of energy I would manifest in this scenario.

"Right, well, if you haven't seen him-"

"But since you are here, you must see the wonders of Heaven!"

Picture every valley girl you have ever met in your life. Mold them into a receptionist and inject that receptionist with 200 ccs of cocaine and sermonizing emotion. That is what I'm dealing with here.

"Well, see, Shannon told me I had a choice, and while Heaven is definitely where I want to go, I don't want to jump the gun before I find my Dad."

"Oh no! You don't have to make your decision just yet! You see, we give you a bit of a guided tour. It's a slideshow and, if you'd like, we can take you inside for a bit as well!"

"Uh...okay. Sure."

It isn't like I don't have the time. I wonder what time it is on earth. Receptionist number two takes me into the room to the right. It has about seven people sitting around as you'd see in a waiting room. They seem relieved that I am there and Shannon #2 starts the projector to show us what awaits us in the Great Beyond.

The projection begins with the most brilliant high definition picture I have ever seen. I guess Heaven can afford such luxuries. The movie shows the allures Heaven has to offer: Drink and eat all you want and never gain weight or develop liver disease; time with your family to do whatever it is that you want to do; go holiday anywhere in the entire earth. Oddly enough, it's a hedonist's wet dream.

As slide after slide portrays some clichéd fantasy of the average human, my eyes fall on the individuals in the room. Each one of them brainlessly staring at the screen with their mouths agape. At that moment, I have an epiphany and I begin to study each one of the participants. Their faces marbled with the pure joy of bliss in eternity and their eyes glued to whatever is being projected. It's almost as if they are numb to the possibly horrible truth. I wonder if they would even care about the truth if it was awful. Something dawns on me, and I can't help but stop the presentation.

"I'm sorry. I'm sorry..." I raise my hand with slight indignation

"Um...Mr. Delaney. You had a question?"

"Yeah, so, what happens when you get bored of all of that?"

"Bored? From Bliss?"

Everyone is looking at me like I'm an idiot. Sure, what do I know? I'm not supposed to be here anyway.

"Okay. So, in my Heaven, I'd probably be around my whole family. We'd vacation all the time, as you said. And we'd always be together and around one another. What happens when we are tired of summering in Santa Barbara? Or, for instance, we get so disinterested in the same old routine that we hate it there."

"Well, you can always change-"

"Right! But we are talking about eternity here. How many times in eternity can we change before we are tired of that as well? And then, eventually, even tired of our family?"

Everyone is looking at me like I just admitted that I started Chicago Fires. Not in the way they were previously, but now as if I was making them think. They hated me for that. People will always hate you for making sense and making them think. Why do I still have to be the one spouting irreverence?

I see their faces turn to indifference and I dig my claws further in, trying to make my point and at least give these people a fair shake.

"Sir," I point to an old man near me "What is your idea of Heaven?"

He takes a moment to answer the crazy man asking questions during the conference.

"I-I suppose it would be out fishing with friends and family all day. Go into our houseboat at night and regale one another with stories from the past."

"Good! But how long could you do that? Really though. How long could you sit around telling stories of your 80 years on this earth? How long until catching that same large-mouth bass bores you? Think about it! We only see Heaven in our lives on Earth as what suits us then! We never actually pause to think-"

"I'd never get bored of family." The old man retorts almost amusingly

I give him a defeated look.

"Sir, I'm sure that-"

"Mr. Delaney...I think you should leave..."

Shannon number two grabs me gently and kindly around my elbow to lead me out.

"I'm sorry, Mr. Delaney, but I cannot have you confusing the patrons of this room. If you would like to be in Heaven, then that is fine. However, make your decision and come back later."

"I'm sorry." I feel bad for a moment, "I'm a Christian. Really! I am-"

"I know Mr. Delaney."

"I was just-"

"I know Mr. Delaney."

"I wasn't trying to-"

"I know Mr. Delaney!"

She walks me out the door I came through, and I sit on a chair near the entrance. The hallway leading to the other afterlives is dark; only the light shining through the transom of each door illuminates the way. I decide to sit and gather my thoughts for a moment. I rub my temples with my fingers.

"Fuckin... Heaven..." I mutter

Let's face it; Heaven is nothing to strive for. It is a cave in which we place ourselves; a distance from reality....an exodus from the truth....

Don't ask me why here or why now I thought of this memory, but it crept up on me like a nightmare.

Chapter 7

I had just graduated High School, and it was early June. I was working day and night at the local steakhouse and making pretty good money. Eighteen years old and I had the world in my hands…but it wanted me to let go.

In summary, I was a 3.6 GPA student that played football, drank on the weekends with my buddies and hooked up with just about anyone who was willing to meet up from MySpace. I was most likely 'that guy' you hated in high school. You'd be right in hating me, but I'd like to think that some people change.

High School, though a time of great disillusionment for most, was a time of frivolity for me. It wasn't hard, and I was friends with all the right people. That's why I'll never forget that night. The night High School became a thing of the past. The night my life started for real. It was 9 PM and nearly closing time at the restaurant where I was the head cook. I worked there since I was sixteen and at seventeen I became the head grill cook of Lone American Patriot Burger. You weren't *technically* allowed to be behind the line until you were 19, but things were different back then. Plus, my attitude toward work pushed me in the right direction — Protestant guilt in action.

We began cleaning up around 10 PM. I had only eaten a peach all day, but back then one single peach and I was working a ten-hour shift. Youth is a Hell of a thing to waste. I already knew where I was going that night too. Quinn, whose friendship I had maintained since junior high, had called me around 3 PM while I was taking my smoke break and told me about how he was house-sitting at his mother's friend's that weekend. That meant a party. That meant booze. That meant a good time. I couldn't close the kitchen fast enough.

Around 11, after I had showered and got changed, I was on the road in my 1985 Ed Bauer edition Bronco to Quinn's location. I loved that truck. I still have that truck. I can only hope they're burying me in it down on Earth right now.

The house (or condo rather) was inside another set of condos off Washington Avenue. This was the kind of place where you'd love to retire. A bunch of old bastards watering what garden they had in the gated front yard portion of their pristine retirement home without a care in the world.

I parked my truck right in front of the house and walked in ready to 'fuck shit up' as Quinn would say. Before long, I was being embraced by an enormous pair of biceps connected to a massive barrel chest. I knew then that Jacob was the first one to greet me. He was the biggest guy I knew. He was six foot seven and weighed around three hundred and fifteen pounds. Hardly any fat was hanging on him. Jacob was the star offensive lineman of our football team and he, Quinn and I were good buddies. Hell, he was the only one on our team to get a full ride to a division two college.

After a moment of shooting the shit with Jacob, my gaze fell on the cute, petite girl that was laughing on the couch as I came in. Cute isn't exactly the right word. Her visage was a divinely carved providence to my eyes. She wasn't a supermodel and didn't have an actress's beauty per se, but her "girl next door" look sent my blood into a frenzy and my stomach butterflies whirled into a tsunami. The only thing that broke my concentration was a husky redhead doing a garbage bag full of whip-its. The mystery girl thought it was the funniest thing in the world. She was beautiful. Why hadn't I ever seen her around?

Before I became distracted more, Quinn pulled me aside to show me where the beer was. Jacob grabbed one, and I did as well.

"Miller High Life" Quinn exclaimed "The Champagne of Beer!"

"At least it isn't Bud," I said shrugging with a smile

One beer always turned into a second. Social drinking is overrated. Plus, I could never have just a few. "A few" is meaningless. It defeats the purpose of drinking.

Jacob dragged me to the other end of the kitchen. I didn't even get a chance to talk to Quinn for long before Jacob was placing me in front of a bottle of 151 Rum. He poured us both a shot. I took the shot with less than enthusiastic results. This shit burned like a napalm catheter.

Okay, so being that I was 18 years old, most of my drinking at that point had been from Mad Dog 20/20, Keg stands, red cups filled with enigmatic panty-dropper, and Bourbon chased with Coors Light. I did not know what 151 Rum was. I did not fully grasp the idea of percentages and proofs or the sole peach (or what remained of it) disintegrating in my stomach. If you don't know where this is headed, turn back now.

We took roughly seven (or maybe even eight) more shots of the 151 within an hour. The rest of the night was just beer for me. When they say "this drink CREEPS up on you," they mean it. I didn't feel any drunker than I usually did, but my motor function skills were definitely below par. Or, is it above par?

I decided to go back to the living room to meet up with Quinn and hopefully get introduced to this new mystery girl, but before I could make it, the fat redhead stopped me.

"Are you okay?" his voice bellowed from the whip-its

I know I have a nasty shitface. I can drink most anyone I meet under the table, but after a few, it is obvious I've been drinking. I'm so tall and lanky that I can hardly manage a sturdy stance after a few.

"How many have you had?" he asked still with a guttural tone

"You think I keep count of that kind of shit?!" I blustered

He shrieked a little and slinked back into his garbage bag and started inhaling again slowly. I got a hold of myself before "Drunk Jack" ruins "Romantic Jack's" chances at meeting the girl on the couch. "Drunk Jack" already fucked "Sober Jack" over last week by misplacing his truck keys while "Hungover Jack" panicked on how to get to work on time.

Quinn greeted me near the coffee table once more, and we exchanged drunken pleasantries. I have my eyes going back and forth from the new girl to Quinn. My attempts at discretion are probably all but working. Her smile has me in a trance. She has the smile of a real girl. Not like those dumbass sluts we usually hang out with on the weekends but a genuine smile. Her face is a little gaunt, and she is thin, but with a great body. I don't know what it is about her. She definitely isn't the normal girl I go after. I want to talk to her. I actually want to speak with her. I don't want to just tell her what she wants to hear.

"Jack!" Quinn says fraternally as the fat redhead near the table huffs down another whip-it

"Quinn!" I yell, drunkenly embracing him

"I want you to meet my sister Annabel. We just call her Anna, though..."

His fucking sister. Of course. Why would the universe want me to be happy?

"Anna, nice to meet you. I'm Jack."

She smiles at me sincerely, and either her presence or my withering inebriated state of mind makes me feel on top of the world. I can't describe Anna's beauty; it is absolutely arresting. She is quite possibly the most vibrant and breathtaking girl I've ever seen. Her brown hair is straight yet curly at the ends. Her stare would send Angels into a jealous rage. I almost lose myself in her smile for a moment. And she is fiery. She is here with all of her brother's friends, and she isn't the slightest bit shy. She drinks with the rest of us. Quinn says she is going to be a sophomore this year in High School. Brilliant. Just when I was starting to like her.

The rest of the night is an absolute haze. I did a few whip-its with the fat ginger and smoked a little weed Anna had brought. A few more shots of 151 with Jacob and we were all having a great time. It is only when Quinn tells me that I need to move my truck from in front of the neighbor's yard that I groan. I stumbled out of the house before fumbling for my car keys. Starting the car was easy. Leaving the neighborhood to go park on the street was easy. Hitting the car parked next to the alleyway was easy. Rushing off in the truck to go three blocks away to avoid suspicion, and walking two blocks back to the party was hard.

When I got back in, all I could muster was a silent 'Fuck...' as I reached for the wobbling wall alongside me. I passed out on the floor long before the party was over (compliments of my virtuous diet that day) and woke up the next morning ready to get the fuck out of Dodge.

Chapter 8

Memories and time are the only things I have left here in eternity.

As I sat in the chair by Heaven, a man came by and struck up a conversation with me. This was utterly unprovoked; I didn't want to talk with anyone.

"Hello, old soul." The man stammered "How's it going…"

I'm trying to be as impassive as possible to cut this thing short.

"You tell me."

His gown was like all the rest of ours. It was long, almost passing his feet, and completely white. We all have the same unstained robes…

"Oh, I don't know. Want to tell me which way my Old Man went? Or maybe you can tell me where Pol Pot is? Probably milling around Heaven no doubt."

The man managed a smirk before looking back at me.

"Genocide is a favored vice of the human race. It is an abhorrent act that men in power have the control to utilize. You'd be surprised what a dead man could evaluate…on his own life."

"Are you trying to be deep or something? Bugger off…"

I roll my eyes and wave him away with the back of my hand.

"Make sure you check out Hell next." He said, ignoring my disdain "I think you'll be surprised. Not pleasantly, of course. No…. no one is ever "pleasantly" surprised there."

I close my eyes for a second to contemplate a *nice* way of telling him to fuck off but, when I open my eyes, he is already gone.

"Stupid, geriatric…fucker," I mutter, struggling for a better insult

Sorry, but I'm getting more cynical by the hour.

I take the old bastard's advice since it is the closest door to me and go through Hell's gate. I don't know what to expect. I suppose, more than anything, it was curiosity that pushed me. I mean, doesn't everyone want to know what the Devil looks like? Is he a goat draped in black attire with massive horns? Possibly an enormous, engulfing personification of a flame that consumes us all. All the while, people behind him are being impaled and slit apart like there is no tomorrow.

The room through Hell is not much different than the one to Heaven. They at least have a mini-fridge with water bottles here. And the receptionist doesn't look much different than Shannon….or Shannon #2 for that matter. God damn…I don't have a choice do I?! There is no choice. This whole thing has been Hell. They're just giving me the illusion of choice. My eternal fate is to walk through the endless doors only to be greeted by a different Shannon. They're all just sinecures of the damned. Each one with their eyes gazing upon-

"Oh! Hello!" a voice from behind the receptionist's desk blurts out

"Hello." I answer ruefully

"We weren't…um…expecting *you*…."

"Why not?"

Stupid Question.

"You aren't our typical clientele is all…"

"Oh…"

I'm confused. The way I lived my life, you'd think they'd be begging to get me in. I've never done anything that bad....just an inherent sense of iniquity.

"That's okay! Care to take our tour?"

"Well, maybe just a slide show.... actually I don't even know why I came here. I don't want Hell."

"Few people do..."

"Right...come to think of it.... why would anyone choose this place?!"

"Admittance has always been low." Shannon #3 takes a second to sigh "Why purge your sins when you can get off scot-free in Heaven. Alas, some actually choose Hell but not that many..."

"People choose Eternal Damnation?"

"Their transgressions are bad but not worthy. I've seen enough real sin to know the difference."

"That's right..." a voice announces

I knew Satan would be showing up soon. This is genuinely what I came for, to get a look at the Big Guy. The Morning Star!

"Hell is the resting place for many tortured souls."

His voice came from the dark hallway behind Shannon #3 and echoed deeply through the walls of the antechamber. Only a silhouette of him is visible.

"Their souls wrought with indignation and their flesh seared with flame."

Not so scary when you know you get to choose though...

"These souls have found an anti-paradise in our lair."

And here he comes. Stepping from behind the curtains. He looks… Vanilla. It is just a man with glasses and a three-piece suit. Way better than my wardrobe though.

"You're the Devil?" I say aloof

"As my assistant said, admittance is low. Nobody wants the torturous eternity that used to be, so we offer something a little classier. A gateway to power and bliss?" he says, questioning the last sentence as if to see if it is what I wanted

"Are you asking me or telling me?" I answer "So, it's like Heaven on fire?"

"You fucking humans with the fire! Always with the fire! Everyone thinks fire is involved! How do YOU know fire is in Hell? Is this because of Dante? Or Milton? God damn them!"

"But you just said-"

"Probably because that is the most painful, earthly punishment you can think of…" Shannon #3 intervenes

Despite his innocuous appearance, his oration is unsettling. His eyes make me uneasy each time I look at them. But with the freedom of choice, and Shannon number 3's ditzy smile juxtaposed behind him, the place loses its menacing vibe.

"There are probably worse ways-"

"It's true." He stops me short with a defeated sigh "You will only find eternal damnation here. There's nothing fun about it. The flames are real, though not entirely pervasive. There is no bliss or power or "Reining in Hell" and people do suffer. I used to be so desperate to get people here I'd beg them to come in but…well now it doesn't matter. Temptation is lost on choice."

"Well, if that's the case, why would anyone still choose to come here?"

"To repent..."

I manage a faint scoff before looking back at Satan.

"Repent? That is what you have to do on Earth...I thought. Then again, I thought there was no choice a while ago so..."

"You're confused? Let me ask you something: How many people deserve Hell?"

"I don't know....a lot?"

"Absolutely! But why come here when you have thirty billion other choices to choose from?"

"Like 4,000 actu-"

"What the fuck ever! Don't correct me you Shanty Irish prick!"

I inhale deeply and cock my eyebrow at the outburst.

"So...no one comes here?"

"I wouldn't go that far. People come." Satan seems flustered at the prospect of explaining it to me, "It isn't the ones that should though. Those who have accidentally murdered others that they truly care about on earth. Those who have created some misfortune so strong they couldn't live with the guilt — a guy who sleeps with his brother's wife, which leads to his suicide. One guy left his child in a hot car and forgot she was in there which lead to the child dying from a heat stroke — that type of 'stuff'. The list goes on and on. This is home to them. The soul never forgets what the mind wroughts."

"So people who are just mentally traumatized with guilt? People who-"

He interrupts my question and waves me off infuriatingly.

"Hell is reserved for those with sin and guilt. Those who do not purposefully kill others or wreck marriages by accident or… well you get the point. Those who do so purposefully…they always go somewhere else."

I only stare at him blankly. Even I am haunted by the corruption. He looks a little disheartened.

"The wicked irony of Hell is those who repent are the ones who are pervaded with guilt. The ones who don't and slip off into another afterlife are inhuman. They show no remorse. Their souls are so black and selfish that they only care for themselves. Those with humanity remaining in their hearts who have shown repentance but cannot forgive themselves come here."

"That is so fucking unsettling. I-"

He interrupts me once again and waves a hand like a man shooing away a bum asking for a dollar.

"Anyway, this place isn't for you, kid. Run along now to Buddha's temple or Alternate realities. I'm sure you'll find what you're looking for."

"I have to find my Dad anyway."

"Is he an asshole?" Satan laughs while crossing his arms over his chest

"What? No!"

"Eh… I thought maybe you and I would have that in common. My Dad is a real prick."

He and Shannon #3 share a condescending smile as I walk out filled with contempt. I didn't like that. I turn to them once more before giving a gracious farewell.

"Blow me," I say before leaving through the hallway door

The afterlife is more fucked up than I imagined. A memory creeps up on me slowly.

Chapter 9

I am in my first year of college. Unlikely as it may seem, I graduated from college. And as much as I may have wanted to, I wasn't going to end up like my Old Man hawking beer for the rest of my life.

I live with a clean-cut freshman who went to High School with me. He is around my stature and likes to party like I do. He isn't a close friend, but Quinn was (is) friends with him, and since Quinn never went to college, he sets us up in a two-bedroom apartment off-campus. Things are going great. We hold a party every Thursday, and we are having the time of our lives. We become pretty close.

Well, late one August night I get a direct message from Quinn's sister, Anna. After some preliminary conversation, she tells me, at great length, that she is interested in me. In all honesty, I had been thinking about her since the party. However, I have my reserves. She is a sophomore in High School. I am a freshman in college. On top of all that, and most importantly, she is my best friend's sister.

Briefly, I had thought about my little sister and whether it would bother me as much. On some level, it would.

She asks me what I'm doing. I tell her not much; the typical text message bullshit adolescents are fond of writing. She beats around the bush for about an hour more before asking to hang out. I'd like to say I contemplated this for a moment, but I was an impulsive teenager, and I was into her. I didn't want to "sleep with her" though. I wanted to see her. So, I took a risk. I told her to meet me that

Saturday morning at the mall to see *The Dark Knight*.

I met her there as she got dropped off by a friend. She was wearing a striped tank top and blue jeans with chucks. She smiled all the way to greet and hug me. It felt good to embrace her. Oh, that smile. That smile could launch a thousand ships. At least, in my mind it could. Objectively, she was just another pretty young girl, but to me, she was everything in that moment.

We went into the theater. No popcorn. No soda. Just us. I had played this game a million times before. I knew what could happen. The movie began, and she whispered a little about Quinn's new girlfriend. I gave my insight.

I really liked Briley. She was great for Quinn. The two of them were inseparable. I mean, Quinn wasn't going to college, and he had been with enough girls, so settling down was the right choice. Right?

We only got to the part where Batman is interrogating the Joker before Anna started to rub my face. She was all over me. All of my instincts die. Don't get me wrong, I'm as hard as a rock, but I can't help but feel like a loser.

- She is too young
- She is still in High School
- She is too naïve
- She is your best friend's sister

And that last one really turned me off. Even if we were the same age, I wouldn't want Quinn thinking that I had to prioritize him or her. I can't do it. I just sit there saying "Hold on" and "This is a good part" while she molests my face with her hands and I subtly push away making the entire ordeal as awkward for both parties as possible. I don't regret it though. I mean, I want to, but I don't. Jesus, just reliving the memory makes me cringe.

The movie is over, and as we walk to the parking lot, I wonder if there is something I can tell her; some sage wisdom to help her understand. Yet, as my critical thinking skills fail me in that instant, I am now tasked with merely taking her home since she doesn't have a car of her own....or even a license.

She seems sad. She looks confused. She seems angry. I can relate.

"I don't understand..."

"Look...it isn't that I'm not into you...it's just-"

"My brother..."

"Okay, well that's one thing. I mean, how am I supposed to drop this on him?"

"He won't mind..."

"Okay, for argument's sake, let's say he doesn't mind. That only brings me to my next part. You are sixteen, and I am going to be nineteen soon. I am about to tell my best friend that I plan on dating his sister, who is still in High School. Plus, Anna, he really treasures you. You have the brother/sister relationship that siblings would kill for throughout their lives. The last thing he wants is his provocative and less than chaste friend going steady with you."

She doesn't understand. She doesn't care. This dilemma is only mine to burden. She is now only angry. She is neither confused nor sad. Only frustration and fury paint her face. Just as she is about to leave the truck she looks once more into my eyes. The overcast sky is dark and decorated with clouds that are the harbingers of the coming monsoon season. A wind comes down and chills her, but she does not shiver. The look on her pained face makes me anticipate her saying something, but she only leaves.

For the next few months, I receive message after message. Each digital parcel is some reasoning for how we can make it work. I want nothing more than to make it work, but I dispel each request.

If only she knew how much I wanted to make it work. She had, in a sense, almost a power over me. The desire to abandon reason, my entire routine and my way of living has never been greater. But I don't.

'Eternal Regret' thy name is Jack Delaney...

Chapter 10

This brings me back to the afterlife, which is getting shittier by the minute. Why wouldn't it be? I'm dead. Everyone is either praying for salvation or waiting on damnation. You never think of an alternative.

I am at an absolute lack of surprise when that one old bastard greets me again. However, this time, he does not say much. As a matter of fact, he says nothing. He just passes by me and nods his head like I was another faceless man on the street. As if I were lost in my own mind and uncertain of what eternity would bring. Unsavable, if you will.

The hallway is empty, and I start thinking that Heaven is more my speed. I reconsider, though, as I see people pooling into Heaven's door behind me like cattle. Why go further, anyway? The rabbit hole is only for the strong. The enlightened. One of which I am not.

A corridor-like waiting room is just past Heaven and Hell. A few wanderers are sitting there, and I find myself sitting once more to calm my mental fatigue. Death takes a lot out of you, and it is only when you realize that you are dead that you start to panic mildly. I place my fingers on my temples and look down the rest of the hallway and see the endless, unlimited options to go through. It is only after focusing my gaze down the hall that I notice I can see further than I thought. Either I can see further, or the end is getting closer. No, it is definitely getting closer. With almost lightning speed, hundreds of doors enclose on one another, and the once endless hallway becomes nothing more than a 50-foot stretch of corridor with a handful of entries and selfsame transoms on each side. I hardly pay any attention to them though, as my vision closes in on the door at the end of the hallway. It is entirely black and has no light shining out of its transom. The lights from the submarine-like windows of each entry almost make a carpet of illumination to this door — a red carpet to some effect.

"It intrigues you doesn't it?" a voice from the chair next to me whispers

"What is it?"

"95% of souls never go past Heaven. However, man is always driven to curiosity by what he does not know and fears what he does not understand. Curiosity and fear then become mutually exclusive." He manages a laugh, "You'll see. If you've come this far....you'll see."

Unvexed, I roll my eyes at the man's cryptic statement.

"Son?!"

I jerk my head to the right of the perpendicular hallway. Already?! Could I have already found my Dad?

"Son! I wasn't sure if you went through to Heaven!"

"Not yet! But, obviously, I'm thinking of it! I mean..." I pause, reflecting on my last statement "I was just waiting for you, Pop..."

"Yeah." He whispers softly

"Well, at least there's a lot of really charming people in the afterlife," I say elbowing the guy next to me while he stares off unimpressed

I try to cajole a laugh from Dad, but his smile turns sour in an instant.

"It's great to see you Jackie. I've been thinking a lot since I got here. Would you mind if we talked a little?"

Oh, great one of these spiritual deviants got to you, didn't they Dad? "It's great to see you."? "Would you mind if we talked?" My Dad doesn't talk like that...

"Of course, Dad. I've been thinking a lot lately about the past as well."

"Good...My Father, your grandfather, was a man I admired greatly. I am the man I am today because of him. I want to tell you about him."

I never really learned much about my grandfather. Dad would talk about him briefly, but the memories were too painful to finish. Dad sat in front of me and leaned forward while resting his forearms on his thighs.

"Of course." I said before looking at the Stranger to the right of me, "Do you mind?" He walked away without another word.

Jack Sr. took a deep breath and began to speak.

"When He was 14 years old, Dad used to go to the train station late at night. He didn't have any direction in life so He figured He'd take the world into His own hands. Things were different back then. You didn't call in a missing child right away. They were working things out, or they were just trying to clear their heads. Young men were treated like adults back then. He used to climb onto trains coming into the station. My grandparents were poor and divorced, but they always made ends meet. My Dad didn't need to run away. He was just, out for a ride."

"He would hitch a train headed south to Missouri and ride it all night long with the hobos.

Dad was like us. Anybody got near Him, and Dad showed his teeth. One time, He beat the shit out of some guy at the train station and pushed his thumb into his eye until the eye matter oozed out. To say the least, He was not susceptible to kidnapping or abuse. He made friends though. That was something He was always good at throughout his life. Dad would ride that train all the way to St. Louis. He would gawk and awe at the city lights. Living in rural Detroit afforded Him little, so He enjoyed the skyline at night and in the early morning. He would smile, foot hanging off the side railing of the train as He chatted up his new homeless friends. And at the train stop, with everyone else taking a break and hanging out, He would get on the next train to Detroit. These were some of the greatest moments of His life."

"In 1942, when Dad was sixteen, He decided to run off and join the Army. As I said before, things were different back then. Hah! Back then, all you had to do was tell them you were eighteen, and they would accept you. We'll probably never figure out how many people fought in WWII from ages 14-17. He served in the Pacific chapter. I'm certain my grandmother was beside herself with grief. See, your grandfather never told her. He just tucked her into bed one night and said:

'I love you with all of my heart. Please…stay happy…'

"He left her a note telling my grandmother where He was going, and He promised He would return. He kept His promise. He survived, and after the nuclear bombs were dropped, my Father returned home with His gear and a katana He had taken off a Japanese soldier He had killed."

"Years later He met my mother, and they had Layla, Michael, Patrick, Otis and I. He worked in construction for the rest of His life. He was divorced twice and finally stayed with my third step-mom Dolly. She was a laugh riot. They lived out on a home that He had built himself by Lake Havasu. It wasn't anything too fancy, but it was quaint in its own way."

"By the time my Father was 60, He was smoking roughly four packs of cigarettes a day. He could finish about a 30 pack and some Wild Turkey before calling it a night. I know others who could drink and smoke more, but I still thought that was pretty impressive. With as much as He smoked, I was certain lung cancer would get Him, but it didn't. He just fell off the bed one night from a massive heart attack. He was 61 years old. Even after all of that, with the death of the Man that I had loved and revered for so long, I kept smoking every day. I didn't care. I kept smoking throughout the 80s. It wasn't until you were born that I quit cold turkey."

Chapter 11

Dad's story reminded me of our family curse; or, rather, self-inflicted ailment. The Delaney Curse is something I had only heard about by sneaking around my house at night when everyone would think I was asleep. 'The Delaney Curse' they'd call it laughing while drunk in the living room, 'it's when you never met your grandfather because he died before you were born from drinking related illnesses.' And this was true. I never did meet my grandfather, my Father never met his and, just as well, my grandfather and many other ancestral Delaney's before them never met theirs. No one would confirm it when I was awake the next morning since no one wanted to scare me. They wanted to keep me safe and secure in this bubble of ignorance they had contrived for me. Even when I had experienced it, and cognitively put the pieces together of every male in our family never meeting their grandfather, they shot me down with systematic and anecdotal evidence. Even at an older age, when they thought I had conformed to the idea that everything was okay, I would bring it up again in jest and Dad would say, *"Oh, it's just a matter of coincidence. I have no idea what you're talking about."* I never bought it though. I just dropped it after a while.

After Dad's story, I felt compelled to keep checking each door with their infinite possibilities. My eyes wandered down the hallway.

"Go on. I'll be waiting here when you get back..." Dad sighed

I didn't bother him any further. It was time to check Door number 3. Buddhism.

As I opened the door, the room was filled with people talking and hugging one another. A receptionist greeted me in the middle of the room. Shannon again…

She looked different from the other Shannons though. She was bald and….well, you get the picture, she looked like the Dali Lama.

"Hello, young one."

"Hi, I'm-"

"We have no names in the afterlife. Though your physical body had a name, it does not matter here. One should stave away from self-identification. You are not American, Republican or Democrat, Teacher, Doctor, Man, Woman, Child, or even Human. Your knowledge is limited only by your capacity to seek consciousness."

Oh boy…

"I don't think this is for me…"

"It is. It isn't. It makes no difference what you feel. It is only in your en-"

"Isn't Buddhism centered around reincarnation?"

"That…" she stops for a second, a little taken back "depends entirely on you. You see, there are several schools of thought in Buddhism. You may reach for Nirvana, which we see as the collective energy of the Universe. However, if you cannot reach Nirvana, you may be reincarnated until your thoughts manifest unto complete enlightenment and understanding."

"So, essentially, I would need to go on a bit of a spiritual journey?"

"If that is how you wish to look at it."

"Thanks for being so helpful..." I roll my eyes childishly

"Irony is one of the many forms of human coping. It has no true meaning here. Of course, your proclivity to being vapid only shows me your lack of desire for our school of thought."

"Touché..."

I'm an asshole...

Too bad. It always seemed like a cool religion...or philosophy. Anyway, as I said, it wasn't for me. Unaware of etiquette or proper parlance, I bowed in front of her to which she responded to with a raised eyebrow before I took my leave. Still, I couldn't shake the memories creeping up on me. It was like all you could do in the afterlife was remember the past.

Chapter 12

I needed something, anything, to get my mind off Anna. Drinking helped but only for the six hours I was conscious. I'd pass out and dream of her. I'd wake up with a headache and think of her. A one, two punch from my brain; a reminder that there is no exit. I wasn't depressed. I wasn't sad. I was….anxious. Christ, I felt like an idiot; I barely knew the girl, and I was going crazy over her. I even started to get short with her in our text messages just to make her hate me.

A few days after Anna's last text, like a beacon from Heaven, a girl we knew from High School came to one of the parties my roommate Clay and I were having at the house. I always had a crush on this girl. I mean a really, really big crush in High School. She was our Chemistry teacher's TA, and I used to stare at her all day. That 3.6 GPA could've easily been a 3.8 if this girl wasn't in class. She was a year older than us though and moved away to college her freshman year. She came with one of our friends who was still a Senior in High School at the time. I was a little defeated at that but glad to see him nonetheless.

"Hey Colin," I said as I walked near him to hand him a beer

"Jackie! What is up? How's college?"

"Not bad; haven't done much yet."

Colin talks for a bit longer about High School and how he is dating this girl now that is about to go to Northwestern.

"Oh, wait, so you aren't with Sara?"

"What the fuck?!"

Colin looks at me like I've just asked him if he were gay or something.

"Wha-"

"Sara?! She's my sister..."

Oh great. Another one of my friend's sisters. I laugh all the same. Actually, this made me laugh more than anything. I have to hold on to Colin's shoulder from laughing so hard.

"Sorry man, I didn't know."

I'm still smiling but trying not to laugh anymore with Colin around. He laughs nervously after observing my mini-attack.

"Yeah. She just moved back after she broke up with her boyfriend."

Clearly I'm not as good of friends with Colin as I am with Quinn or I would have known this.

"Hey, you should introduce me."

I raise my brow a bit. Colin rolls his eyes but still smiles. Sara and Clay are talking now at the other end of the room. Clay raises his glass as he walks past me, and we both smile.

"Yo, sis, this is Jack. An old friend of mine."

"Jack. Yes! From Mr. Raymuell's class."

She remembers me.

"That's right! Can't believe you remembered."

"How could I forget?" She says flirtatiously yet clearly drunk

She goes on a bit about how her ex-boyfriend was an asshole and how she wants to get back at him. I nod my head to seem interested while I modestly check out her body and try to make gawking at her bosom as discreet as possible. She laughs and seems into me, and it is helping alleviate the sting of Anna.

Colin and Sara leave together at the end of the night and Clay and I are sitting on the couch talking about the girls at the party.

"Honestly though, Sara is smoking. I've had a thing for her since High School." I announce out of the blue

"Really?" Clay asks

"Yeah. I don't know; I might even kind of like her." I laugh a bit after saying it

"You really like her, huh?"

"Yeah." I nod my head for a moment while looking up at the ceiling, "I do."

"How about Brittany and Chanice though? I heard they are down for whatever. I'm definitely going to be going after that."

I give him a nod of approval and continue to think about Sara for a bit longer. Do I like Sara? Or am I just lonely? Or maybe, I am trying to fuck a girl to eradicate any puerile feelings I had during my time with Anna. Fucking can be an effective form of pain management. Contemplating this, Clay and I drunkenly pass out on the couch.

Weeks later, I was sitting in my room behind the computer working on an essay for *The Bell Jar*. I opened with the instances where the novel could be considered a roman a clef. I was also making connections between the 1950s era role of feminism and how it is comparative to our modern times but, even after heavy research, I had no idea what the fuck I was talking about. Samuel Delaney once said, "Literature survives on fertile ambiguity" but, of course, in my draft, every line was as typical as you'd expect from a freshman using a cliché thesis to impress his English Professor. Hey, I had to cut my teeth somewhere. While writing my second paragraph, the phone rang. Clay's number pops up, and I answer it.

"Hey, what's up dude?" I said

"Nothing. Just hanging out with Colin. Are you home?"

"Yeah. Just working on a paper. What's up?"

"Hmmm. Nothing. Just checking I guess. Um, alright, I'm heading home soon. I'm pretty tired. I'll probably go right to bed."

"Okay. See you later."

Looking back, I remember thinking how odd of a call that was. It was weird. Why check up on me? Just come home and go to bed.

About a half-hour later, I can hear the keys from Clay's keychain jingling in the door. I was finishing my third paragraph when I turn around to face my open door and greet him from inside my room. Clay gives me a quick head nod and walks briskly to his room. Behind him is Sara. She sits at the counter by the kitchen for a moment facing Clay's room. I'm confused. I don't say anything, and I can hear Clay whispering to her as she moves out of my vision into his room. I walk over to my open door and see his shut. It can't be. I sit at my desk for a moment to gather my thoughts. Am I dreaming?

I try and work on my paper for a bit longer, but the redness of the shame and the intoxication of anger drown my senses. I hear a movie start loudly from Clay's room. I think it is *The Meteor Man*. Clay was always playing weird, old videos. It didn't take long until I began to hear the sounds of fornication rushing through the air. I have chills. I am pale. I had spent the last few weeks pining over this girl. For once, I can't say anything. The only thing I do is work on my paper like an idiot while the sounds of sex and James Earl Jones's voice give me a soundtrack. I have always hated James Earl Jones's voice after that.

I grab the two bottles of malt liquor I had in my fridge. I go outside for a cigarette and play music from my mp3 player to pass the time while the sounds of ecstasy fill the room behind me. The first song to come on is "Lean on Me". A soft laugh pushes its way out of me somehow, and I marginally move my head. I am grateful to laugh. I didn't think I had it in me at this point. Time to grow the fuck up. I light the American Spirit and inhale. I wonder what Anna is doing right now.

"Dysphoria" thy name is Jack Delaney....

Chapter 13

It was Christmas of 2008, and I had just started seeing a girl from my old high school. She was fun enough. Quinn was throwing a party that night, and I was on Winter break for three weeks with the next two days off of work at the Irish Pub. The Pub was a lot closer to home, and the pay was way better than the steakhouse.

At Quinn's apartment, some old high school friends are here. Dylan, Nick, Tom, Michael, and the rest are all swarming around the beer pong table and the kitchen to grab what they can of the action. Quinn meets me on the patio with a beer and a cigarette. We talk about school and work and how nothing important is going on. Until, of course, Anna walks in.

She is wearing a Santa Clause hat, and a hoodie that reads:

"I'm a Drinker. Not a Fighter."

It had a shamrock separating the two lines in the middle. Merry Christmas. It's good to see her again. Yet, the sight of her holding the hand of another guy arrests my merriment. Jealousy is an eight-letter word. She shows off her new boy to everyone at the party — he looks like a real cunt. I'm bigger than him. I'm way better looking. He's just a kid. Then again, so is she. I have a girlfriend anyway. Let it go Jack...

Anna turns to come outside and locks eyes with me immediately from the open patio door. She is only there as a reminder of my happiness; a specter of my shame. Awkwardly, I attempt to make it seem as though I wasn't staring. She gives Quinn a big hug and proceeds to provide me with one as well.

"Guys, this is Gio."

Quinn, being the gallant brother he is, greets him quite hospitably.

"Hey…" Quinn nods as he releases a furious belch

"Gio this is my brother Quinn and his best friend, Jack."

"I'm gonna get another beer. It was great meeting you Tio."

"Gio, Quinn, Gio…" Anna says

"Right. How foolish of me." Quinn says disingenuously as he laughs and walks away

"Babe, I'm gonna grab one too. Want anything?" Gio smiles timidly

"Whatever you're having."

Thank you Universe for putting me in this position. No really, I love being at this party with Anna and having nothing to show for it. Just Brilliant.

"So, how have you been Jack?"

"I'm getting by."

"Yeah? I heard you're dating someone."

This was not the same girl I dropped off after the movies. This was a much stronger and thoughtful girl. This was a girl reborn from the ashes. A girl who will never let me hurt her again. She must hate me.

"Yeah. Her and I have been talking for about a month."

"Is it serious?"

"Why does everybody always ask that when you date someone?" I say as I laugh a little

She breathes out a faux laugh.

"Well, I hope things are going just splendid for you."

Great. Anna's passive-aggressive tone is palpable. I speak three languages fluently; English, Maudlin, and Truculence.

"Oh, I'm doing just fine Anna. And you? Your boyfriend seems great. He left a great impression with Quinn."

"Yeah. Well, ya know, Quinn can't be friends with all of my boyfriends…" Anna says raising a "Fuck You" eyebrow but with a lack of contempt

"Bully for you, Anna…" I sneer

It only takes a moment, but she ceases any austerity she had before staring deeply into my eyes. I can't tell whether she wants to hit me or kiss me.

"Are you happy?"

And just like that, I don't know how to respond. I take a second and breath in the cold December air. I contemplate the question while losing myself in Anna's eyes. There are only a few clouds in the sky before I meet her gaze once more.

"I guess. I don't know. Yeah. No…"

A wind from the clouds blows her hair up as she manages a saccharin smile before heading back inside.

The rest of the night is a haze after Anna leaves. She doesn't get drunk. She only dances with Gio for a bit before they head out. Great. Now I can get shit-faced.

I stand over the counter and exhale with a terrible grimace on my face and a beer in my hand. I pour a shot and chase it with the beer. I have another and one more before Briley runs screaming and crying out of the apartment. Quinn sits at the table expressionless. Tom puts a tray of Christmas cookies in front of Quinn. Quinn pounds the table before yelling:

"I don't want cookies! I want another drink!"

Quinn looks around, and the focus is clearly on him after his fiancé just left. His face turns white and pale before flushing red as he struggles for an excuse to tell the party. I've seen that face before. The look of a man who just told the girl he was seeing that he fucked another girl.

"I-"

"I need a drinking partner!" I yell laughing, in an attempt to divert attention away from Quinn "And! A beer pong partner!"

Quinn smiles slowly before raising his hands with a shrug.

By three o'clock I'm too hammered to care about whether there are DUI checkpoints on the local streets. Quinn and I cut through the night in my truck looking for any fast food restaurant that's open. Of course, it took much longer than usual as Quinn and I waited for 45 minutes at a stop sign waiting for it to turn green.

In all that excitement, I realized I didn't need anyone other than my friend. I realized that I probably got into a relationship just to feel whole and fill a void. That same night, after dropping Quinn off, I went to break up with my girlfriend at 4 in the morning. My breath smelled like eggnog...

Chapter 14

I'll let Dad stew a bit longer. He seems a bit more distant than usual. I mean, we're dead... it's understandable. I want to talk to him and tell him I'm sorry; I'm sorry for killing us. There will be a time. However, my intrigue and curiosity are far too great right now. Plus, some guy is talking Dad's ear off from what I can see.

The next door is sanguine and striking. It has a feeling of life and adventure in ephemeral bursts. I walk through, and the room is adorned with plants of all types. There are deer grazing and birds flying from pillar to pillar. This has to be some weird metaphysical shit. The receptionist does not move so much as she floats. As she passes through the darkness into the light, I give a weak smile when I notice she is another one of Shannon's duplicates.

"Hi there!"

"Hey. So, what is this place?"

"This is the realm of spirituality. Don't let the decorum fool you. There are both dark and light spirits here."

"Ahhh, I see. So, like, ghosts?"

"Well, yes. That is one way you may see it on earth."

"Interesting..."

"I think you'll be captivated with what we have here. You see, we live in realms in this afterlife. The Third Realm, as we call it, is the average deployment for most souls."

"Why the Third?"

"The Third Realm is the AVERAGE. If your soul is dark or 'evil', *your words not mine*, it goes to the First or Second Realm. There is an infinite number of Realms to ascend to! Even those in the first two realms can achieve a higher domain."

"Do they ever?"

"Not usually, no. Not because it is so hard to achieve the ascension, but …well, your soul is the same as it was on earth. Humans are, well, stubborn. Repenting is the most difficult thing for them to do. When you enter our afterlife, you enter with your duplicate body, your memories, and, of course, your character. Humans are funny. You could promise them all the knowledge of the universe, Heaven, or any other assortment of beautiful scenarios they could live in eternally, but they go with what is familiar. Those in the first two realms live out eternity in pain and suffering. We cannot guide them after they have entered. They know the rules; they choose to stay where they are."

I don't know what to say, so I simply nod my head and wait for her to talk again.

"Of course, one of the great appeals of our afterlife is the ability to view and even, momentarily, communicate with the living."

"No shit?"

"Yeah! You have to enter the Seventh Realm to get there, but it is possible. Actually, you can even get past that realm, but by that time, most of the spirits' families have passed on, and they would only be seeing their great, great-great-grandchildren. People lose interest in continuing their ascension after that and usually stay put…"

"Shannon, or whatever your name is, this is by far the greatest afterlife I have seen so far."

"Thank you!" She remarks gleefully "And how many have you seen?"

"Uh, four…"

Her smile turns sour with disappointment.

"Anyway, most people who make it past the door to Heaven choose spirituality."

"I'm gonna go check on my Dad, but I might be back."

"Great! We'll be right here."

"Don't die waiting for me," I say, pointing to her sarcastically

She reciprocates by floating back off into her realm.

I leave the room through the door and head back to the hallway. That guy is still talking to my Dad, and I figure I'd save him.

"...and we are really all powerless if you think about it."

"Hey," I chime in as the man gives me an exhausted glance, "You doing alright?"

"Hey Jackie. I was talking to Paul here." Dad gives me an almost bewildered look "He's been going over the philosophy of AA with me."

What a joke. Dad has probably been placating this guy just to stick it to him with a clever jab in just a moment.

"Hello Joe." The man says with a warm smile

"It's Jack." I say in an austere tone, "What're you guys talking about?"

"Your father and I were just talking about how there is a higher power and-"

"A Higher Power?" I snort a laugh through my nose

"You know that there is one, right?" the man says almost parodically

"Only too well..." I scoff, "And we needed you to tell us that? We are all dead and choosing between Heaven, Hell, and about a billion and a half other afterlives regardless of our station in life.

We don't have enough to go through here? What kind of dipshit do you take my Dad for? You're wasting your fuckin' time."

I nudge my Dad to join in, but he is just sitting there looking up at me. Christ. They've already brainwashed him. I'm staring down at a child lost in a supermarket. A child who knows he has strayed far from home, and it is his own damned fault.

"I understand humor is your coping mechanism." Paul smiles

"Oh, Jesus, not this again...."

I'm about to turn and leave before my Dad puts his hand on my shoulder.

"Do you remember your Uncle Otis?"

"Of course I do. He's my fuckin' uncle." I look at Dad as though a microcosm of his former self is still behind the eyes that he and I share "Steel Cut Oats you used to call him. Why?"

"Did I ever tell you about how he died?"

"It has to be more enlightening than this bullshit..."

"It was 1998, and it was not long after your mother and I separated. Otis was the second youngest of our family, only older than me amongst our siblings. When we moved from LA and I met your mother, Otis was the only one who started his own business. I was the traveling beer salesman, your Uncle Michael married for money, and your Aunt Layla tried to find God. He could have started a bar or a distribution factory, but I couldn't talk him out of a small liquor store on the east side of town. I visited Otis's liquor store on a weekly basis, but my visits had become increasingly sparse as weekly, turned to biweekly, and so on. The smell of stale beer and wood shavings was inescapable in that place. Even now, in death, I can still picture the paint chips falling off of the walls and the faint smell of day-old Schlitz on the floor. Every time I walked in, there were the same customers, roaming the grounds, looking for their usual. Frat boys were up at 6 AM to get a deal on a keg. Transients would haggle with Otis over the price of a bottle of Thunderbird. I remember approaching that liquor store, and every time there would be homeless people outside. They'd have three dollars apiece. They would buy Thunderbird for two-fifty, then go to the Circle K across the street, get a stick of butter, eat it and then down the entire bottle of Thunderbird in one sitting. With that stick of butter in their stomachs, they wouldn't chuck up the Thunderbird and let it go to waste.

 Of course, Otis was always sitting there in his high stool behind the cash register eye-balling each patron. That bottle of Blackberry Brandy was already half gone by the time I'd get there in the mornings. It wasn't the cheap shit either. It was some rare import from Germany or something. Fifty percent alcohol by volume. That was his diet; 75 percent Blackberry Brandy, 15 percent Coors and 10 percent bread.

 I remember us going out near the mountains one night to check out a dive bar that was getting a lot of attention. On the way back, Otis was swinging wildly in the truck. We couldn't hold him down. So, I cold-cocked him with that empty bottle of Blackberry Brandy he left in the back and threw him into the bed of the truck. I was driving seventy miles an hour down the freeway, drunk as a fuckin' skunk, and this motherfucking brother of mine gets up in the bed of my truck and starts sloshing around. Literally, doing spins and twirls while I'm

driving the truck down the freeway. Each time he'd
fall, he was an inch away from dropping over the
side of the truck. He'd manage his way back up,
hold on to the railing, kick the back of my window,
and fall a centimeter within the truck's barrier. I
finally had enough. I waited for him to get back up
halfway and I threw the brake down as far as it
would go. He smashed his head face-first into the
back window and passed out from the booze. I
could've killed 'em, but he only lost five teeth.

That was the level he was at when I dropped
him at his front door that night. Day and Night. The
prick could drink like no one else even when we
were kids, but this…this was different. That's when
I started visiting him more and more. The more I
was there, the more he wanted to party. The more
he partied, the more yellow he turned until finally
his skin no longer blinded me with paleness but
instead repulsed me with yellowness. Not only was
his skin turning yellow, but his eyes and fingernails
too. I'd come over and be looking at Death himself.
I had seen some bad shit before and felt remorse for
friends and family I'd lost, but I never felt sick the
way I felt when I talked to him for the last time."

"Otis… how you doing bro?"

He's lying there in his rocking chair still
skulling the bottle of Blackberry brandy.

"How do I look?" He manages with a grin

"Maybe…I don't know; maybe we should
get you to the doctor."

I was only able to look at his wife for a
moment as she began to cry and leave the room.

"Ah, Jackie…."

He wanted to laugh but he couldn't. His
smile turned to a marginal simper.

"I've been to one. It'll be dialysis for me."
He laughed before taking another sip of Brandy.

"Dialysis?" I had said, a little relieved,
"Well, that's not death."

"I'm not doing that shit!" He barked
instantly

"B-but don't-"

He took hold of my knee so hard it
interrupted what I was going to say. His empty,
yellow eyes stared into mine before he spoke.

"Jackie, if I keep drinking, I will die. If I
stop drinking...I will die."

Those were the last words Otis spoke to me.
I left shortly after. He died within a week. His wife
found him wrapped in a blanket with blood
covering the front of his chin. A few of his organs
had ruptured and he was announced DOA at the
ER."

Chapter 15

Not exactly the story I was hoping for today. Dad always said Uncle Otis died of a rare congenital disorder. I guess I don't really know my family that well. I'm just glad I didn't know him like that.

"Thanks for that, Dad…"

The guy from AA is still sitting there with that stupid fucking smile on his face, and I say:

"Shouldn't you be going off into Heaven?"

"I'm trying to help-"

"Help who?!" I stop him "Do me a favor and go help yourself by going to Heaven and then go fuck yourself you twat."

"My life is not yet complete, and I am continuing the work of-"

"Your life IS complete you moron! All of our lives are COMPLETE!"

I take a moment to compose myself before starting again.

"Yeah, see, the problem with your philosophy and reasoning is that it never takes into account humans. We cannot live our lives by some moral set of laws put in place thousands of years ago. We still constantly ask the question 'What is the meaning of life?' and never stop to think that life is void of meaning for us. That life does not need us. We take only what WE need first and then try and pass on our understanding of what we think is right next."

"You only think that way because you are pessimistic about the world. It has hurt you. It is understandable-"

"No. I'm not pessimistic. I'm enlightened. See, you have this AA philosophy that puts forth this system of a higher power. Sure, okay, there is a higher power. Look around you. We're in it. But it doesn't encompass meaning you blundering idiot! You can't judge someone because they decide to go to a bar alone to cool off from a stressful week and then say 'Fuck 'em! They're damned!' all the while you feed off of what people find attractive. If I wasn't dead right now, I'd be having a FUCKING STROKE JUST FROM THE RESTAINT OF NOT PUNCHING YOU IN THE FUCKING FACE!"

"Your nihilistic point of view-"

"This isn't Nihilism... this is realism."

I'm not letting up on this guy. I've never seen my Dad reduced to such a state. I'm pissed.

"Alcohol has clearly-"

"Alcohol is for the strong. That's the truth. If you can't handle it, don't start drinking. It's a fucking test of your will power. Your FREE WILL POWER!" I enunciate in his face, "And if you start and can't quit, you're shit out of luck. Figure it out. You wanted pessimism; you fucking got it..."

"What did you ever give up for Lent?" he says, smiling that same damned smile

"We aren't Catholic you cunt..."

"Neither am I. The act of Lent is an act of contrition that binds the spirit and soul to the body. So, again, what have you given up for Lent?"

I stare at him for only a fleeting moment before answering with a scoff.

"My faith..."

His smile never wavers. He just sits there grinning while trying to figure me out... like I still have so much to learn. I won't engage him anymore; I refuse to reward his vacancy with time. I decide to move on down the hallway and check on the remaining afterlives. Of course, like always, a memory approaches.

Chapter 16

My twenty-first birthday was one for the books. It was unequivocally my metanoia. It had been a day I looked forward to my entire adolescence. Of course, being underage never stopped me from having a good time. It only prevented me from reaching my true potential.

"You were born under a blood moon in the fall..." My Father used to tell me every year for my birthday. I suppose it's only fitting my 21st fell on the day of one as well.

I woke up promptly at 8 AM. As I opened my door, the cool October breeze beckoned me to live. My first stop was the DMV. It seems stupid now but getting your license changed from vertical to horizontal was a rite of passage. No one had ever been happier to arrive at the DMV than me on my twenty-first birthday. At 8:30 on a Wednesday, I was the only one there. That was a first...

After I got my new picture and ID, I began cruising towards University Ave. I rolled the window down and waved a middle finger to every bar that had kicked me out for using a fake ID. I traveled further north for ten miles to the Liquor Depot in the Foothills. It was an enormous, leviathan of a liquor store. It was the first 'legal' spot I wanted to enter. However, as I parked, I turned my head to see Mcgee Liquor Store. Nostalgia washed over me. It had been my Dad's most frequent stop on the north side. Dad had become good friends with the manager, and he frequently hung out with him on the weekends. As I stood in the parking lot holding my keys, I looked north to Liquor Depot before looking northwest to

Mcgee Liquor Store. I headed northwest before entering the store.

The door had an old-fashioned bell that rang over my head as I entered. The shop hadn't changed a bit since my childhood. The floor was scuffed with footmarks, and the counter was filled with cheap, portable shots of B-52. The man behind the counter leaned from his seat to lazily greet me.

"How can I help you?" he said adjusting his glasses while turning his attention back to the newspaper

"Just looking around," I began, "My Dad used to distribute here."

"A lot of distributors distribute here," he whispered distractedly

I returned a careless nod as I turned away.

"Yeah. How's business?" I said while traipsing around the store

"Shit the last few years since Liquor Depot moved in."

"Does Tom still own the place?" I asked

Though I said it loud enough to hear, the length in his pause made me think otherwise. I turned to see him staring directly at me.

"How old are you?" he asked firmly while staring at me behind his paper

"21..." I said ready to pull my ID out

He stared blankly.

"Prove it..." he insisted

I pulled out my ID and gladly presented it to the cashier. I eyeballed him carefully while he examined my license for a few seconds. After a while, his eyes slowly crept up to meet mine.

"Jack Delaney..." he mumbled with a low, dull surprise

"Do I know you?" I asked

The cashier that I now realized was around my age, lifted his newspaper back over his eyes before cracking it straight.

"Tom Mcgee Sr. is dead..." he said letting the word slowly roll off his tongue

"Yo- you're Tom Jr.?" I asked quietly

He snapped the newspaper straight even louder this time.

"Tell Jack Sr. I said hi..." he orated stoically

I left the liquor store and went back to my truck. I never went to Liquor Depot. I decided to drive back down to University and go to Jett Liquor. It was the unofficial liquor store of the college dorm rooms. I had bought beer at Jett countless times with my fake ID. They still ID'd me every time though. I grabbed two 40 oz. of St. Ides and placed them gingerly on the counter.

"Alright Thaddeus," the cashier said laughing, "You know the drill!"

I greeted his laugh with one of my own and placed my license on the counter. For a moment, he looked confused. He picked it up for a closer look. His confusion turned to annoyance as he held a flashlight under it to check the authenticity of the ID. I paid for the beer and left him with a sheepish grin.

Back at the campus apartments, I was all alone with my two 40s. This was the price you pay for playing hooky from work and college on your birthday. I opened the first malt liquor and took a healthy drink. It was 10:16 AM. Before finishing the rest, I turned the TV on and flipped through the channels. Dr. Phil reruns were the only thing on the television. I shrugged and took another prodigious sip. It was 10:20 AM. Dr. Phil was lambasting a couple for getting high and pushing their elderly grandmother down the apartment's trash chute. I finished my first beer. I fiercely drank the second. 80 oz. of malt liquor and some pseudo-psychology was enough to get me feeling jittery. "Drunk Jack" body-slammed "Pragmatic Jack" off the 8th floor of the dorm and took off down the hall with my truck keys. In my truck, I turned the ignition on and put the vehicle in drive. The dashboard clock read 10:29 AM.

I wasn't sure where I was going. At a pleasant cruising speed, I made my way towards the east side of town. My phone rang at a stoplight, and Daniel McGuire was on the other line. He and I used to cook at the Irish pub before they fired me to make room for the owner's son. At his behest, I was compelled to go to the pub for my 21st. He'd buy me a shot. This day is good for one thing every year…free liquor. I stopped at yet another liquor store along the way. I grabbed a tall can of Mike's Hard Lemonade and a plastic shot of something called "Snake Bite". I downed the snake bite first. It tasted terrible, but the Mike's washed that away. When I arrived at the Pub, I got two text messages. The first was from my mother, who was reminding me that we were eating dinner at my favorite restaurant with Dad later. The second was from Quinn, who was reminding me of the long night of drinking we had ahead. Quinn hadn't been to the bars yet because his birthday was four days before mine. He promised to wait.

At the Irish Pub, I walked in as if every patron would recognize me. Then again, I never worked on a Wednesday morning, so I was really just another idiot who had turned 21.

"Jackie!" Daniel yelled from the open-air kitchen, "What'll you have!"

I looked at the bartender. Her name was Wendy.

"I'll take a Smithwick's and a shot!" I yelled back to Dan

Dan looked at Wendy and nodded his head up.

"Hook 'em up with a Listerine shot." Dan laughed

Wendy laughed and shook her head.

"Sounds appetizing…" I mumbled sarcastically

Wendy put the shot and beer in front of me. The shot was as dark as my beer. I took the shot and almost threw up.

"Jesus Dan!" I yelled, "What the fuck is in that?!"

"One part Goldschlager, one part Jagermeister, two parts Orange juice." He laughed

"You sick fuck…" I said, wiping my mouth.

Before he could answer, I heard a voice yell over my shoulder.

"Wha cha fouking mouth ya cunt! I got me fuuucking wife 'e kids in 'yearrr!" the man said pointing to his pregnant wife who was drinking a glass of wine

I was drunk enough to fight, and I knew the establishment wouldn't call the cops, but the state of this guy was enough to turn even the most ravenous dog sick.

"Buffalo shot next!" Dan shouted as he tossed his towel over his shoulder

"No!" I said sternly, "I'm not fucking green Dan! You think I haven't been where you are a thousand times before and seen people take that nasty shit?"

"Fine..." Dan laughed, "Give him a... hmmm... oh yeah! Smoker's Cough shot! One part Everclear, and two parts warm mayonai-"

Voices soft... breathing decelerated... vision truncated...
Dark... dark... dark... dark conscious... dark....
Brain descending...
Everyone biting...
Dark...
Dark...
Dark...
Light...
Small light...
Smell ascending...
Vision returning...
Breathing accelerated...
Time moving...
Hell manifesting...

In a jolt, I shot up out of the driver's seat. The bell that indicated a door ajar began beeping frantically. My vision was receiving images two times slower than my head was moving to see them. The smell was putrid. There was vomit all over. Door ajar bell ringing frantically — chunks of vomit everywhere. Empty beer cans lined the interior of my truck. My phone was completely dead. How? It had a full charge when I got to the pub. I turned the key that was still lodged in the ignition. My truck's battery was dead. I looked up and saw Thirsty's Bar and Grill. I hadn't been here since Halloween when I was 6. It was the last Halloween my parents were together. How did I make it here? I don't remember driving. I blacked

out. The thought was too frightening... even for
myself. I turned away from the light and plunged
myself into a world of ignorance. I never left the
bar.

The time was 5:01 PM. It was well over an
hour after I was supposed to meet my family for
dinner. I ran around frantically in search of a phone
to call them. Thirsty's had a man at the door that
wouldn't let me in. The vomit all over my shirt did
not help in the least bit. I ran after three different
people who all ran away at the sight of me as if I
were a rabid coyote at their heels. Finally, one man
lent me his phone to use. My Father would be
furious. He drives two hours to see me, and I was
nowhere to be seen. The dial tone drilled in my ear.
On top of that, they had no way of reaching me and
probably thought I was decapitated in my truck after
a drunk driving accident. The phone line trilled
once more. Fuck. Dad answered.

"This is Jack." a calm voice announced
"Hey Dad..." I said meekly
"Happy Birthday Jackie!" Dad cheered
"Dad? Thanks? Sorry about-" I began
"Your mom is pissed, but I figured you were
out having a blast and lost track of time." He
mentioned casually, "I was 21 once too..."
"Thanks Dad," I said, disappointed in
myself, "I'll make it up to you."
"Just have a good time." He insisted once
more, "And call your mother when you can."

I hung up the phone and handed it back to
the man. If my Father knew what I was really doing
that conversation would not have gone down so
easily. I ripped off what remained of my vomit
soaked shirt and threw it in the bushes. I buckled
my jeans and walked into the Tex-Mex taco stand

next door. While staggering, I ordered a 1-pound burrito and one of their Large Shirts to wear. The white shirt had the establishment's mascot on it. Their mascot was a nearly anthropomorphized chicken smiling with a toothpick and a silver front tooth. The time was 5:06 PM.

Still reeling from the day, my mind reminded me how much it is at war with itself. I feel as though it plays tricks on me. My conscious is continuously at ends with itself. Sitting on the curb outside Thirsty's, I take a minute to rub my temples and watch the people coming and going. The Spiritus Mundi of which I am wholly apart of now. As I wait for Quinn to pick me up, my eyes rest on the incoming sunset while the blood moon rises higher and manifests itself into a light crimson.

Quinn pulls up about ten minutes after I finished eating at the Tex-Mex restaurant. He smiles through the driver's side window and pounds the side of his truck.

"What the fuck happened to your truck? And are you wearing a Buoy's shirt?!" Quinn asks laughing, "Happy 21st by the way."

"Long story," I said, rubbing my eyes and opening a beer on the floor, "Happy birthday to you too."

Quinn drives off toward University. I was there no more than 8 hours ago. Usually, I might call it a night, but I'm still a little drunk from the day, and my hangover hasn't kicked in yet. Plus, something in me is changing. The desire to go fuck myself up all over again is ever-growing. My tolerance is nonpareil as alcohol is a hot blade that I have tempered. I owe it to Quinn to have a night out anyway. I catch him up on my day, and he laughs the whole time. I knew he wouldn't judge me. We've always been the same.

Quinn arrives at a spot called The Buffet. It's the oldest bar in our town and my Old Man's favorite. He used to distribute beer here every weekend. Even though it was his smallest location to deliver to, it bought the most kegs. The most massive bar he distributed to would buy 35 kegs of Coors; the buffet would order 73. The bar could hold no more than 50 people, but they sold pints for 2 dollars a pop and mixed drinks for 3 dollars. They were open from 6 AM to 2 AM and had an eclectic group of frat boys and homeless men and women waiting outside each morning by 5:45 AM. Needless to say, it was our town's premier dive bar.

Inside, Quinn and I ordered two pints and a shot each. There are two plaques above the bar. The first, and most prominent, reads 'To Teddy Behr. Thanks for all your service.'. The second, just below it, reads 'To Jack Delaney. The man who made it all possible.'

Peggy, the 90-year-old owner, recognized me right away.

"Jackie?!" she squealed

"Jesus… I can't believe you recognize me." I said

Quinn stared in amazement.

"I can't believe I'm still alive to see you drink here." She laughed, "All drinks for you are on the house tonight."

Quinn nearly did a backflip off of his bar stool.

"How's your Dad?"

"Good." I said in a blasé tone, "Ya know, surviving…"

I shot the shit with Peggy for another minute or two before Quinn ordered a few shots for our birthdays. He asked the waitress what was good. She gave him something called Gorilla Puke. The Native American man at the end of the bar was reading the newspaper at seven o'clock at night while drinking a pint of Coors filled with ice and shaking his head at both of us. It was an ounce and a half of Bacardi 151 and an ounce and a half of Wild Turkey. Overserving was clearly not an issue here. She gave me a Three Wise Men shot. It was an ounce of Jack Daniels, an ounce of Johnny Walker and an ounce of Yukon Jack. Quinn looked at me with momentary dismay before we said "*Sláinte*" and drank them both whole. As the shot poured down my throat, I wondered how many times I would puke tonight.

After a gummy bear shot to settle our stomachs, Quinn and I settled at O'Reilly's next door. The bar was outside in the open air, so it was usually a popular spot. However, tonight, O'Reilly's was desolate. I expected nothing less during the middle of a midterm week, but it still threw me off guard. I ordered a Bloody Mary and Quinn ordered a Whiskey and Coke. I stared at Quinn while he went off on a tangent about his most recent triste. I ate the olive and celery from my Bloody Mary and nodded in agreement with everything he said. The bartender approached us with two shot glasses.

"We didn't order those," Quinn said before she could get a word out

I slap Quinn's arm with the back of my hand and give him a lazy look of disbelief.

"But we'll take 'em." I implored

"Actually, they're on me!" The waitress said smoothly

All of a sudden, I could feel her foot feeling up and down my leg from the opening in the bar. She made her way up and down my pant leg, and I stared back with a coyly raised eyebrow.

"Happy Birthday boys…" she said as she walked away

"Jesus Christ… She know your Dad too?" Quinn drawled as he clinked his glass against mine

"No." I said, lifting my glass up to meet his "But if she's lucky, she can know me."

Quinn and I howled like wolves in unison at the sky before inhaling the shots. I turned the shot glass upside down and pounded over and over again on the bar.

"Fuck me! Are you trying to poison us?!" Quinn wheezed

The bartender just laughed. I drank the rest of my Bloody Mary in one gulp.

"One more of those!" I yelled from across the bar

The bartender was quick with our order. She brought our check too, and I paid it while leaving my number under the signature line.

Quinn and I took the shots. I slid the shot glass towards the end of the bar. I felt saliva building in my mouth. Within an instant, my eyes shot open like that of an owl's. My cheeks puffed out. God damnit…

"You okay?" Quinn asked quickly

I shook and jerked my head suddenly to indicate that I was not. Quinn wasn't catching on. I dashed through the door, and, as soon as I was out, I opened my mouth. Vomit came out immediately. It wasn't projectile. I had saved myself the embarrassment of puking on the bar. I didn't even think it was possible. I laughed manically, and Quinn joined in while he attempted to throw his arm over my shoulder. We stood there for a second.

"Should w-"

"To Dirtbags!" I interrupted

A smile grew on Quinn's face.

"That's what I'm talking about." He answered

Dirtbags was our last stop of the night. Dad used to distribute here too, but I doubt anyone Dad knew was still here. It was more of a fraternity bar, but when the frat boys weren't there, it was a pretty cool spot. Of course, there were only two people inside of the bar; a female bartender who looked younger than us and a toothless man drinking a beer while thumbing a rosary.

"What can I get you gentlemen?" the bartender asked politely

"We're trying to get as fucked up as possible before 2 AM!" Quinn yelled in excitement

"I think I have just the thing…" she answered deviously

She walked off toward the bathroom.

"Not exactly what we had in mind…" I said in a bemused tone

Quinn and I scratched our heads before looking at one another and shrugging. I walked over to the jukebox and played "Mother" by Danzig. I began playing the air guitar before I was interrupted by the clacking of heels on pavement. The waitress came back out in a candy striper negligée. At the sight of this, I slowly dropped my invisible guitar in disbelief.

"How about a flight of shots?!" the bartender said in a licentious tone

"They make you wear that to serve a flight of shots..." Quinn asked in disbelief

"No." She answered casually, "But guys do tip better."

"That can't be up to code!" the toothless man yelled

He was ogling the bartender and becoming visibly aroused. He made absolutely no effort to conceal his erection.

"Great..." Quinn said while his eyelids sank

"Don't worry about Cheetah." The bartender said, "He's harmless."

"Cheetah?!" I asked before bursting into tears laughing

"So, I can only give you guys two shots at a time, but I have it down to a science... or art... one of those!"

The candy striper bartender began mixing the liquor and handed us both two shots. The first was just completely black. I smelled it and winced. Quinn and I briefly made eye contact before downing it.

"That was the Black Death!" she said excitedly "Two ounces vodka and one-ounce soy sauce!"

"Jesus!" I yelped while sticking my tongue out, "No wonder Cheetah is so hard over there!"

"Next one!" she chirped while handing us a clear glass with a brown tint

We downed it.

"That's my personal favorite," she said while stroking the striped material of her lingerie, "It's a Candy Cane. One part peppermint schnapps, one part cinnamon schnapps, and a dash of chocolate syrup."

She waited with bated breath for our verdict. My eye twitched a little as I was reminded of the Listerine shot from earlier. I struggled to hold back my vomit for the third time. Within seconds, I could hear Quinn utter:

"*I hate peppermint...*"

I looked at Quinn as he turned green. He and I both wasted no time shooting up from our seat and running to the enormous trash bin just outside the front door. In unison, both of us were evacuating the schnapps from our stomach, perfectly into the container. We wiped our mouths before giving one another a tired glance and sitting back down at the bar.

"This one is liquid steak!" the bartender yipped with glee

We didn't ask what was in it. We both took it.

"Tastes like the first one!" Quinn gagged

"Two ounces 151 Rum and two ounces Worcestershire sauce!" she said nodding

"This one is called Cement Mixer!"

Once again, we took the shot.

"One part Irish Crème, one part lime juice, one part tequila!"

The room was spinning. Quinn held onto the bar with both hands.

"Last one!" she said

"Thank God..." Quinn slurred

"Infected Whitehead! One part-"

I held my hand in front of her face to interrupt her.

"Lady," I began, "We've come this far..."

We threw back our shots and Quinn paid the waitress. I left her a twenty for having to deal with 'Cheetah' and make that nasty shit. She gave Quinn and I a pitcher of Guinness on the house for our birthday and to thank us for the generous tip.

"Fuck!" Quinn drunkenly exclaimed, "It's already midnight."

"I don't really want to stick around here, but I don't really want to bar hop either," I said

"You know," the bartender said while stuffing the twenty into her bra "There is a place that is pretty exciting around here even during midterms. The owner doesn't give a fuck about anything! Of course…"

She leaned in close as if she wanted the information clandestine. There was no one there other than Cheetah. I don't think she was playing with a full deck…

"…you guys would have to be pretty open-minded in this place."

"What? Is it like a gay joint or something?" Quinn asked

"No. Not at all." She retorted

I rubbed my eyes for a moment.

"Bartender" I began, "we just took a flight of six shots that I'm certain are not street legal or at the very least break some health code. How open-minded do you want us to be?"

"Alright," she said with a certain allure "The place is called 'The Meat Rack'…"

"I thought you said it wasn't a gay bar…" I chided

"It's not!" she took a moment to adjust her candy striper outfit before continuing the proposition "It's two blocks east. If you aren't too drunk, you can get there in a couple of minutes."

Quinn and I wasted no time finishing our pitcher. Before leaving through the front door, I heard the voice of Cheetah shout behind us:

"You only have one life! Don't waste it!"

Quinn and I stopped at the convenient mart next door to Dirtbags. The bars were closing in less than two hours, and we were only half in the bag. We grabbed two Four Lokos in the beer aisle and proceeded to poke holes in the can after paying for them. Outside, we kept the flavored malt liquor steady with our index finger under the tab.

"I hear they're banning these things," Quinn remarked, "People have been dying from the caffeine or some shit."

"Hmmm," I grunted in reply

Without another word, we both popped the tab and shotgunned all 24 ounces. I was the first done, but Quinn was close behind.

"That's nothing," I slurred a little as we threw our empty cans to the side and began to walk

"Huh?" Quinn responded absently

"Remember, in Mexico last year? I did the six beer beer-bong. And two shots of tequila on top!"

"What'd'ya want? To measure dicks the whole way to the Meat Rack?"

"Sure," I teased "I'd win that too…"

"I remember you passing out in the middle of the day while we pushed your truck out of that sand trap…"

"Fuck you," I laughed

After a few minutes, we finally arrived at The Meat Rack. The small shack was painted yellow and red with a cheeseburger cartoon in front of it. The only light outside was like that of a heat lamp that keeps fries warm in a restaurant. There was only one car; it looked like a foreign electric car. It too was all yellow with a pink stripe down the middle and a face on top of that. The face was of a bald man with a goatee mustache. The mustache twirled off in six directions on each side of his face. Quinn and I gave one another a confused glance before heading through the front door. There was no one inside.

"That bitch fuckin' lied," Quinn commented

"Hello?" I yelled

In a truly horrific manner, a pair of eyes were instantly opening from behind the bar. Like a leopard's glare in the tenebrosity of night, these eyes had no face. The eyes said nothing. The head that they belonged to was barely visible and swayed eerily in and out of sight. Quinn and I gave each other another, more serious, glance. The walls of the antechamber to the bar were covered in a mural of photos. Above the bar, there was a sign that read "Beach Bar". The entire ceiling was adorned with bras of all sizes. The eyes still stared at us. They never blinked.

"I think we made a mistake," Quinn whispered

"Hey," I said, my tone implying that I was confused "You guys still serving?"

The eyes examined me for a moment. Silent. Finally, as if from a nightmare, a happy face revealed itself from the other side of the counter.

"Hell yeah brother!" the man gushed. "What can I get you boys?"

The man slid down a menu. At least, I think it was a menu. It looked like a bunch of laminated notecards bound together with string. Page after page labeled cocktails ranging from 'Turbo Slut's Revenge' to 'Anita Dickinme'. The last two pages only had a few words on each side. The second to last page read:

Beer:

PBR

The last read:

Food:

Cheeseburger

"You guys must get a lot of aristocrat types in here, huh?" I laughed

"That's a good one friend!" The man said pointing, "I'll have to tell Prophet that one."

"We'll take one Irish Bullfighter," Quinn interjected

"You sure you don't want a Clitty Litter?!" the bartender asked "It has Amaretto, Gin, Vodka, Eagle Juice, Cherry Brandy, Milk, and-"

"No!" I yelled at first before calming down, "No. Just the bullfighter please…"

Quinn and I took a minute to look over the place. It was a dive bar to be sure. There was a gong hanging above the bar and just above that was the largest brassiere I had ever seen. I couldn't imagine the chest of the woman that wore it.

"Here ya go!" the bartender blurted, placing a pitcher of green sludge in front of Quinn and me on a coaster made from the cover of an AA pamphlet

"What the hell is that…" Quinn asked in disbelief

"The Irish-"

"No." I laughed, shaking my head in my hands, "Why is it in one pitcher with ten straws?"

The bartender contemplated the question for far too long before shrugging.

"Welp! My shift is over. That'll be eleven dollars."

"It's 12:45. Aren't you going to close?" Quinn countered

"Oh no!" the bartender laughed. "Jim will be closing. You'll love him."

"I doubt it..." Quinn said, handing him a twenty

"Fuck it..." I remarked before sipping one of the straws

I immediately twitched.

"Christ! There must be at least ten shots in there!"

Quinn sipped it immediately after me and winced.

"Close. It's only eight." The bartender said handing Quinn his change

"Aren't you worried about overserving?" Quinn asked, "I guess we should be good until 2 AM..."

"2 AM? Overserving?!" the man said, shocked for the first time before putting a fake smile on once more. "Oh, boys...I just knew you were new here..."

The bartender left through the front door. Within a few minutes, the same bartender walked through again. He wore a backward hat and glasses. His face seemed longer, and he had a scowl. He stared both of us down the entire way to bar. Placing both hands on the counter, he leaned in close to us.

"Well, you already got your fuckin' drink," the bartender snapped "You want some fuckin' food or what?"

"I'm scared..." Quinn remarked

"Two Cheeseburg-"

"Oh yeah!" the bartender said, throwing both hands up in the air "Two fucking cheeseburgers for these cunts right here! Coming right up! FUCK!"

"Are we on Candid Camera?" I said, feeling drunker by the moment

"Are we alive?" Quinn countered

In an instant, lights went on behind us. Quinn and I turned in distress to see that there was a full kitchen.

"What the- was that here before?!" Quinn shouted while rubbing his eyes

"Play that Funky Music White Boy" began to play as a manifestation of the drawing of the man from the car outside came out from behind the open-aired kitchen. Robed with a cook's apron and an enormous goatee twirling on both sides, the man twirled a spatula in each hand as the fire from the grill rose to the roof.

"Welcome…to the Meat Rack!" the bald man bellowed

Quinn and I looked at one another for what seemed like an eternity. Our feelings of malaise finally subsided and transformed into a drunken stupor. In an instant, we were hysterical and laughing all over the bar.

As the bald man grilled behind the bar, two girls in short dresses walked through the front door.

"Finally…" Quinn yelled

They weren't alone. Following them were two elderly people. All four of them sat at the opposite end of the bar facing us. This night just kept getting better.

"What can I get you Methuselah?" the bartender said, deriding the elderly couple

Taken aback, the elderly woman put her hands up. The bartender flipped off the elderly couple before switching his hand around and making a cunnilingus remark to the two girls with his tongue and fingers in the shape of a "V". He

backed off as a bell dinged in the kitchen. The
bartender brought us our food. We had finished our
cocktail pitcher, and it was 1:07 AM.

"How's the food?" the bartender questioned

"I could use some mayo…" Quinn blurted

The bartender reached behind the bar and
threw three mayo packets at Quinn. They hit him
directly in the face.

"Another pitcher?" the bartender said, staring
us down

"Just PBR for now…" I laughed

"Whatever butt boys…" the bartender
scoffed

"Yo, are we gonna fuck this guy up or
what?" Quinn said laughing into his hand

I laughed lightly and stared in disbelief.

"I'm wired man," was all I could manage

The bartender went back to the elderly
couple with the two girls. He had his arms crossed.

"It's after midnight! It's officially my 21st
birthday!" the girl finally squealed

"Good for fuckin' you," the bartender said,
grabbing a huge piece of butcher paper from
underneath the bar "Is it your kink to fuck old
people or something?"

The girl laughed a little nervously.

"Excuse me! This is our granddaughter! She
brought us to this God-forsaken place because it
may well be our last year in this world. How does
that make you feel now you…nasty man!"

The bartender did not acknowledge the
elderly couple. Instead, he kept writing on the
butcher paper with a felt pen. Finally, he fashioned
the paper into a hat and placed it on the girl's head
like a crown. I could barely make it out, but it read
something like:

"It's my 21st birthday! It's also the 21st time I've gotten fucked tonight."

He fashioned one for the other girl as well. He must have been running out of inspiration because it only read:

"Cum Slut"

"This is bedlam…" I whispered to Quinn, who was laughing uncontrollably

"That's it!" the elderly woman screamed, "I know my granddaughter said this place was lewd, but this is too far. I want to speak to your manager!"

The bartender leaned on the bar with his forearm looking at them. A genuine smile was painted across his face for the first time all night. The older woman attempted to lean in closer with a glowering look. Quinn and I, with our arms crossed and eyes wide open, leaned in closer as well.

"You wanna see the manager?" the bartender said, never losing his smile "You got it…"

Quinn and I each raised a single eyebrow in shock before looking back to the bald man in the kitchen. The bald man had no expression on his face. He had his arms crossed and was leaning on the wall of the kitchen staring at them. Quinn and I jerked our heads back to the bartender. He was pressing a button underneath the counter. In an instance, a school bell rang throughout the entire bar and the circus music "Thunder and Blazes" played as loudly as the speakers in that shanty could handle. Confusion sprung eternal for all but two in the bar as we searched far and wide for the manager. Finally, a door busted wide open near the entrance. As I adjusted my eyes, I recognized a midget, on a unicycle, dressed and painted as a clown, with a metal clown horn in each hand. As the clown approached the patrons on his unicycle, he began honking each horn. He stared directly at the elderly couple and began chanting:

"*Faggots! Faggots! Faggots!*"

He synchronized each horn honk with each utterance of the word "Faggots".

If Quinn and I's jaws could become unhinged and hit the floor, they would. Normally, people might say "I feel like I'm on Acid!" but all I could say was:

"*I need a shot of Thorazine...*"

The elderly couple left shortly after the clown wheeled himself back into his room. Quinn and I shot up at the feeling of thunderous hands falling onto each of our shoulders. We looked back to see the portly bald cook staring back at us with an enormous grin.

"We use that for uh... profilin' purposes," The bald man laughed "You boys haven't shot your load yet, have you? It's only 1:39 and we got plenty of party left."

Quinn and I had half a drunken smile on while nodding our heads.

"C'mon," the man waved "I'll give you the rarest of things; a tour of my palace. I'm Prophet by the way. That bartender over there is Mark...or Steve...I guess it all depends on how he's feeling."

"Your name is Prophet?" Quinn snickered

"Got it legally changed," he said as we walked to the antechamber entrance, "you probably know me as James Andy though!"

He smiled at Quinn and I waiting for a response. Quinn and I shook our heads. He was a squat man. Beefy and short. I was six foot three, and I always thought Quinn was short at five foot nine, but Quinn even towered over this guy.

"Well, you guys were probably too young. I ran for Mayor in this town years ago. I was gonna get the city to pass a bill to have no overserving and go lenient on the drinking age. I also wanted bars open 24 hours."

"I don't think Mayors can-" I began

"Influence!" he interrupted, "Influence is everything."

With that, he began showing us the place. He pointed to the mural of pictures that littered his antechamber. He showed pictures of him with other famous and influential people. One picture was of him and Arnold Schwarzenegger and a cocktail waitress. He had his arm around the waitress, and Arnold was openly fingering her. I would have thought it was a fake, but the picture was a polaroid. He showed us pictures of him with Jimmy Carter and Sean Hannity. There was a picture with Barney Frank and him shotgunning a beer. One showed him and James Caan painting dicks on Robert Redford's face. He had a picture of a girl blowing him. He swears it was Sarah Palin, but you really couldn't tell.

The next room took the cake. It was his "Pleasure Room". It's one of those places you feel immediately dirty in as soon as you step through the door. In the corner, there was a cage with an enormous blow-up doll squatting down to the floor of the cage. Several photos on the wall showed women spreading their sphincters. One had Rosie O'Donnell's face pasted on it. There were sex belts and love swings galore, but the one device that admittedly stood out was the piece of plywood, shaped like an elephant, with a vibrating dildo on it. He called it the "Aunt Eater". Before leaving the room, I noticed a picture of a woman tied up and naked that read 'Prophet Made Me Do It'.

We finally moved to the main area as Prophet walked us over to a wall. The wall was solid oak and had a caricature of his side profile carved into it. The bartender, clearly not faking his ailment, was heating a poker in the kitchen.

"What's with the poker?" Quinn asked

"It isn't a poker! It's a brand! You get my face branded on you, and you'll get twenty percent off your drinks for life!"

Prophet outstretched his arm and displayed the wall with several different badges on it.

"This is my wall of shame," he began "Each height has a different chip from an AA member. You turn in your chip…you get a drink. If you're sober one day, you get a shot. If you're sober a week, a shot and a beer. If'n you're sober a year, you drink all night for free."

Quinn and I were perplexed on how to respond. Instead, we both finished our beers, opened a new one, and settled for saying:

"*Damn…*"

Prophet moved to the bathrooms. The men's bathroom was nothing special, but he snickered the whole way to the woman's bathroom. The bartender moved to the gong hanging above the bar.

"Check this out," he said, shutting the door to the women's room behind us "It's completely soundproof."

And with that, he opened the door to the bathroom. In an instant, the ear-piercing scream of the bartender rang through our skulls. He shut it and opened it over and over again. I thought the poor bastard at the bar was going to have an aneurism.

Quinn and I stared blankly at the man. He left the door open this time.

"That's not the best part!" he said, pulling two quarters out of his pocket and placing them in the condom machine "When a girl is frisky and needs some protection, this is what happens."

He turned the vending machine, and a red alarm went off just over the women's bathroom. He stepped out of the bathroom, and the bartender hit the gong while "Cherry Pie" played in the background.

"Well," he laughed to himself, "You guys have been good sports. Here's a little souvenir."

He handed us each a yellow keychain with a caricature of his on it that read 'I'll ruin your life. Signed, Prophet'

"I'd show you boys my room with the mirror on the ceiling, but it's time for business."

I checked the clock. It was 1:59 AM.

"Shit," I said, weighing my beer, "I guess we should finish these."

"Hell yeah!" he bellowed "And get another one! The night is young!"

"But-but it's 2 AM..." Quinn scratched his head

He was halfway to the bar before a swarm of people, young and middle-aged alike, rushed in through the entrance. He looked back at us with a confident look before uttering lightly:

"Blood Moon Mother Fucker..."

The night... or early morning rather, was a blur. Patrons charged through the entrance after 2 AM like a starving stampede. We took drinks outside. We did keg stands inside. We smoked cigarettes wherever the fuck we pleased. I had had more alcohol in 24 hours than I had ever had in 72 hours up until that point. The girl, whose 21st birthday it was, snuck back in around 3:47 AM. She and her friend blew the bartender in front of everyone while he yelled invectives at them and doused them with liquor. Music blared through the bar speakers as if we were at a concert. Life was spinning out of control. The crowd, clearly drunk for hours, had begun their own chant; a mantra to invoke the anti-muse. Quinn and I snorted a line of cocaine off of the bar top before falling over on to the girl riding the Aunt Eater. One guy finally took a triple shot before getting branded on the arm. Prophet did the honors before tempering the iron in a pitcher of cocktails and drinking the whole thing in one gulp. It's a fucking white-trash bash. The clown midget rolled through the bar over and over again. He had a 40 ounce of malt liquor taped to each hand and hopped over people passed out on the floor. Quinn finally jumped the bar and hung on the ZZZ sized bra before falling on top of the bartender. I ripped one of the half-full malt liquors from the midget's hand before yelling:

"Anyone who can drink more than me is a fucking alcoholic... and anyone who can't drink as much as me is a fucking pussy!"

Quinn and I finally stumbled outside at 5:27 AM but we were too pissed to call a cab or drive home. We just walked. We walked about ten yards before running into a man. He said nothing. He handed me a book. It was the same book the bartender placed our cocktail pitcher on in the bar. I eyed it before giving it to Quinn and looking back at the man.

"Imagine what you could do with all the extra time and money you would have," the man said in a lighthearted tone, "The wage of sin is death…"

We stood staring at him for a moment. We were undoubtedly shitfaced and haggard.

"Usually," I slurred "When I have extra money, and free time, I get a case of beer and go out drinking."

Quinn guffawed. The man jerked his head slightly to the side before walking off.

"Your life of flagellation will not end in remuneration!" I shouted

Quinn and I went in the opposite direction. As we stammered away, I could hear the man chant familiar words:

"We grow accustomed to the Dark —
When light is put away —"

The morning sun was rising. It was my last memory before waking up the next morning behind a gas station three blocks away from The Meat Rack. Quinn and I were sleeping five feet away. I peaked at the sun and figured it was around 9:30 AM. I wasn't hungover yet. I lit one of my cigarettes. I puffed for a while before shaking Quinn awake. Quinn shot up and looked at me while struggling to keep his eyes open. I smoked my cigarette once more before flicking it to the curb and gruffly saying:

"Party's Over…"

Chapter 17

The afterlife is really nothing more than man's desires and demands. We demand every base desire on earth and, regardless of our wasted time, we always get what we want. I know I'm not one to talk, but the thought alone turns my stomach sour with a vitriolic rage. They used to tell us in Sunday School that life after death will 'hone our moral consciousness' and bring us closer to God. The only thing this place has done is hone my misanthropy.

Staring down the trafficked hallway, I begin dreading every memory that approaches. My mind coils with each passing second, and all I can think is:

"I'm too young for this shit..."

As my present conscious returns to me, I begin to walk door to door. Looking for any signs of fulfillment, my eyes lock onto a door that has souls leaving it by the boatload. Each person going back through the hallway has a scowl on their face a mile long. With a shrug, I open the door. The first thing that hits me is the smell. It's almost like deodorant mixed with a new car air freshener and sweat. I grimace before searching for one of the Shannons. Plugging my nose, I move across the antechamber and into a clamorous uproar. The noise is like a swarm of cicadas moving in and out of my head. In an attempt to stifle the cacophony, I run my fingers from my nostril orifices to my ears. Before long, I recognize the origin of the blustering noise; humans arguing. I shift back on my left foot and crash into the receptionist's desk for this room.

"Welcome, welcome, welcome!" a voice from beneath the desk begins to shout

I back up again as the people arguing grows more bearable.

"Yes, sir!" the voice roared louder "Step right up and join us in the greatest eternity known to man! Look no further than the resting places of those sowers of discord! God have mercy! We may have a live one here!"

I finally put a face to the voice as one of the several Shannons appeared from behind the desk with a fake mustache and a carnival barker's outfit on. Equipped with a cane and loudspeaker, Shannon bellowed her cheer while the attendants of the antechamber began to yell back and forth at one another again. I simply stared at whichever number Shannon she was until she spoke once more.

"Now I know what you're thinking!" she spat "You're thinking: *Boy! These are some really annoying twats!*"

She leaned in close to me and raised an eyebrow while I hung on to her level of energy with a crooked and confused grin.

"Well, Mr. Delaney, there are more than just politicians here!"

She was undoubtedly the most vociferous of the Shannons.

"This afterlife harbors the best of the rhetoricians!" she paused for a moment and picked her front tooth with her fingernail "Okay... maybe not the best. But God Damn! If you like arguing, this is the spot for you!"

"Why would anyon-"

"You sure ask that question a lot!" she heckled, "Too coarse for Heaven! Too pestiferous for Hell! The only place that will harbor the atheists, congressman, pastors, celebrities, scientists, and aaaaalllllll the philosophers you can find is right here in Magniloquence Manor!"

Each second she spent orating was another second my ears blistered from the onslaught of nonsense the dead were yelling at one another. I glanced around and stared at each person in their hooded, white robes. They were almost robotic. They never stopped. While one yelled at another's face, the other yelled at their neighbor. It was a bucket brigade of bedlam and madness. I guess people will spend an eternity trying to prove they are right.

I began to slowly back up out of the door. I gave a pity wave goodbye to Shannon before turning around into the antechamber.

"You'll be back!" she wailed

I looked her way once more and met her eyes.

"Prove me wrong…" she laughed.

Chapter 18

This is the memory I dreaded. A remembrance polarized by calamity and delight. Yet, in death, I cannot help but reflect on this moment.

In January 2011, my uncle and cousin came to town to stay with my mom. I was beyond ecstatic. My cousin was always like a big brother to me. I never had a big brother, so having him around filled that void. Thankfully, now that I was 21, I could go out with him. He was twenty-seven, but, despite our age difference, we were very close. I raced to the East Side of town around 7:30 at night. It gets dark early there. I still had my 1985 Bronco, and the top was off. On the older Bronco models, you could literally take the top off so everything from the backseat to the bed of the truck was exposed. It was stupid, but it did turn heads riding down the street. Of course, once it rains, you're shit out of luck.

At Mom's house, Uncle Chase was already sitting in the kitchen drinking a Wild Turkey on ice. Uncle Chase was the Sr and Chase Jr we just called Bubba. My cousin Bubba was tall and bulky, with a fair amount of muscle on him. His face was filled with freckles, and he always wore a backward snapback hat. Bubba was hanging around the kitchen close to my Uncle Chase, and my mom was catching up with them while asking how the weather was in California. I walked in and greeted everyone with open arms. Uncle Chase was stoic, as usual, and didn't talk much but asked how everything was going. I nodded my way through the entire minutia ad nauseam. Gave them all the rundown; College, no girlfriend, working at the pub still, etc. Eventually, Bubba and I were off. I told him that we would hit University and see if there were any parties afterward.

I took Bubba to where all the College students hung out. Obviously, we started at The Buffet. From there, we went to O'Malley's and Maloney's and The Shanty and Whispering Wick's White Tavern. We were only out for about three hours before we decided to pack it in and head home. Our conversations weren't too engaging. I didn't expect much of course; we were both out drinking and hadn't seen one another in a year. What are you really supposed to talk about?

Bubba asked if I wouldn't mind stopping at the Taco Bell across the way before we went home. I obliged him, and we sat in our car for around ten minutes talking while he ate. I turned the engine off. I'll never forget just how much I enjoyed this moment. The way Bubba turned his head to eat the taco and the laugh he made while I told him another dirty joke. It seems like bullshit now, but this memory sticks with me vividly to this day.

As we pulled out onto the nearest cross streets, I idled my truck at the red light while a cop pulled up going the opposite direction. Normally, I wouldn't care. Yeah, you're a cop, the big dick in town, we all bow before you. However, instead of just making his right turn, he simply sat there. He waited. He could go. But he just…waited.

Once the light was green, I went off past the cop and headed home. It wasn't five seconds later that the police car was pulling me over. Quick! What's the protocol here?!

- Pour out any remaining beer on the floor
- Get as many sticks of gum as possible and chew them….I think a penny works too…

- Look at yourself in the rearview mirror
- Size up the cop as he gets out of his car in your side view mirror
- Roll down the window
- Look at yourself once more in the rearview mirror
- Breathe…

"How's it going?" the cop says shining a light in my face

I'm fine. I honestly haven't had that much to drink.

"Well, officer. How can I help you?"

"I noticed your front lights were off."

For fuck's sake… my lights. I turned them off when we went to Taco Bell. For the uninitiated, having your lights off is an automatic pull over and check for a DUI. I have no clue why. I guess it's the last thing a drunk thinks about turning on. If I could have just gotten past those crossroads to the other side, I would have noticed how dark it was and turned the fuckers on.

"Oh…"

What else could I say?

"Have you been doing a little drinking tonight?"

And there it is. I was waiting for it. Well, not really. I was actually hoping it would go more like one of my other traffic stops. "Sure thing officer" "Thank you, officer" "Won't happen again, officer"

"Drinking, sir?"

What gave it away? The smell of Mickey's Malt Liquor retching up from the floor? The conspicuous amount of gum I had lodged in my mouth? The fact that it is January and I have the top of my Bronco off in 38-degree weather wearing nothing but a white t-shirt? Or was it maybe our all too chipper reaction to seeing a police officer this late at night?

"Yes. Drinking."

"No sir!"

"Why don't you step out the truck for me..."

I don't need to tell you the rest. If you've been pulled over for suspicion of DUI, you know the rest of the story. If you haven't, it isn't anything too special really. I passed my field sobriety test with flying colors, but the part that kills me was my BAC. Do you know what the legal limit is? Roughly four beers, which registers about a .08 BAC. Do you want to know what mine was? .09... .09! My buddies and I have a breathalyzer where, just for the hell of it, we measure our BAC on those real gladiator nights. The winner gets another beer. The loser also get another beer. You wanna know what my record is? .37!

I never saw my cousin again....

The DUI had marred me. I was forced to ride the bus to school each day, and afterward, I would go to the Quik Mart and pick up alcohol to drink the night away. I drank, and I drank. Most people would become sober after a DUI leaves you unable to go anywhere, but I drank the boredom away. I had to go to court-ordered AA meetings, but when the instructor told us we could save money by not drinking and asked me what I would do with the extra money, I only answered:

"I would buy more beer...."

On the night of Christ's birth, my routine had become volatile to my spiritual health. I was especially fucked up on that night. I could feel my body deteriorate day by day from the poisons that consumed me. An entire bottle of bourbon and a twelve-pack of beer was my only solace. My walk was becoming increasingly staggered as I stumbled drunk to the bathroom. With no money from the DUI to afford heat in my house, I watched as my own breath took physical form. Ominous, dark bags rested underneath my eyes as I stared at myself in the mirror. Moving sluggishly, I pressed my right hand on the mirror. I looked into my eyes intensely. I struggled to envision some sort of spiritual revelation, yet none came. As I stared, I waited for a response from my reflection. I stared once more at the bottle of liquor before speaking nonsense to my reflection drunkenly.

"One day...." I said as I struggled to speak to myself, "one day I will kill you. The world has hurt you, and the world will hurt you again. They wish to watch you suffer. Your death would be too final. I am your greatest enemy and your greatest friend. Your misery will end at my hands. You will die at my hands.....one day......one day soon my old friend."

I grabbed the bottle by the sink and clothed myself in the sweater that hung over the towel rack. I walked to my car and started the ignition. It was at this moment I knew I could never be saved. I lacked remorse, and redemption would fall through my hands like sand in an hourglass.

The sky's darkness engulfed the stars above so that no light was shown. I drove my car and went to the local church while grasping my bottle that left many dead memories floating among its abyss of liquefied amnesia. As I parked the car, I took one final drink from the bottle before resting it on the passenger's seat. The cross was lit brightly. Its illumination and radiant light flooded the parking lot. I, only able to open one eye, stared for a moment at the light before walking towards the entrance.

The journey seemed endless. The memorials of the dead, plastered all over the side of the church, spoke no words yet stared at me as I continued throughout the courtyard. The music stopped just as I arrived. I warmed my hands and blew one final cloud of breath before opening the two giant doors to the cathedral. Just as I opened the door, the familiar pitch of the organ played the start of *God Rest Ye Merry Gentleman,* and the congregation of the sermon stood at once. I stood by the only lonesome pillar that was not visible to the rest of the church. The hymn's transcendence sent chills down my spine. The entire church kneeled while I sat in the back, with my flask and a lit cigarette and listened to the harmony that would either save or kill me.

> *God rest ye merry gentleman*
> *Let nothing you dismay*
> *Remember, Christ, our Savior*
> *Was born on Christmas day*

I stared at the choir, all singing in perfect harmony. I remembered the church from when I was young. My eyes moved to the alter as I observed the sacraments being laid out.

> *To save us all from Satan's power*
> *When we were gone astray*

I solemnly crept my vision to the crucifix. The head of Christ was cast down. I rejoiced that Jesus could not stare at me at this moment.

"*I'm sorry*" I whispered to myself while fighting back a drunken tear

O tidings of comfort and joy
Comfort and joy
O tidings of comfort and joy

I took one last look at the church before leaving with a confusing tear in my eye. I wonder how long I'll have to sit in my backyard and drink and smoke alone.

Chapter 19

It was time at last. I had evaded this room long enough. I needed to see what was behind the door of the black room at the end of the hall. Its appearance was sinister yet inviting all at the same time; a juxtaposition of inclination and damnation. As of yet, no one has informed me of what lies beyond that door. As a matter of fact, I haven't seen anyone come out of it. There was that one guy who went in, but he never came out. People are continually coming and going through all of these doors, but only one man went in that door. The ebony handle and pitch-black hinges gave off a foreboding tenor of things to come. I stare once more at Hell's door and then at the Pitch-Black one at the end of the hall. What could be more ominous than Hell? Hell gives me a "Danger/Caution" feeling, and yet the black door gives me a different sense; fear. There is a distinction. One I can avoid. The other I cannot.

I stand up from my seat. I could just as quickly take ten steps to my left and ask Shannon about the door, but I decide against it. I just keep ambling down the hall to unearth the mysteries of the undesired and unwanted door. As I get closer, I notice a sign I hadn't seen before. It was just above the door and impossible to read from that far back. It simply reads *"Time Died Here"*.

I can taste my breath. The same taste as when adrenaline pumps through your veins, and you get a waft of it through your throat. I eye the doorknob and lock on to it. Souls push their way past me ten at a time. Some gasp and awe as I make my way deeper and deeper down the corridor. My eyes are fixed on the void of sable wood that is my destiny. I reach slowly to open the door. I take one final breath before opening it with my eyes closed.

Nothing. Quiet. Dark. I open my eyes and see three gentlemen standing in front of an empty receptionist's desk with their heads down. All three are wearing gray hooded robes in lieu of everyone else's white robes. I take a moment to look around the room before all three promptly look up at me without saying another word. Their faces are still dark enigmas that I cannot solve. Their hoods shade what visage they may have.

Only busts made of marble occupied the hollow space of the room. There was a painting on each side of the room as well. One was by the second door in the room and the other by the entrance. The first one, near the entrance I came through, was innocuous and even somewhat boring. A sailboat with a man, barely visible, floating in the ocean towards the shore that resembled a type of Monet oil painting. Though well done, the structure of the oil painting left something to be desired; it had a pleasant and calm feeling, and though it washed one with comfort, you knew it wasn't real. It lacked... pain.

The other horrified me. I stared at it acutely. Fear like I'd never felt crept all over my body. The terror had seized and paralyzed me, yet I needed to look more. It almost felt like my eyes were supernaturally glued to the painting, and yet I convinced myself this is where I wanted to stare. The depiction was realistic. The most realistic art I had ever seen. It was a woman with her back to me. I couldn't see her face. I could only see the shadow of her body on the wall, two feet in front of her. My breath stuttered as I searched every inch of her to find a clue about her, hoping that she would not frighten me further and turn around. Rationality was removed from my reasoning. This must be a dream. I could only see the creamy smooth skin of the back of her ear. Futility had finally crept over me as I felt that time truly had died in this place. I didn't want to see her face, but I had an overwhelming desideratum to find out what she looked like. I felt ready to lose my mind as the painting wouldn't move... it just wouldn't mov-

"Welcome," one man said grabbing my shoulder abruptly

The greeting jolted me back to consciousness.

"What is this place?" I stammered

"Frightening isn't it?" the man in the gray robe answered turning his head to the painting

"I can't keep my eyes off of it. I almost find myself becoming lost and terrified in the nothingness of the art. It's just a simple painting though…"

"Simple to most, yes. However, it represents something much more primal than that. It represents the unknown. It represents a skewed philosophy all men must either confront or avoid. What does her face look like? Why is the background so bleak? What century was this painted in?"

"Yeah" I lightly muttered with understanding

The other two robed men just stood near the reception desk. They did not lean casually, nor did they keep themselves busy. They just stood there, dutifully, with their hands crossed around the torso of their body. It was only then that I noticed a man in a gray robe lying down on an almost casket-looking couch. I stare for a second before seeing a quarter of some sort on each eye.

"What is this place?" I manage again

"It is a place of finality. It is a place for the truly enlightened. Yet, it is also a place of superficial and spurious horrors for the rest of mankind. It is, in short, a rest to the toils of life before and after. Some call it Hell, others call it Heaven, but most know it only as Oblivion."

"Nothing…"

"In a manner of speaking."

"Oblivion" I whisper once more almost tasting the words of death in my mouth "So, this ends it all. This cuts everything off immediately."

"Once you choose to step through our door here, you are abandoning all hope of any future in the afterlife. Your existence is only briefly remembered by those few on earth and then, eventually, no one. You cease to think, live, love, hate, and speak. You are as you were before you came into this world; nothing."

"You guys must be popular with the people around here…."

A little levity is always a good thing, but I can feel my whimsical nature and wit dissipate every moment I'm in here. I feel myself leaving a state of denial and sarcasm I had previously tried to hold on to this entire time. I suffer an old, intimate emotion of wonted somber. It falls over me and reminds me of just how bad I was before I started my story. But, it is only for an instant….

"Hell receives more participants than we do Mr. Delaney."

"I wonder why?" Sarcasm again "Why would anyone want to be here?!"

"The desire to die is man's first step in truly understanding."

"That…. sounds familiar…" I say pondering the statement

"One of our acolytes once wrote that in a journal on Earth. You see, mankind sees the inadequacies of life. He knows that he is nothing more than a mole; a being that is born complacent and dies in melancholy, all while trying to germinate life for future cycles to the same drudgery. It isn't death we should fear Jack but, rather, life. A life where our only purpose is to amass wealth on whatever ostentatious scale we see fit to justify living in a world that never wanted you there in the first place. We desire meaning and resist destruction, yet toil with the evils of the world. And what do we cling to? Why do we cling to it?"

"I-I don't know…" I say while vacillating my tone of voice

He laughs but only lightly and for a moment. He still has yet to smile.

"Well." He says as he stares me dead in the eyes, "You saw how many people charged on through the other afterlife doors. Quick to decision and careless with choice. The laws of man are dictated by religious values and men constantly shout '*Fight the System*!' and yet, when one acts on their rebellion, they are lambasted for it. That is the way of man. There are more things in Heaven and Earth, Jack, than are dreamt of in their philosophy."

"Yeah," I say as I take a minute to look out the transom at all the countless people running around

"This is what all of mankind has in common. No matter how different a person can be, we all experience a loss of innocence. Whether you

- 115 -

live in a comfortable home and never leave and never need to work for anything, or whether you are born into poverty and die of an illness before you are even a teenager, we all discover it. It is our one bond that we as humans share, yet we deny ourselves the privilege to connect with it. Time is the essence of Hell. What we once thought was horrible and unbearable at a younger age will eventually become acceptable to us."

I look into his eyes vacantly. I bite my lip and try to find something, anything, to say.

"Humans don't have much longer anyway." He rubs and scratches his face for a moment while looking at the wall behind me. "We reached the apex of our evolution some 50 years ago. It didn't happen overnight, but the decline has been perpetual. Throughout the years, parents have labored measurelessly to raise their children. And still, categorically, the end result has always been an acceptable product in the end, barring a few rotten eggs here or there. But now, as is human nature, people take a perfunctory approach to the nurturing process and their child's social well-being suffers. Humans are lazy, Jack. We always have been. Since man was first conceived, we have found ways to avoid tasks at an excelling rate. The only steadfast virtue humans had was caring for their offspring. And yet, inevitably, as we evolve, so does our idleness. Whether through excuses, or technological advancements used as babysitters, or even just plain apathy, parents have sent a generation of their brood into the world unable to care for themselves. Of course, there are always exceptions to the rule."

For the first time since meeting him, a genuine smile is painted across his face.

"The enlightened will examine their place in this world and note the unavoidable tragedy. The aforementioned group of 'people' will sicken them, but they know that their overpopulation is ineluctable. Then, they will say a phrase I'm certain you have heard before… '*I won't bring children into this world.*' And they will willingly sterilize themselves to end the line. Eventually, when the enlightened men and women have removed themselves from the population, those still paralyzed by ignorance will realize their ruination. Those poorly evolved remains of mankind will not persevere. Their greed, dishonesty, cruelty, self-obsession, close-mindedness, hypocrisy, manipulation, irresponsibility, materialism, impatience, immaturity, spite and ignorance will be too much for their forebearers and themselves. And when it is all too late, and we have halted and inversed our progress as mankind, they will look only at the monster they have contrived in themselves and sterilize their race through celibacy or suicide. And, rather than change their ways, these options will be their only ones because they can never evolve from their one true malcontent… idleness. Human history is stagnant and will soon come to an end. We are past the paramount of our evolution Jack; we are reaching the cornerstone of our dégringolade."

"You seem pretty sure of yourself. You must think you're right about everything…"

"Everyone thinks they are right!" the robed man howled fiercely, "That's why humans hate one another…they can never be wrong."

His words have, on some level, resonated with me. He's right. At least, I believe so. I just have a hard time agreeing with someone like this.

"Well, you said it yourself, this place gets fewer attendees than the others. It's not for me."

"No? Or are you afraid of the gravity of this possible choice? The afterlife can be summated in that picture you fear." He says, repositioning my gaze toward the painting "You can search eternally for the face, and yet you will never conjure it to move. So, will you quell your will to go on? Or will you live endlessly? Are you a mole, Jack? Or are you a panda?"

"I haven't once seen God while being here. Isn't he anywhere?"

"You needn't look too far." He began with a coy smile "But that is just it. Your God simply does not know how to find you. Your God is omnipotent; a fact proven by creating you. Your God is omnibenevolent; a fact proven by giving you a choice in the afterlife, regardless of your moral apathy. Your God, however, is not omniscient; a fact proven by staring into your eyes. Your God does not, in fact, love you."

I return a pragmatic glance to him and his friends.

"Why didn't you just shoo me away when I got here like Satan? I am one of those fucking people you're talking about!"

"You might be," said another faceless robed man, "but you made it this far."

"Jack," the lead robed man says, grabbing my arm "People are tortured here in the afterlife. You know this. You might have been a degenerate while on earth but you, like so few, saw the reality of it. You recognized that all those who go to Heaven, will eventually desire a taste of Hell and everything else in between. They are no different than people who are sexually orthodox but grow

tired of their unadorned fantasies before becoming
BDSM tolerant. The only difference is that those
who go to Heaven will never be able to act of their
impulses and desires for death! They fucking chose
based on a lie!"

As the robed man became increasingly
aggressive, I instinctively retorted.

"Your cynicism mocks your own
philosophy." I shake my head and stare
disapprovingly at the ground before speaking once
more "Your...your curtailed nihilistic belief is the
only reason people don't drudge through here."

"Cynicism?!" he scoffs in disbelief for what
I believe is the first time in centuries "You want the
truth? The truth of what all manner of men have
been seeking their entire lives. That four-letter word
people curse and cling to with no understanding
whatsoever while they allow it to control their lives
and simply call it 'fate'? The REASON you are
here, Mr. Delaney, is because your parents
copulated at just the right, or wrong, time. A week
before your conception, your father, reeling no
doubt from booze, crept away from the bed your
mother and him shared and sat on the toilet to
masturbate to a penthouse that was left lying
around. He could have just fucked your mother, but
she was on her period, and they were wary about
sex without any birth control. Frustrated sexually,
your father, with little regard for the bathroom floor,
ejaculated all over the toilet seat and tile. In an
effort to clean this up, he smeared his ejaculate all
over the tile where piss and dirt had been resting for
eternity. A week later, and that would have been
you there on your parent's floor of infinite filth. No
longer a twinkle in his eye, you and your unborn
brothers would have melded eternally into the abyss

of rancorous grime and soot without a thought in anyone's mind. And while you are the lucky one to survive such an internecine oblivion, you wallowed your days away at the bottom of a bottle with unsavory characters and reprobates alike. THAT is your GOD. That is your gift. Life. And while you mocked it, ridiculed it, and stuffed it neatly into a social commentary of pseudo-existentialism, you left behind a piece of reason that you should have observed all along. That YOU.....WERE....ALIVE... How is that for cynicism, Mr. Delaney?"

After his oration, I exhaled. I gave him a face that I only showed to people I was about to fight. I took one step back.

"I have to find my Dad."

"Of course." The robed man said with an almost mocking glance, "Bonne Chance..."

Chapter 20

Life in the Southwest was a real bitch. The one reprieve we always had was being two hours from Mexico. With the start of summer approaching, Quinn and I made plans to go to Puerto Peñasco. Unfortunately, we were never really great with plans… or timing for that matter. Anna was finally graduating high school, and Quinn promised his mom that he would be at the graduation party tomorrow morning.

"We could just go the next day," I tell Quinn as I light up a cigarette in the passenger seat

"I can't. I have work the next day," Quinn says, exhaling deeply through his nose "Fuck!"

"You know, we could probably pull it off…" I say, shrugging

Quinn laughs, and a smirk grows on his face that reveals his contemplation.

"Remember Vegas?" Quinn says, lighting his cigarette "We were drunk, at Kerry's pad, and just up and decided to drive to Vegas at 3 AM."

"Drank a case of beer on the way there too," I laughed "It's only a two and a half-hour drive to Mexico. What time does your mom want you there?"

"Nine," Quinn said indignantly

"God damn," I sigh, breathing out smoke, "Well, it's your call."

Quinn didn't contemplate long, and within the hour, we were on the road. The path to Mexico is a shrine to the Navajo people. Sand makes a seemingly infinite Ocean of heat and regret. The drive doesn't take long, but you almost always get lost in the vast emptiness of hills and lost dreams.

Before even getting to the border, there have always been a few, neighboring, Sonoran cities that make me laugh. *Why* is the best one. The town is actually called *Why*. It is, without a doubt, the most confusing town in the Southwest. Then there is *El Pozo de las Mujeres Muertas* which naturally translates to "The Well of Dead Women". Oh yeah! And, of course, my favorite is *Salsipuedes* which means "Leave if you can". The mind boggles to think of their origins…

About a quarter of a mile before the border, American Border Patrol officers slow us down. Quinn rolls down his window to talk to them.

"Officers," Quinn stammers, trying to sound natural

"You boys headin' in?" the lead officer asks

"Yeah," Quinn answers nonchalantly, "Just for the night."

The lead officer ignores Quinn for a moment and lowers his sunglasses. He focuses his vision on to me in the passenger seat. I give him a half-hearted wave and smile.

"Got your passports?" the lead officer asks

"Yep!" Quinn and I say in unison while raising our passports

The officer readjusts his glasses over his eyes.

"You boys be safe," he mutters in a guttural, disapproving tone

The border is a fucking trip man. If you frequent Mexico, I'm sure you're used to the way the border works. However, if you have only seen Mexico on TV or flown into Mexico, you wouldn't believe it. Or maybe you would… On the left-hand side of the border to get into America, there is a line of cars as far as the eye can see. The border has armed guards all around it, and there is an anti-acceleration lock built into the gateway. The border patrol checks under your vehicle, they do a sweep of your possessions with a canine unit, and sometimes they even lift your car. On the right-hand side, one guy is sleeping in a chair with a hat covering his face and another guy waving you through the parking garage-esque security gate. Their gate is literally a single bar that is raised by a motion detector. I have seen malls with better boom barriers.

Once we're across the border, there are endless battalions of homeless people rushing your car to wash your windows for a nickel. Not all of Mexico is like this, but just about every border town I have been to is. Rocky Point is really lovely. Sonoita is not. Locals cover their legs in the hopes that some naïve American will think they are an amputee and give them money. All the same, Quinn and I always give them change. A lot of people say that homeless people in the USA can change their life around. That might be true. Homeless people in Mexico cannot.

"Jesus!" Quinn shouts before braking, "That guy is fucking dead!"

I shoot my eyes to where Quinn is pointing. There's a man lying half in the street half on the sidewalk.

"There's no fuckin' way," I say in disbelief before continuing "What am I saying? Of course there's a fuckin' way…"

Quinn drives cautiously around the corpse before heading down the mile-long stretch of road known locally as "The Valley". It resembles more of a miniature canyon than anything else. The houses are like impoverished high-rises that reach up toward the sky and could crumble at any minute. Most of the locals stay away from here due to the high levels of cartel activity.

Once we are through, Quinn stops at the closest liquor store. It's a real dump, but it's the only one before we get to Rocky Point. As we pull up, I notice a suave, black SUV next to us. I slowly lean forward to peek inside of it and see two men dressed like the agents from The Matrix.

"*Shit...*" I say under my breath as Quinn begins to notice them too, "Federales don't dress like that. They where ski-masks because of people like that. We're too close to the border. We're not supposed to stop here. It's like an unspoken rul-"

"*I know that Jack!*" Quinn whispers combatively

Quinn reaches slowly towards the steering wheel to shift gears.

"Too late..." I say, stopping him "Too suspicious. Just get out and come in with me."

Quinn nods, and we open our doors as naturally as possible. As we pass the SUV, the passenger gets out and follows us into the liquor store. With great haste, Quinn and I grab a twelve-pack of Tecate Light and a bottle of whichever tequila is cheapest. We pay the cashier five American dollars and leave. As I open my door, a voice from the driver's side window of the SUV makes me turn around.

"No trouble now," the driver of the SUV says expressionlessly

I give him a look of understanding and nod my head. Quinn and I both light up a cigarette and race down the highway out of Sonoita. About 20 miles in, a familiar thumping noise can be heard coming out of the back of the car. This noise is then accompanied by a vigorous bumping that forces Quinn to pull off to the side of the road.

"Please tell me you have a spare tire,"

"Of course I do," Quinn responds, "Damn… fuck off."

Quinn and I search the back for the donut. We find it. It's flat. The only other useful thing Quinn has back there is a moving car jack. At least we can push the car.

"Shit," I say "Well, maybe we can find a tow servi-"

"A towing service?!" Quinn said panicking, "Jack! Do you know where we are?! Do you know what they do to young, white men who are stranded in the middle of the road, in the middle of nowhere in Bumfuck, Mexico while the sun is going down?!"

"Alright, alright let's regroup," I say calming him down with my hands

Flustered, I lean on the car and take a moment to think.

"Grab me a beer, will ya?" I beckon to Quinn, "And get yourself one while you're at it."

"No shit," Quinn laughs as he begins to calm down

After about two hours, the entire twelve-pack and a third of the bottle of tequila was gone. I couldn't tell if it was from nervousness or thirst that we had drunk so much, but we were rocking back and forth by sunset. We had to start pushing the car before we were swallowed alive by the darkness. Every quarter of a mile or so, Quinn and I passed the bottle of tequila back and forth and took a swig. We made it a mile and a half.

"You bring any food?" I asked, "Or water?"

"Nah," Quinn slurred "Jesus… we've never been so unprepared."

"It's my fault," I sulked

"Look!" Quinn yelled, jumping out of his stupor

As I adjusted my eyes, I saw a sign that read: *"El Burdel"*

"You speak a little Spanish, right?" Quinn asked

"Not much dude," I admitted, "It says something…under… hmmm. I don't know. Oh! 'Cantina'! Bar!"

"Well," Quinn said, staring at the waning sun "We're not making it to Rocky Point tonight. 'Any port in a storm' as you'd say."

We pushed the car faster than we'd ever pushed a stationary vehicle before. In no time at all, Quinn and I were in the establishment's parking lot.

"Does that look like a pair of tits to you?" Quinn asked, pointing at the Cantina's sign

"Yeah," I responded

"¡Hola! ¿Como estas?" a nameless man behind us shouted

"Hola… uh… Hable despacio por fav-"

"It's okay my friend," the Mexican man responded, "I speak English as well. Not very good, but probably better than your Spanish."

Quinn laughed.

"Fuck off," I said to Quinn while laughing as well, "So, what's your name?"

"Jesus," the man responded

"It's pronounced like Hay-Zeus though right?" Quinn asks

"No, no," Jesus says, "Just Jesus."

The sun had finally set, and darkness fell over the desert. There wasn't a home for miles. The only thing visible that was within walking distance was an outhouse, the bar, and a giant open-aired taco stand. The parking lot was a third of the way full and almost blended into the desert mountains as sand covered the ground. Jesus stood there smiling. Quinn and I, half in the bag, returned the gesture.

"Amigo," Jesus began again, "I can fix your car's tire. We have a spare here. It's only five dollars."

"Oh, you're the mechanic?" Quinn asked

"Mecánica, parking lot attendant, security guard, you name it," Jesus shrugged

A man with one crutch and a single leg hobbled through the parking lot to the outside of the bar. He had a red and blue Spiderman shirt on. One other, more defeated looking man, lit a cigarette and stood next to him.

"Locals?" I ask

"Yeah," Jesus answers, "The guy on the right is Spiderman. I don't know his real name. The guy to the left of him is David."

"David looks like he's been snorting coke from dusk till dawn," I respond

"He probably has," Jesus laughed. "You guys want any drugs, you find them."

I watched as the two men struck up a conversation outside the bar. David looked very timid. In an instant, Spiderman stood on his only leg and cracked David over the head with his crutch. David hobbled inside of the bar as Spiderman gave him a foreboding stare all the way in. I turned back to Jesus.

"How's the pay?" I asked while placing the empty tequila bottle into the backseat of Quinn's car

"Not bad," Jesus said, "16 bucks?"

"16 bucks an hour. Not bad at all," Quinn answered

"Oh no," Jesus laughed as he put the car onto the jack "16 dollars a night."

Jesus put on a jacket that read "*Security*" and headed off into a garage to grab a spare tire.

Quinn and I gave one another an uneasy glance. This man was about to serve us beer and fix our car while watching our vehicle overnight. Jesus was saving us.

Quinn and I made our way to the bar. Already drunk, but losing our buzz at an alarming rate, we ordered whatever they had on tap. To no surprise, it didn't take long for the mariachi band to play something a little more risqué. It didn't take long for women in string bikinis to fill up the stage behind the bar. It was a titty bar. The girls were interesting, to say the least. They weren't horrendous, but you just knew that so many broken dreams rested on that stage. They were the Wednesday morning girls in our town, and our town's best girls were the Monday morning girls by Las Vegas standards. And, of course, their pimps were David and Spiderman. They were relentlessly propositioning us to take the girls home. Quinn and I were adamant that we wanted none of that.

With nothing left to do, Quinn and I drank, drank, and drank until our optic nerves began to twitch and blur our vision ever so gently.

"Why do we drink?" Quinn muttered, staring into his glass

"To get drunk," I answered and laughed after finishing my beer

"No, like, honestly, why do people get drunk? Why do we? Cause it feels good to stumble around and not know where you are? Like, people like the dizziness and stuff?"

Quinn is clearly in his cups. I'm getting there. Quinn isn't dumb, he knows why. He's just fucked up is all.

"To feel better," I say, "It makes you not care about what you are, what you have become, and what you may be. It is, essentially, a momentary nirvana. It's why drunks stay drunk. Who would want to leave Heaven?"

Quinn just stares into the reflection of his pint glass.

"Of course, once you wake up the next morning, you know it was all a lie, and you have to face the truth."

Before either of us could say another word, the sight of a barmaid walking around the half-filled Cantina with a beer bong that was larger than any I had ever seen arrested us. The tube to it must have been ten feet long. The barmaid began blowing a whistle and abruptly grabbed me by the elbow. I resisted at first, but my drunken logic had started to fail me. The bar roared in jubilation as the barmaid guided me out the front door. Outside, the surrounding crowd chanted "*Chela, Chela, Chela, Pomo, Pomo, Pomo...*" as they pointed up at the enormous church bell that rested at the top of the establishment. From above, the barmaid had returned and dropped down the lengthy beer bong. Jesus laughed and handed me the nozzle as the barmaid began pouring beer after beer into the funnel.

"Rite of passage, wey," Jesus shrugged

Quinn and I drunkenly stared at the barmaid on top of the roof before shrugging indifferently.

"How many beers is that?" I asked

"Seis," Jesus said, crossing his arms

As I lifted the nozzle to my mouth, I noticed another person at the bell tower for a moment. I shook my head and chalked it up to pink elephants in my drunken flurry. I downed the beer and fought back throwing up for almost five minutes. Finally, as I had held back my vomit and after I had won the respect of the locals, Quinn went next. This time I was sure I saw another person up there. Quinn didn't spill a drop.

Back in the Cantina, Quinn and I are a beer short of a massive stroke. We sit next to the only other white guy in the bar. Before we can even order a drink, he begins to talk.

"What truths do you know," a dark voice whispered from two seats over. "You don't belong here, gringo..."

Quinn and I didn't answer.

"I've seen things, man. Things you'd never imagine," the man said, attempting to hide his meth-head appearance by seeming sinister and moving closer to us "I saw a man get his genitals torn off by a pit bull while the cartel held him down. But, he deserved it. I saw a man get his face and hands cut off. They poured salt all over him. What the fuck do you think they'll do to you? Huh?! What do you think I'll-"

On a drunken impulse, I swung on the guy and landed a right directly to his temple. Quinn, out of instinct, began kicking him while he was down. I don't know why I attacked him. I don't understand why he talked to us. My head feels funny.

We break bar etiquette and are kicked out when I threw a pint glass at the guy behind us for laughing. I thought he was laughing at us, I guess. Two large men approach us. I thought there were only 2. Both of them, the size of NFL Linemen, are holding us underneath their arms like children struggling to get free from their parent's grip. While walking, the men punch us both in the face with their free hand every time we fight to get free. Landing flat on our faces, Quinn gets right up and lets the expletives fly as he backs up and trips over himself. A hand grabs Quinn by the shoulder. Quinn rears back and punches the unknown person in the face. I look over and, much to my chagrin, see two Mormon boys with black helmets and bicycles. They frequent this place, knowing how bad the clientele is. Or, I think… Quinn reaches down to apologize profusely before one of the large men shoves him on his face and demands we walk the other way. Wait… that's not right… is it?

Quinn laughs and falls as we wallk aimlllessly to the dessert while the adrenaline rush starts to wear off and weeeerrreee left with noting but aan extremly high liquor level on….on? Quinn never gets this drunk. Back up, back up…e nver gets this dunk. I don't want you to think my old boy Quinn is a softie cause he aint. No, as is in a matter of fack, Quinn fuck with what we say the best of 'em. HAHA! No, no, no! Quinn is the best men. just, just he never is like Blackout hammered. I can't tell if he holds his own or if he is just thinking something where he doesn't want to drink like how we drink. Um, Quinn is my best friend.

Fiannly! After years of travelling the desert, we lot get done arrived back at the bar with the chooch bell on i. But, and I meen, this big ape standing at the door won't let us in…

"What do you have to say?"

"Fuck off. No more admittance for you drunk fucks!"

"Our duck plucks?! C'mon it's only, fuckin, 1:59... look!"

Quinn is now doubled over smashing his brains out. Funniest...thing...ever... Fuck... mayve weve ban druged? I've had an idea that is mawn-you-mental! Okay, so we've herad to the side of the bar.

"Quinn...Quin! ....HAHA!"

"Oh, shit..."

"Quinn, switch shirts with me. He'll neverrr be the wiser...."

It didn't work....

A ring in my ears heralded my waking life. With a deep gasp for air, I wake up next to the side of Quinn's car. I am, unbelievably, sober. Did I just dream all of that? The bar is closed, and every light from the taco stand to the outhouse is turned off. A coyote passes by me about 15 feet in the distance. The moon barely reaches over the mountain and gives me little light. My clock reads '2:07 AM'. Had it only been 8 minutes? Or, possibly, 24 hours and 8 minutes? Did we miss Anna's graduation? I'm wearing Quinn's shirt halfway around my neck and—fuck...

"Quinn! QUINN!!" I shout at the top of my lungs, thinking the worst "QUI-"

"What?!" a voice just above me demands

As I look up, Quinn's head is staring down at mine from the backseat window.

"You're alive?!"

"Jesus..." Quinn mumbles

"Yes?!" a voice in the desert answers

I stand up. Quinn is beginning to shake a little. I open the door to the car and get in. Quinn locks the door, and we promptly fall asleep.

Chapter 21

People often say, "Life is funny". That is a cliché. People say it in the most absurd and undignified scenarios. "Life is funny,"…no it isn't. It is utterly fucking hilarious. I cannot tell you how many times I have laid in bed, with anxiety about everything, staring at the ceiling and laughing my fucking ass off.

Why?

I don't know. Maybe that is the only way to comprehend life. Honestly, I just sit there trying to sleep, and I think of about a million things that have happened in life so far, and I almost die laughing. I literally sit up and curl over because I am laughing so hard. Why is that?

Why am I asking why? Is there an answer?

Too fucking funny…

Life really isn't any different than those ambitious nights out drinking. Your conception is the idea that is planted into your head that you are getting wasted that night. Your birth is giving the bartender your card to open up a tab. Your first steps are your first drinks. Much like life, you start out the night optimistic and ready to take on the world. You find acquaintances in your drunken flurry that you probably would never have talked to given certain circumstances. After your eighth beer, you find the love of your life, only to be rejected by her. You become depressed and decide to settle for any girl who will talk to you. You have sex and afterward vomit on her, much like you may vomit children back into the world. Finally, after that girl has had enough of your shit (and subsequent puking), she leaves you. And you are left in your bed, with no one around (except maybe your cat) to keep you company while you slowly fade into blackness.

Do you want to know when you are an alcoholic? I can tell you. It isn't after you've struck your mother for crying after your third arrest. It isn't after you've thrown up on a live Skype conference call with a business associate because you had six vodkas before the meeting. It isn't after you argue with yourself the morning after a bender about whether committing suicide is the prudent choice of action. About whether a cold dead nothing is better than drinking like a maniac. It isn't any of those. It's when grain alcohol is more palatable than the other liquors. When Everclear at almost 100% alcohol is more pleasant than Bourbon at 40%. When it isn't the percentage that holds you back but rather the "notes" of the alcohol. The notes of bourbon (the sting after drinking) are what keeps us alive. Once you drink Everclear (which is practically rubbing alcohol) and you don't wince, you are deep-six invested. It's over. You've gone too far, and there is no turning back. It's because at this point the alcohol is a part of you. If grain alcohol is 95% alcohol, the other 5% is inconsequential. You are used to 50% or even 60% that is not alcohol that stings and hurts you. No. Everclear has no burn now. It is the quickest and best way to get drunk. To reach the peak of what everyone wishes they had. To enter a state of acedia. Immortality.

Chapter 22

It's incredible how alcohol immediately gives you split personality syndrome. You wake up a different person. You aren't your drunken texts. You aren't your previous statements. You do a complete 180. You reach a state of enlightenment when you are intoxicated. You accept the unknown and the nonsense of life. A particular song plays, and you are in touch with the world. Your only regret is that you will wake up sober and go on living the way the rest of the world does; as a different person

Still 2011. Still May. Still Anna's graduation party to attend. I wake up, and my head feels fine. No hangover. I'm still drunk no doubt. I take my Dad's old advice and grab a beer to stifle the incoming migraine. The last major hangover I had was at the lake. I drank 26 beers the entire day on the water, and when we got off, I chugged a whole bottle of white zinfandel. By all accounts, I should have died.

I look out onto the desert's sky, and Quinn is still passed out in the driver's seat. We didn't make it home. As paranoid as we were last night, we managed to sleep for a few hours. The sky is beautiful, and I have a front-row seat to the sunrise. The sun warms the desert as it elevates its illumination amongst the sky, yet it tries valiantly to fight off the incoming clouds. I nudge Quinn and wake him up to drive to his mom's. He takes a moment to look out at the desert.

"Fuck me..." is pretty much all he can utter.

We don't say a word the entire ride. Quinn drives slower than normal to avoid any unnecessary contact with the donut tire. It's about a 2-and-a-half-hour drive back into town, and we can't think of a thing to say. We just concentrate on our irregular heartbeats from dehydration and the slow creep of an imminent headache. I still didn't throw up though.

At Quinn's mom's, there are several balloons and streamers with a large "Congratulations Graduate" sign near the driveway. We walk, or rather clumsily sashay, into the house to greet Quinn's family. Everything is in perfect order. People are happy and laughing at one another's jokes. I feel like shit. However, I don't feel like shit in the traditional "I drank too much last night, and my head hurts" shit. I feel like shit like I usually do after a night of drinking. The type of "I hate myself right now" shit; that feeling of anxiety for no real reason and depression when everything is going well. The sense of impending doom when you know nothing is wrong.

Quinn's mom greets us, and we hug one another and tell her congratulations. She offers us some food, which I cordially deny and Quinn graciously accepts. At this point, I wish we had stopped at the apartment first to get some different clothes. The entire party is in their summer's best, and we are wearing our usual jeans and a t-shirt. On top of that, I just realized I'm still wearing Quinn's shirt from the night before, and it reeks.

Anna comes in with a smile on her face and greets us both. She seems very happy, and I notice Gio in the back yard talking with the other guests.

"You guys have fun last night?"

"Yeah…" Quinn mumbles as he shakily takes an Advil

There is a daunting moment of silence as Quinn leaves the room.

"Did YOU have fun last night?" I break the silence

"Oh, it was a blast! We went to Jay's and stayed up almost all night." She exclaims while staring at me with a smile "Truth be told, I got hammered like a motherfucker. No one else was really drinking, but I just figured fuck it."

"Now Anna…what would Quinn say?!" I try not to laugh while giving her a grave stare

"Right," she rolls her eyes in jest, "If you were to ask half the people you, Quinn and I know, they'd say we have a drinking problem."

I gaze at her for a second more.

"And the other half?"

"The other half would be our drinking buddies."

I manage a laugh before changing the subject.

"Any plans for college then?"

"I'm thinking Vet school but maybe just a vet tech. I don't know yet. Let the chips fall where they may."

The window to the kitchen is wide open, and a cool summer breeze is fighting the overcast sky as Anna hops back onto the counter near the sink.

"How is…what are you studying again?"

"English Lit…"

"Right! How is it?"

"I can't complain. Just like high school, but I'll probably just end up working some labor job after college. Who knows…"

"Right. Well, if it means anything, I think you deserve better than that."

"It pays well…"

"Yeah, but will you enjoy it?"

The wind comes in through the kitchen window. It pushes Anna's hair past her face and makes a veil over her light green eyes. She smiles. She cannot help but smile. I do the same. Looking at her gives me infinite bliss.

"Are you happy?" she utters under the wind

I knew that was coming. I don't know what to say. Instead, I eschew the question and stare deeply into her eyes once more before calmly walking over, and giving her a robust and embracive hug. We stare at one another for what seems like an eternity. Our faces are close, but instead, I lean casually into her ear and whisper:

"Congratulations Anna…"

My cousin Bubba died of a seizure a week later.

Chapter 23

In death, you cannot dream. As ethereal as death is, there is no sleep. And yet, sitting there in the foyer of the afterlife, I felt my mind slipping into a phantasmagoria of dreams past. My consciousness steadily became the hallucination of nightmares and nuance.

A black background filled the room, and all that was left was a bulldog sitting upright and staring at me. With each breath that this beautiful canine respired, the colors of all the nebulae manifested behind him. Each inhale was a flash of crimson and yellow that surrounded him like an aura brought to life. The world was then behind him, and pillars of man's greatest creations seemed to bow at his feet. This magnificent beast's eyes were continually betraying his true feelings and his unwavering happiness towards a random and chaotic world. This world, he knew, was unfair and unkind. Yet, in all his majesty, this ball of fat resolved to find happiness in even the most decadent of arenas. The background colors and landscapes grew and grew with every breath, and the world was his. He didn't care what you looked like. He didn't care how you spoke. He didn't care about your intellect for his was far greater than any ever known. He only cared for his next pat on the head. He only cared for the next time you wrestled with him. He only cared about his next meal. And in an instant, as the world used him up for his endearing ugly face, he was abandoned and deceived. He was exiled and dethroned by the very world that had loved him so. Each breath now only revealed dark shades of black and white. Man's greatest inceptions then grew angry, for no reason, and tried to cast the marvelous, beauteous English Bulldog to the corners of Oblivion. I cried. I cried and yelled for the world to save him. I demanded recompense for the dog. And in the midst of the clamor and clang of this vision, the bulldog's smile never faltered. Categorically, the dog was happy to only look into my eyes. Each breath he inhaled become few and far between. His eyes slowly shut as the colors and world around him disappeared. I tried once more to reach for him, but I was stuck. I could only stare at the dog who had become my best friend. I could only stare as the landscape of my dream faded to black. The dream felt like an eternity...but it only lasted ten seconds.

Chapter 24

I'll never forget that night. The night my Father cried. The ubiquitous smell of liquor in the air. The constant sorrow perpetually drowned by the next glass of whiskey.

O'Leary, my Dad's best friend, had gone to Seattle to get a final bill of health for his kidney. He technically didn't need to go to the hospital as his cancer was in remission, but he figured a final checkup with his "specialist" doctor was necessary. I was actually headed to Seattle myself for a cousin of mine's wedding when this happened. I texted O'Leary to catch up. He never texted back.

When I got back to town, my Dad told me that O'Leary had fallen ill on his return. He got an infection when his doctor removed his portacath. He went to Seattle for instant hope and left with a slow death.

Dad visited him day and night at the hospital. It would be midnight before he got home each evening. This was a big shock considering Dad always woke up at 3:30 to get to work. I would always ask him how O'Leary was doing, but Dad only shook his head and went off into his room. To think, he didn't even need to go to that doctor...

One night, Dad had texted me telling me that it looked bleak. He said He'd be home late, and He didn't know if O'Leary would make it or not. I got to Dad's around 11 that night. Dad got home at 12:30 AM that morning.

The front door opened, and I stayed on the couch for a moment. I heard the bludgeoning of his keys and wallet as he put them on the counter. He sat in the lay-z-boy, still in his work clothes and attempting to take off his shoes. I decided to get up and ask how O'Leary was doing.

"Not good.."

Dad fought back a sob

"Ughhh…He just…"

Dad couldn't finish a single sentence. His voice cracked and whimpered and, for a moment, I thought he was an imposter. I thought he was joking and fighting back a laugh.

"Well, these things happen…"

Dad had lost four or five friends to the bottle. This was different. O'Leary never drank. O'Leary was a Vietnam vet that got kidney cancer from Agent Orange. He was a vegan. He did yoga. He was, in every single way, the antithesis of my Father.

"He's gone…"

And with that statement, my Father broke down and cried, his boot still halfway around his foot. My Dad could not bring himself to cry in front of me before, but he was powerless. The constant sound of His wailing and Him trying to stifle them made me feel uneasy, so I did what I needed to do; I grabbed my Father and hugged him. He gave me a quick hug before he headed to the kitchen—both boots now off.

Dad pushed the tears off and shook His head as if His previous outburst had never happened. A moment of history wiped clean. He reached under his liquor cabinet and brought out a handle of Jameson. He poured two scotch glasses up about two-thirds of the way. You run out of fingers at this point. He simply said, "Cheers," and without thinking, we drank. I noticed that he wasn't sipping. As I looked down the bottom of my glass and struggled to finish the drink, I saw my Father mourning the death of his best friend, and I knew it was time to grow up. He poured another, more conservative drink this time and only two minutes later, we were downing that. I rushed to the garage to grab two beers. This would help us get through whatever mayhem my Father was planning. With a Coors light in hand, we took another drink from the glass.

I'll never forget the drinks we took. They weren't so much sips as they were gulps. As I saw my Dad lift the scotch glass taller, I followed. He saw me match him, so he raised his higher until we were both finished with our drinks. I saw my Dad lower his for a second before I watched and started to finish mine. Dad then finished his. The surge and thrill of drunken danger pulsed through me with each drink. I put on "Stone the Crow" by Down.

Dad and I drank beer and finished the handle of Jameson. An entire handle vanished, like the memory of my Father crying. I remember telling him stupid stories about Quinn and me. I'll never forget how hard he laughed. Stories about all the time we struck out with suburban girls at the bar that wanted nothing to do with us before settling for some other trashy girl. Stories about passing out in an alleyway after a bachelor party. Anything to laugh and get his mind off O'Leary.

This is the vicious cycle of my Father and I's life. You and your friends drink. A few friends die. You drink even more.

I remember finishing the Jameson. I don't remember the vodka. By the time I came to, my head felt like it was swelled up the size of a melon. It wasn't so much a headache as it was a thirst for water.

The next day, my Old Man and I said nothing of O'Leary. We already knew. We understood what his memory meant to us.

Chapter 25

Happiness and eternity can never exist mutually. The waking world will always be feared. Disabuse yourself before supplicating for the end.

Chapter 26

Though life moved on, I still couldn't shake Anna from my mind. But shit, why stop my vices? They were the only thing that kept me going.

One night in June, I found myself at a Country bar with Quinn. I can't stand Country music. It has become the Pop music of our generation. I almost gag every time I hear a Country song. The songs consist of one of three things:
1. Fishing
2. Drinking
3. Women

Sure, I love all of those things, but there has to be a limit to how many songs you can make based on them. Honestly, each song is an homage to a woman he loves and how she reminds him of Tennessee whiskey, and he might as well cope with her leaving by drinking and fishing. Brilliant...

Well, Quinn somewhat fancies the Country bars. He is my best friend, so I decide to go along for the ride. There is a bar we frequent every Friday night that has one dollar beers, making it an excellent choice. I just hate dressing the part. I have to get a button-up shirt and blue jeans that were "Country-like". You can't wear a hat and you can't wear shorts. Ironic that a genre that makes its bones off of a total lack of decorum would have such strict etiquette at its watering holes. I never wore boots though. I might try and fit in with a new shirt and pants, but I'll be damned if I'm going to wear boots.

Luckily, for that one night in June, it was "Beach Night" and I could wear my gym clothes and shorts, and no one would look at me cross. We start out at the top bar, and there is a small crowd for a Friday at 10 PM. I order a drink from the bartender, Crystal, who is here every Friday and Saturday. She may be the only bartender in the area that actually does not know my Old Man, and that gives me some sense of accomplishment. She is in her late 30s (or maybe even early 40s) and is the object of lust for everyone in the bar. You could tell that Crystal was a bit older, but she was so stunning you didn't care. I can't even begin to tell you how twenty-something-year-old Adonises would have gladly given up red meat and their annual subscription to Boot Barn Monthly just to sleep with this Aphrodite. She was blonde, thin at about 105 pounds, and had fake breasts. Her skin was tight too, like that of a woman in her late 20s. The only way she showed her age was in her eyes. Those seasoned eyes gave her away almost immediately. The eyes of an adroit, sophisticated woman who would fulfill your dreams before haunting them eternally. Her eyes interpreted her life.

I never fancied her though. I marveled at her physical beauty, but I never really tried to make a move. She was a bartender. It was her job to be kind. She even admitted she would pull in around $500 a night on Fridays and Saturdays from tips alone. If she were to flirt with me, I'd laugh it off, tip her, and move on. I wasn't falling for that one…

"Hey Chrissie. Two Coors Lights."

"Jackie! Coming right up! And two for Quinn?"

"Yeah. Sorry, forgot about him for a moment."

Quinn is over there warming up two girls while I'm getting the drinks. I'm sure you've figured that I am not getting four beers for the four of us. I am getting four beers for the two of us. Crystal brings back the drinks, and I pay her promptly with five dollars before heading over to Quinn to see who he is talking to.

"And is this your friend?" says Girl number one

"He has great arms," says girl number two

Great, these girls are already fucked up.

"Hey, I'm Jack."

I give them a nod as they introduce themselves as Brandy and Amber.

"Jack here lives on the other side of town, down the block away."

"Oh, well, it'll be hard getting back to your place tonight." Says Girl number two...I mean Amber

You should know that girls on our side of town are very fast. We never had problems in High School getting laid. Matter of fact, I can recall a story of my friend telling another girl to sleep with another friend of ours because he was in a bit of a rut. She said she would as long as she could sleep with him the next day (since she was really into him). He agreed. True story.

We talk up the Brandys and the Ambers for a bit longer before Quinn heads off to the dance floor to two-step with Nicole... or whatever her name is. Brandy smiles and yanks on my arm for me to come to the dance floor. I hate dancing. I am the epitome of a "bad time". I can be a great time, but I hate dancing, and I don't really care about impressing this girl. She gets fed up and runs out to the dance floor by herself.

I spend most of the rest of the night drinking with old High School alum and some strays at the bar. I'm actually having a great time. We are laughing, joking, and drinking for easily three hours straight. Someone tells me that Quinn has left with both Nicole and Amber and I buy everyone at the bar a shot of well bourbon so we can cheers his accomplishment. I hardly ever get lucky here…

It isn't long before I am out of the bar. Outside for a smoke, back inside for a drink. This routine goes on until about 1:30 in the morning, and I am ready to blackout. I love that feeling. Everyone will tell you that the worst thing to do is blackout. That couldn't be further from the truth. That feeling of warmth in your brain as your inhabitations are emptied almost as easily as your bladder. The euphoria of being able to smoke a pack of cigarettes in an hour and a half while food is magically consumed at a triathlon rate. Yeah, the next morning sucks when you wake up coughing up a lung with a distended stomach that will take a week of clear liquor, chicken breasts and a thousand crunches a day to burn off… but in that fleeting hour of liquor induced nirvana, you are free.

About this time, I turn around at the bar. There is a girl, can't be taller than five feet, staring at me. I am ready to fall over at this point, so I don't know if I have seen her before. She looks familiar, but she just stares at me.

Have I talked to her already?

She smiles, and I walk over in my state of drunken bravery that has been fueled with liquid courage. I tell her my name is Jack. She tells me she knows. I talk for a moment and get her laughing before I lean in for a kiss. She pushes me away at first. I take it as a slight and turn back around towards the bar apathetically to get a final drink. I order, and she is hanging around me for another ten minutes. I play hard to get since she has already snubbed me and she keeps talking my ear off about this and that. I couldn't be more disinterested. She asks if I would like to split a cab and I answer "Sure" while I sway back and forth.

I finish my drink, and we leave the bar. She is now holding my hand and rushing to the Uber she just called. I am confused. I am drunk. Just a moment ago she denied me a kiss, and now she is fawning over me. Did I say something to attract her? Is she just mental? Knowing the girls in my town, it is probably a little of both. I tell the Uber driver my mom's address since it is closer to this part of the city and she is out of town. She is gripping me the entire ride, and I am just swaying.

At my mom's house, we leave the car and go through the front door. At this point, she cannot keep her hands off of me. I do my best to find the key to my mom's house while she is pulling on me for another kiss. I finally find it, and we go at each other with pure ecstasy. I feel nothing towards this girl, and yet I want to get her into bed as soon as possible. I throw her onto the couch as all of my mother's animals spread away in surprise. We have sex. That is all I can remember.

It is the next morning, and she is asleep next to me on the couch. I don't know her name. It all happened so fast. She wakes up, and I cut right to it

"So, you dating anybody?"

I look at her as though I know something and I want her to fess up to it.

"No. I just broke up with my boyfriend about a week ago. Actually, he broke up with me."

How convenient…

"Oh?"

If I press her, she might leave faster.

"He is in the military. Last night was a bit of a 'new experience' for me. I've only ever had sex with him. He's had sex with a lot-"

I tune her out. I was not expecting all this information at once.

"I see." I say yawning "I was just asking."

"I know you..."

"I don't think we've ever met..."

"No. We haven't, but I know you."

Great a stalker...

"All of my friends do. We have always thought you were hot. We went to school together."

She is blonde and a bit superficial. She's not really my type but I'll fuck anything when I'm drunk.

"Oh, well, nice to meet you."

Stupid thing to say but I don't know what else to say. I offer to take her home, but she says she has to get to work. I call her a cab.

A month later, on the Fourth of July, I get a SnapChat from Leah. She is driving home from work and under the chin of her smiling selfie it asks:

What're you up to?

I'm at a BBQ with Quinn and about ten of my other friends from High School. I skip the selfie bit and just respond to the message:

At a BBQ. You?

She responds:

Want to hang out?

No... but I'm already at the point of blacking out so I acquiesce.

Sure.

Don't sound too excited.

What's your address?

3723 E Kopecky Ave

- 151 -

I know the area. I head over after a few more drinks.

For a few months, I hook up with her from time to time. Finally, in October, while at a Halloween party, I get a text from her to come over. I'm not getting any luck at the party, so I head over.

I arrive at her house and tip the cabbie. I walk in, and we cut right to the chase. I take her clothes off, and she takes mine off. We get to it straight away, but I am actively disinterested. I just… don't like this chick. Every girl I've ever slept with has been the same:

- I get to see her naked
- She says something kinky that I've heard a hundred times before
- I stick it in her

This is the wrong time to be pondering, but I just don't even care about sex right now.

She moans, "Ohhh, Jack!"

I say, "Ohhh yeah."

She screams, "Please cum Jack!"

I say, "Ohhh yeah."

She begs, "I want to feel you cum! I want that explosion breaking through every inch of my walls!"

I don't even know what the fuck that means…

Impassively and a little freaked out I say "Yeah…almost there…"

She yells, "Fuck me!"

I say, "Oh yes, Sarah!"

Shit. Everything stops. I can't believe what I have just done. I just said the name of another girl I had been screwing. I want to feel bad for Leah. I want to scold myself. I want to do something, but in an instant, Leah pushes me off of her and is infuriated. I don't blame her. If the shoe were on the other foot, I'd be hot too.

"Sarah?! What the fuck Jack!"

"It's a girl from the store! I was thinking about groceries..."

Good! Good Jack! What a save! How do you come up with these things on the spot? Genius... And here I thought you couldn't think on your toes. At least I didn't pass out drunk while fucking.

"Yeah fucking right!"

My shame cannot be hidden. Quinn and my other friends would be laughing their asses off, but at that moment, I can only feel pity. I knew she was getting attached to me, and I felt terrible. The only humor I saw in the situation was that I wasn't even thinking about Sarah. I didn't even like Sarah. It was an accident.

"I fucking hate you..."

"Look, this wasn't really go-"

"No! In the morning, I'll drop you off, and I never want to see you again."

I feel bad for her, but I couldn't be more apathetic. Just another girl I don't have to break the news to. Just my luck, she did it for me. I don't have to break her heart now when I tell her it's over. This is for the best. At least she hates me.

"Fine by me..."

"Anna lucked out not getting you..."

Stop everything...what did she just say?

"Wha-"

"Yeah. She did."

"Who is-"

"Don't even! Anna...Quinn's sister! Yeah, she is a friend of mine. I figured enough time had passed and she was dating Gio so it wouldn't make a difference. Well, now I don't want you. I hate you."

For fuck's sake, I don't want you either but I didn't know you knew Anna. I feel like shit...

Solitude thy name escapes me right now....

Chapter 27

Walking back down the hallway to the entrance, I pass by a door's transom and the sight of people in a frenzy catches my eye. I peek my head through the door and see another Shannon in a chef's outfit alongside a mass of Hindu people eating steak ravenously. I try to enter the door a little before a man shouts loudly:

"Baahar jao! Baahar jao!"

I wasn't going to stick around to find out what that meant. I found a seat near the entrance of the hallway. Like always, an intruder decides to interrupt my momentary peace. She looks like she is still in High School.

"Hey," she says indifferently

"Hi," I say, looking away, "What can I do for ya?"

"Nothing" she looks at me vacuously

I raise an eyebrow and continue to look away in the hopes that she will get the hint.

"I think like-" she begins before staring at me for a moment, "You used to like, teach at my school or something…"

My gaze locks onto her immediately.

"I used to be an English teacher." I say in dismay, "You weren't one of my students…"

"Nah. I just had friends who had you. I used to meet them outside of your door after fifth period. Or something…"

"Oh, well, good to see you?" I question my own response

"Yeah. Well, see ya…" she remarks before turning away

"Wait!" I say with an almost irascible tone, "How did a kid like you end up here?"

"Oh…" she thinks for a second again "Yeah, well, I was giving my boyfriend a blowjob, and we had heard of that auto-erotic asphyxiation, so we decided to try it. In the middle of the blowjob, I started losing air, and I guess I just died."

"What?! Isn't the guy supposed to be the one being asphyxiated? What the fuck am I saying… Of course he is the one that is supposed to!"

"Huh?" she says looking at me with vacant eyes

I rub my face in frustration before finally saying:

"Heaven is down that way."

She shrugs before moving down the hallway.

Before I can even gather my thoughts and manage a laugh, a maniac of a man confronts me wildly. I shoot back in my chair as he leans a little closer to my face with a raised eyebrow.

"Hey!" he shouts, leaning his head back and wringing his hands "I have something to change your FUCKING MIND about this place!"

For a moment, my skepticism turns to curiosity and I nod my head reluctantly.

"Did you know-" the man smashes his face in with his hands before he wildly jumps on the chair next to me as if to give a liturgy "Did….you….know…."

He's getting even closer now but in a non-threatening manner. Even for the afterlife, this crackhead's noisome breath was unbearable. I finally screamed:

"KNOW WHAT?!"

He looked at me oblivious once more before saying:

"That Jesus was gay."

I exhale deeply and need to remind myself to never come back to the entrance of this place.

"Oh, Jesus…" I sigh, cupping my hands in my lap.

"Yeah!" he began again "That's exactly what Paul was saying!"

"That's not what I meant God damnit! Leave me the fuck alone!"

The man backs up from the room, locking eyes with me the whole time, before running down the hallway.

"I used to live near the sea." An elderly man mumbles to me in the waiting room as I shake out of my stupor

"Christ," I said softly, "Where are you people coming from?"

"So, what are you here for? You're quite young."

"Yeah. Car accident. Go figure."

"Was the driver drunk?"

A take a moment before answering him indirectly.

"Yeah. He was…"

"Young man like you that dies before his time; it's a tragedy. What did you do in the other life?"

I knew someone would ask me eventually.

"Well, I'll give you a hint. That girl who just walked away used to be friends with one of my students."

"You were a teacher…"

"An English teacher….yeah."

"Oh, wow. I wouldn't have guessed. You're so young. All of my teachers were always so-"

"Old? Yeah, I hear that a lot. Well, I used to hear it a lot anyway. The baby boomers started retiring and made room for the spry, young educator that you see in front of you."

He laughed.

"Want to hear something funny?" I asked

"Sure."

"I made about 1000 dollars every two weeks. One time, one of my students came to me and said she made 150 dollars as a hostess in one day. She works five days a week. You can do the rest of the math…"

Before the man could respond, I was interrupted by a hand on my shoulder. As I turned around, my Father greeted me.

"Hello, son."

My Father was changing. I couldn't pinpoint it, but the afterlife had changed Him.

"I found out some information on the car crash." He continued

"What's there to find out? We're dead right? Or is this just some hallucination I'm having while in a coma?"

"It wasn't our fault."

"The other guy was drunk?"

"No. It was just his fault. He was sober, and he survived. These things happen."

"But, if I were sober…I may have been able to see him and…"

My Dad gripped my shoulder tightly. He stared deeply into my eyes.

"Stop," he managed to say before releasing his grip and walking briskly away down the afterlife hallway.

Did he blame me? I could see in His eyes that this was my fault.

Chapter 28

It's July, and I was a month away from my first year teaching. I was also two weeks away from quitting my job at the Engineering plant. Money was tight, so I didn't think twice about house sitting for my Dad's friend that lived in a million-dollar home in the Foothills. All I had to do was feed their poodles and stay at the house. Helluva gig.

The family was so lovely, and when they were giving me a tour of the place, they even insisted I sleep in the Master Bedroom. California King Bed with a Jacuzzi in the bathroom. I had heard about people that lived like this, but I'll be honest, I'd never seen it before.

I'd like to tell you that I wasn't that guy that called his drinking buddies over to piss on your armoire and light your couch on fire. I'd like to tell you I was the guy you wanted house sitting your place. I wasn't. The first thing I did was call Quinn. I told him about the deluxe house I was watching over. I'd have it for two weeks while the family was in Europe. He knew the angle and told me he'd be down on Thursday. I caught a bit of flak from work for asking to come in late Friday, but I'd been working there for two years, and they grudgingly accepted my charming request.

Thursday was there in a flash, and I couldn't wait to hit the bars with Quinn and the others. The occasion? We were celebrating our buddy James's engagement to his longtime girlfriend. We received an invitation in the mail that asked:

"Would you be my Groomsmen?"

At which point we had to get down on one knee and chug a liter of Smirnoff Ice and film it for him. Most people drink a standard bottle when they get iced, but no, we had to down an entire liter of that shit.

I was really excited to get into my routine early. See, I had this process. As long as I don't drink Sunday through Thursday, I'm good. I'm not an alcoholic. I am clean and sober for five days of the week. I drink like a fish Friday and Saturday, but as long as it doesn't carry off into my working days, I'm golden. This routine is reserved to be broken on special occasions such as this…and Spring Break….and Christmas….and obviously Thanksgiving and Halloween.

Quinn brought two guys from our crew. Martin was a good friend. I'd call him my best friend next to Quinn actually. He's a great guy. We've been buddies since High School and even played football together. He always wears a Stetson hat and boots on our nights out. He is the sole reason I've been to more country bars than I care to admit. John was the second. John was Quinn's other best friend beside me, and he was easy to talk to. John was Hispanic and looked like a guy that just got out of the can. He had a goatee beard and that thousand-yard stare you'd see in a Vietnam Vet. He was a good drinking buddy though.

Our night started out at the house. We each drank six beers by eight o'clock before searching the high-class liquor cabinet while a cab was called. After my DUI, we became a bit more responsible with our driving habits. Live and learn. We found a bottle of Glenfiddich 50-year-old scotch. John remarked that it was probably expired. Quinn and I laughed nervously as we hoped he was joking. We each took a shot and left the bottle on the counter as we rushed out to our cab. I took one look back into the house before petting the poodle and locking the door. I felt happy. For the first time in a long time, I felt happy. Even with work in the morning. I had been sleeping around and living life to the fullest. I was about to start my career, and I literally felt on top of the world.

We knew exactly where we were going. We were dive bar dwellers, but on a Thursday night, there was only one scene that would be lively and full of women; College Quern. A mile-long street with nothing but bars next to one another. There was a bar with a live keyboard player every night that is downstairs. There was an upscale bar that all the white-collar college girls went to. Adversely, there was a bar where all of the college dropouts that had not yet told their parents that they had failed, sat and drank on their mom and dad's dime. There was a bar with old arcade games lining the walls that you could play. There was a bar with an entire backroom dedicated to billiards.

Our first stop was a two-story open-air bar called "D'teach". I felt it was apropos so we went to the top. Girls were dancing with white 12 oz. tumbler cups in their hands that read "No Need for a Beach. Come to D'teach." to the latest pop songs spliced together by the DJ with other pop songs. We all decided to order beers. Each of us went to the bar and ordered two of our favorite beers. We always figured that people ordered double shots of whatever they were drinking, so why not order a double beer.

We finished the beers quickly because Quinn and I were not in a dancing mood and decided to hop from bar to bar. We went first to the billiards bar, then the keyboard place, then the arcade joint, before finally landing at a country bar in the very back of the Avenue. Martin was right at home. He had heard about the place from a friend and had wanted to come here. I did the math on country bars. Country music plus drunk people from the city who think they are "Country Folk" plus a mechanical bull that everyone thinks they can ride because they are "Country" equals a probable hookup. Quinn and I unenthusiastically went along. We walked through the door, and the wooden dance floor harbored what seemed like a thousand people in cowboy boots and plaid shirts. They were dancing back and forth, side-to-side, same old same old. If a guy was getting laid in this place though, he needed to know how to spin, flip, and twist his dance partner around. It's all really complicated stuff.

I walked to the bar with Quinn while Martin and John two-stepped to the dance floor. We ordered a boilermaker and followed it with another. After a few minutes, Quinn asked if I'd buy him a drink and meet him outside. I agreed, but only if he was buying the next round. I proceeded to order four Coors Lights and walk out to the bar.

The fan from the outside blew slowly as I pushed through the door. I turned around and around looking for Quinn before I spotted him at the table. I guess I shouldn't have been surprised when I saw Anna and Gio sitting across from him on the outside table. I expect to be more startled, but I am not.

"What's up guys," I say as I hand Quinn his two beers

"Nothing much just thought I'd come to see Quinn while he is in town," Anna responds

"I texted Anna when we were back at D'teach," Quinn says, looking at me

Of course he did.

"Awesome!" I say unenthusiastically

Anna is receptive of my demeanor, and I don't give a fuck at this point.

"So, Bell, how's it going?" I say

"Great! Gio and I just moved into a nice house, and I started my residency for Vet school." At that moment, a girl brushes past Quinn, and he follows, leaving me with Anna and Gio.

"We'll catch up tomorrow sis."

"Well, I'm happy for you guys..." I say staring into her eyes

I am past her. I don't even care. I used to walk around eggshells when I was around Anna, but now I am acting smarmy as all Hell

"Thanks, Jackie. How are you?"

"Oh, you know, just living the life."

I'm too drunk and insincere to care about this conversation.

"You know what I'm talking about right Gio?" I say ironically

Anna shoots me a cold look as Gio gives a courteous smile while staring off into the distance.

"He's such a sport," I say being a dick

Anna just keeps looking at me, upset. I don't care. I'm on a roll.

"Shit Gio, we are trolling for tail tonight if you want to come along..."

Anna is fed up and stands up to leave. She grabs Gio to stand up as well. I am just smiling confidently. She can't help but be angry, but I can see in her eyes she wants to keep talking. She looks at me one last time before leaving.

"Are you happy?!"

For the first time since she first asked me that she seems fiery and pissed. She doesn't know whether to punch me or kiss me. She wants to scream. And for the first time, I answer honestly.

"I'm right as the rain baby! Matter of fact, I have never been better. I am on top of the fuckin' world. I am afraid of the next chapter in my life cause nothing can beat this fucking feeling Bell!"

Anna says nothing else as she grabs Gio and heads out. I say nothing else as I grab my two beers and finish them before heading to Quinn.

Quinn is inside watching John and Martin dancing while he finishes the last beer I gave him. I pull him to the side.

"Let's get out of here and get some pussy."

He nods his head in agreement and finishes the beer with nothing else said.

We walk back to "D'teach" and the place is packed. We don't even make it to the front before I see a bunch of people I went to Teacher's College with. One of them is a girl named Kiki that all our cohorts thought was a lesbian, but I always thought she was hot. Naturally, I make my way towards them.

"Key!"

"Jackie!" Kiki says drunkenly

"What are you guys up to?"

I confidently make my way to her side and look down upon her. She seems happy that I am there.

"Just bar hopping. Why are you here?"

"To see you, of course."

My eyes don't move from hers. She loves it. I know how to get them home, and she is into it.

"Oh, stop it," Key says smiling and blushing

"Yeah, Jackie, stop it..." Lauren, a history minor from our cohort, says unimpressed

"Well, which bar are you guys going to?" Quinn says trying to pour oil on troubled waters

"Don't worry about it!" Nicole, an English major from our cohort, says while pulling Key away

They pull Kiki away as she waves and blows me a loving kiss. I wave back.

"That's a bitch..." Quinn mutters

"Let's go back to that country joint Quinn."

We walk back to the Country bar at 1:45 AM, just before the bar closes. How fortuitous that we would run into John and Martin on the way back. It isn't only John and Martin though. They are each with a girl. Here is a first; Quinn and I aren't going home with girls and our friends are. We link up with them.

"Ready to head back?" I say

Martin is drunker than I expected. He can hardly walk.

"Let's get a cab..." John responds

We stand on the sidewalk for a minute, waiting for a cab. I observe Martin nodding in and out of consciousness. The girl he is with trying to keep him stable. I've been there before.

We finally get a cab to take us back to the foothills. The girls assure us they'll pay the way. I don't pay much attention to them. I already know that when we get back to the house, Quinn and I are planning on drinking ourselves to Oblivion. The cab pulls off into a local gas station so that we can buy more beer before 2 AM.

We sway through the gas station store like a bunch of zombies moving slowly and sporadically for what seems like an eternity before grabbing a case of beer. The Indian clerk is disenchanted when we pay for the beer. I can see that John wants to make a comment to him, but Quinn stops him quickly as he grabs the beer and goes back outside.

Outside the girls are talking to a fat, short guy with a beard. The guy is leaning up against his truck. He seems to be talking to the girls and the cab driver at the same time. I think that I am about to get into a fight from the tone of the guy's voice.

"Shouldn't be charging that!" the fat guy says

"Why do you think he is?" Martin's girl yells back

"What's going on here?" I chime in

"He says the cab driver is charging too much!" John's girl tells me

"I not charge too much!" the foreign cab driver shoots back

"Thirty-five dollars?!" the fat hillbilly counters from his whiskey-infused breath

I am so confused.

"That is standard rate!"

"I'll give you guys a ride for ten bubbas." The fat guy responds while burping

"Let's go!" the girls say in unison

I pay the cabbie for his services as everyone piles into the bed of the drunken hillbilly's truck. The cabbie is not pleased. I am not either, but it saves us a buck. Quinn takes the front seat, and I want to ride in the front also, but he only has front seats and the bed of his truck.

We get on the freeway and pick up speed to about 105 MPH in a 70 MPH zone. I know I should be worried. I know I should be talking everyone out of this, but I can't. Instead, I am as rowdy as everyone else; shotgunning beers and singing along to shitty country songs. Once again, alcohol has taken its effect. There are so many things that run through your head when you are sober that make you fight to live, but when you're drunk, you accept death as an inevitability. Throwing caution to the wind and falling into a state of apathetic drunkenness, I can see Quinn and the driver sharing a flask, and I drink even harder. All the while, the girls are yelling and laughing while trying to show us how tough they are. Martin is now officially passed out.

We make it to the place safely, and I find out why this guy only charged ten "bubbas". He is trying to get with one of the girls, but they thank him for the ride, pay him and go inside promptly. Quinn and I stand by the passenger door with a look that tells him, wordless, that he is not coming in. He speeds off.

We help Martin into the house, and he passes out on the couch. Quinn has now officially stolen Martin's girl. She didn't come here for nothing. We take a shot from the Glenfiddich. I could have just put water in the bottle, but this is a 50-year-old scotch. I'm not stupid. I'll just eat it from the owners. We all grab a beer and head to the pool.

I manage a deck of cards to play "King's Cup". Actually, it was supposed to be a game of "King's Cup" but we were too fucked up and just played "Never Have I Ever" since that's what the girls really wanted to play. For those unfamiliar with the game, you put five fingers up, and linearly, you say a statement that you have never done. If you are guilty of the mentioned statement, you have to put a finger down. If you haven't you leave a finger up. The last person remaining with fingers held up wins. Quinn and I always lose.

After two games of this, we got bored. John's girl had her foot on my crotch. She was doing this right in front of John. He noticed but didn't say anything. I looked up to her immediately and saw that she had a "I want to fuck" look in her eyes. There was no denying it.

"We should skinny dip!" Martin's ex-girl, now Quinn's girl, says.

She had tattoos all over her body. She looked about thirty years old but was sexy in an "I've been around" kind of way. In an, "I've fucked a lot of guys, but you'll fuck me too because I'm here and I want it" kind of way.

"Yes!" says John's girl, now sliding towards me

"Fuck it..." I say, dropping trou and jumping into the pool

Everyone else laughs and follows suit. They are all in the pool. John's girl is now officially straddling me, and I watch John out the corner of my eye while he floats through the pool. I have a moment of apprehension, but I'm really too drunk to care while I notice that Quinn is openly humping his girl in front of all of us in the pool. John swims to the deep end of the pool while I pick my girl up out of the pool butt ass naked and walk to the kitchen. We stop and grab the 50-year-old scotch and move to the master bedroom. We drink a few pulls from the bottle while drinking light beer. I hear a knock on the door as she begins to blow me and I get hard. I walk to the door fully hard, not caring who it is.

"What?" I say while answering the door with a massive erection

It's Quinn. Thank the lord. I thought it'd be John.

"You should let us in so we can all use the Jacuzzi they have in the master bathroom."

Damnit. I'd like to fuck Quinn's girl too, and I guess to get that much closer to Quinn to say that we had a foursome, but I just want to fuck and sleep right now.

"Ugh. Dude, I just want to fuck right now."

"So do I! Dude, I just fucked this girl in the ass…"

Alright, now I'm really considering it. I feel like being a real piece of shit right now.

"I'm fucking this girl first then I'll let you in. Give me ten…"

"Try two you pussy!" Quinn laughs as I give him the finger and shut the door in his face

Okay, so it only lasted eight minutes, but I was in a hurry. I walk to the door, still naked, and let them in. They were both naked too while they were fucking in the hallway. Quinn laughs as he helps her up and brings her into the bathroom. Alcohol you deadly bastard.

I start to fill the Jacuzzi with warm water. This takes around five minutes or so. We obviously cannot wait as the water marginally fills the bath and we all begin to get to business right there on the floor. Quinn lays on the ground while my girl rides him from the top. Quinn's girl gets on her knees opposite my girl just above Quinn and starts to kiss my girl while I get on her from behind. I think about fucking her the way the good lord intended, but I quickly remember what Quinn said and move my cock from rubbing her pussy to fucking her in the ass. It slides in after a bit of a push, as the wetness of her pussy helped. I worried briefly about her fecundity and decided to shoot my load on her face as I forcefully pulled her hair back and readied her face for impact.

After we all had finished, the Jacuzzi had been overflowing for nearly ten minutes. We get in and soak for a moment while our respective girls rest their heads on our shoulders. To be honest, we have had so much to drink that at this point I've forgotten which one was mine originally. Quinn takes a pull off of the cheap bourbon he brought in and passes it to me. He looks at me and laughs, and I laugh too. We have sex with both once more before darkness crosses over all of us in the cooling tub.

I wake up at precisely 9:17 AM. I need to be at work at 10:00 AM. The girls are still there passed out with their heads awkwardly propped up on the marble slab of the Jacuzzi. It's a shame we didn't drown. I get out quietly and dress quickly. Quinn will probably take them both in the morning, but I could care less. I need to get to work.

I get to work at exactly 9:57 AM. I sit behind my desk and start opening emails. I get a text around 10:43 AM from the girl from last night. She wants to hang out this weekend. I tell her I don't want to get a girl I barely know pregnant, and she needs to get a Plan B pill. She never responded after that, and I never heard from her again.

Chapter 29

The deterioration of any language is the decay of any moral society where in the language resides. If people don't know how to communicate or are limited within their own language, then they will act merely on impulse. People's shortcuts are ultimately their undoing.

-see Orwell, George
-see Oblivion

Chapter 30

New Year's Eve 2012. Everyone always asks what you are doing on New Year's. Well, this year, my plans are set. Anna is getting married. Of course, I am invited.

What's the cordial thing to do? I decide to head to Costco to get them one of those enormous bottles of wine. You know the kind that is ridiculously big that tourists from Mexico bring back just to say they have them. That's the one. I don't get that though. I bitterly go about the liquor section and grab a bottle of champagne. This should do.

I'm with my current girlfriend and all of a sudden I don't care that I am on vacation. I am pissed. I am just in a right pissed mood. She, obviously, is in a good mood to go to a wedding.

"Does this look okay?"

"Should I wear this?"

"Should I bring this?"

"Should I talk like this?"

Fuck it. We aren't going to the actual ceremony. I plan it so we just go to the after-party. In hindsight, I knew exactly why I was in a bad mood. I just didn't want to face the reality of the situation.

We get into town around 5 o'clock and I break the "news" that the ceremony had already ended.

"Well, what was the point of me dressing up then?!"

"We are going out later anyway. It's New Year's Eve…"

She doesn't say much as we drive to the L.B. Saloon. There is a two-hour break from the ceremony to the reception so Quinn is waiting there with a girl he recently started dating. She is cute and thin, but not much in the personality department. We drive up and walk through the tattered doors of the once prominent 90s dive bar. Actually, this place looks a lot like The Buffet... only shittier... if that's possible.

I introduce my girlfriend to Quinn's girlfriend, and they hit it off right away. I can't stand that really. Quinn and I grab our beers and head to the bar. We get a drink for each of the girls and ourselves and catch up from the last time I saw him. He explains how his girlfriend is completely enamored with him. He doesn't know how he feels about her, but hey, it's a good deal for now. I couldn't be more empathetic. It is about 5:30 and we drink for about two hours before heading to Quinn's mom's house.

At the house, the place is packed, ear-to-ear, with all of the friends and family Quinn has. I'll let you in on a secret... it's a lot. Old men and young men pack around the bar to get a few fingers of bourbon before perusing the party to talk to one another.

It isn't long before Anna comes through, and everyone applauds. The applause was not ill-conceived. She is magnificent. She is beautiful. She is wearing a white dress that is modest yet absolutely breathtaking. White and unblemished like no other cloth you had ever seen before. Around her shoulders are drapes covered in a completely white feathery gown. She looks as though she could fly away. As if she had wings in that very moment. She elegantly greets everyone at the party and smiles from guest to guest. I just take a sip from my drink and watch her for a moment.

Truth is, I really hadn't talked to her in years, but I couldn't help but ponder over what could have been.

In the backyard, Quinn and the others are going on about what to do later that night. They talk about how alluring Anna's dress was, how cute Gio was at the wedding, how amazing the finger foods are. Without noticing, they look to me with a dumb smile for confirmation.

Yeah, she looks great. So, what're we doing tonight?

The J&B is running low from all of the outside families crowding the bar, and I am just trying to get over to Matt's Pub across the block.

"Well," Quinn said, "Since it is so close I figured we'd go to Matt's Pub."

You read my mind.

"But wait!" Quinn's mom interrupts "We HAVE to take pictures! You can't just leave on your sister's big day!"

Ah shit. Pictures. I hate taking pictures. Unless you hit a significant milestone in life, I don't see the need for them. Honestly, they're just self-fulfilling snapshots of how good you looked on that day. People are taking them for literally anything.

- Road trips
- Bar Trips
- Finished my hair
- Ate some cereal
- Opened my front door

I guess a wedding is as noteworthy as milestones get and I am Quinn's oldest friend. They start with just Quinn and I raising our glasses. Okay, next is one with the girlfriends. For a second, I almost say:

Okay, that's enough. We're done here.

But I don't, and the photographer keeps going. Next one with just Quinn, his girlfriend and I. Next, one with just my girlfriend and I. Next, one with only Quinn and his girlfriend. I felt like this goes on for an eternity. Finally, we head inside to pilfer one last glass of champagne. Anna walks in to talk with us. She talks with us, not with her normal free spirited banter, but rather a reverent tone.

"Are you having a good time?"

"Is there anything I can get you?"

"How are the finger foods?"

Jesus Christ. I am miserable. I feel like the whole thing is a façade. So, I break it up a little. I start asking her how things are going on the other side of town. I break the tension with a joke.

"You know, Anna, we were just outside, and the photographer was asking for pictures. He asked all the married men to stand next to the one person that has made their lives bearable for the last few years. I think they nearly killed that bartender."

Everyone laughs. A pat on the back. Great, everyone is buzzed enough to laugh at my humor. My Old Man told me that one.

Ten minutes pass, and Quinn is pantomiming towards the door. We give Anna a hug and grab one of those smaller bottles of champagne for the road.

"Wait! Can you guys help me put our presents in the back of my car?"

No reluctance here. We start grabbing oversized gift after oversized gift and place them in the trunk and backseat of Anna's car. For a moment, it is only Anna and I, and she just looks at me and smiles. I look back with the same reassuring smile. The sky is completely vacant and clear, and there is no wind blowing at all. I wait and wait.

"It's great to see you," she says
"You too, I'm happy for you."

She heads inside without another word. I'm left alone outside, with a substantial pink-ribboned box in my hand billowing to and fro.

We finally arrive at Matt's and not a moment too soon. It is already 11:30 and the lights from the Off-track betting parlor are practically blinding. The bar has a line that has elongated outside of the door. But, you guessed it, I know Matt. Well, my Dad knows Matt. The little Bijou strikes again. Plus, I worked with the bartender, Lacy, at the Irish Pub years ago. I think she had a thing for me. And, for a moment, I wonder if my friends only hang out with me because of my exclusivity at the bars. It doesn't matter. Quinn and I have been friends for longer than we could step foot in a bar.

It is 11:45 PM, and we have our pitcher of Coors Light. A Hispanic woman walks around and is selling flowers. She must be spoiled for choices here. Every Tom, Dick, and Harry at the bar would buy the most expensive bulb for their bar bitch that night in the hopes of getting their dick wet.

She passes by me, and I take the bait and buy the whitest flower in the lot. I am getting a little happier as I take pull after pull from my beer while Quinn slaps me on the back and laughs. I present it to my girlfriend at the time. She blushes and excitedly takes the White Rose from my hand. She laughs as it starts to shoot out blue and red neon lights. I must have had more to drink than I thought.

Turns out, the flower was a fake. I didn't know or care to know during the purchase. I just took it because of its pure, white color. It gave off a false perfume scent and shot neon lights. She loved it, so it didn't matter.

TEN!

The bar crowd around me has erupted into chaos as they shout the number, and I realize what is happening next.

NINE!

Madness ensues as I lock eyes with the girl I'm with.

EIGHT!

I wonder what my Father is doing.

SEVEN!

I manage to force a smile while I look into her eyes.

SIX!

I take a sip from my beer.

FIVE!

I wonder if Anna is still entertaining her guests.

FOUR!

Still in her mom's living room watching the ball drop.

THREE!

It feels as though we are counting down to the end of the world.

TWO!

Two more seconds of staring.

ONE!

I have lived an unexamined life…

HAPPY NEW YEAR!!

We kiss and the hoarded masses surrounding us lose their minds once more.

We stay around Matt's for a little while longer before I decide it's time to go to a more secluded pub. I tell Quinn that we are headed to

Thirsty's and to meet us there. He nods and gives me the thumbs up.

At Thirsty's, it is just my girlfriend and I. I haven't been here since my 21st. We sit at the bar with about five other losers surrounding us. I manage saccharin smile after saccharin smile while I slowly drink myself into a blackout state. I wish Quinn would hurry up. At least I'd have something to talk about.

Of course, like any other night around this town, some oaf comes up to us and starts to talk to my girlfriend. I just sort of roll my eyes, but I can tell she is waiting for my reaction. She indulges him, and I inconspicuously listen in as I take another drink from my Killian's.

"Are you having a good time tonight?"

"Oh, yes! Thank you for asking!"

"Is this your boyfriend? Or…"

"He is."

"He doesn't seem to be having a good time…"

I have a primal instinct for confrontation. It's in my DNA.

"I am." I say, beginning him to continue his charade

"Well, why aren't you talking to your girl more? She looks lonely."

Why? Why are there people like this? She told you I was her boyfriend. Move on. Don't get your ass kicked over it.

"Aren't we all lonely in this world?" I began

"Ummm…"

Yeah, I didn't think so dumbass.

"Look, I just…" he continues

It is around this time I actually look up at him. Probably early 40s, pathetic looking, and most likely trolls this bar once a weekend for any piece of ass he can find. I would feel bad for him if he wasn't smiling still and wearing that stupid fucking straw hat.

"Look, you were just finished." I say

Here it comes.

"I'm just saying…"

"No, you are just looking to get your ass kicked."

Please fight me. I haven't been in a proper fight in almost a year.

"What's your problem? I'm…"

"No, you were just about to leave us the fuck alone! See, cause you are pathetic. You are a nobody, and I am a somebody. Look at you and look at me! You are nothing!"

I am towering over this pathetic loser, and at this point, I'm assuming the bartender is asking me to leave. I wait for him to swing, but he just stands there unsure what to say. I take off outside and light a cigarette. After five minutes, my girlfriend storms out the door and leads me to the side of the road. What the fuck would she know about getting into a fight? Or hanging out at these dive bars. She's got money. Both her parents are still together. I don't really care. I don't. I just wish Quinn would show up soon.

"What the fuck is wrong with you?!" she says, shaking her head and walking down the street.

Each step of her heels makes a loud *clack* on the sidewalk before she abruptly stops and turns to me.

"Why can't we just have a good fucking night?! It's New Year's Jack!"

I'm barely standing still as the alcohol has reclaimed its place in my body over the adrenaline.

"Who gives a fuck?! That guy was a prick!"

An argument in public; the cornerstone of any healthy relationship.

"There is more to life than fighting and drinking yourself retarded and-"

"Not to me!" I got even closer to her now "I don't want life damnit! I don't want this! I don't want to be an alcoholic, but I don't want to wake up sober and hate myself and my life and feeling of impending doom that ALWAYS follows it! I want it to end! I don't want happiness! I want nothingness!"

Nonplussed, my girlfriend remains silent and waits for the cab as I stood there, reeling in and out of conciseness. We didn't last a month after that.

Isolation is a gift.

Chapter 31

Bars are really quite interesting. I'm not talking about the typical, packed, college Saturday night bar, but a real-life bar. Take your run of the mill dive bar. You walk in, and it either has people lined up for drinks, talking about their crummy week at work or maybe there isn't even anyone in sight. Go into your local pub on a Wednesday at around 12 AM, and you'll see what I mean.

You walk in and to your left is an empty pool hall. To your right is a cigarette machine that hasn't been touched since Reagan was in office. All around are empty tables and remnants of a good time. The lights are dim. So dim that you cannot help but wonder what universe you are in.

Am I dreaming? Is this real? There will, no doubt, always be two people whenever you go in though. A bartender that is cleaning old pint glasses with an even older rag, and a sorry old sod who is taking advantage of their "Wednesday Night Special" just to keep the lights on.

You sit at the bar and are immediately greeted by the bartender. You look at her and immediately examine her life. She is probably 40, she has two kids and had a rough life. She finished high school with a 2.3 GPA and hopped from waitress gig to bartending job before landing at this bastion of sorrow. She looks at you with weathered eyes and glasses that haven't been replaced in ten years.

"What'll you have?"

"The usual…"

She does everything in her power not to roll her eyes while she pours you a drink. You examine the room once more while "Your Cheatin' Heart" plays endlessly in the background. You try and relate to Hank for a moment. You try and envision how he dealt with pain and sorrow and confusion while he was alive. You try to think, but you are interrupted by the bartender putting a napkin down before placing your drink on top of it. She doesn't bother asking for payment because she already knows you. Yet, she stares at you for a moment. You keep examining her. "I'm So Lonesome I Could Cry" comes on now.

How could she stay here? How, after night and night of serving only one or two people for five hours, could she not look for better employment? Has she ever taken a moment to reflect on her life? On what might be? Has she ever taken a moment to laugh at the world? At what little it has to offer?

She moves on, and you look around once more at the dismal, empty pool hall. The cigarette machine that still has Scotch Boy cigarettes in them. It feels like a prison; a prison you could escape, but you don't want to.

Now, think of all the things happening in the world. Good, bad, neutral things that are happening in the world. Students studying for their final exam. People watching the evening news. Syrians fighting for a chance to survive in a better country. Celebrities taking their yachts out. Disc Jockeys preparing for their morning radio show. Think of that and realize that this place exists. It exists here and now. Does anyone ever wonder what is happening here?

The bar lacks any unified value system of morals and identities. It is a phantasmagoria of lofty goals, and faltering will power. The wall behind the bar that cascades itself with endless choices of liquor is only representative of your choice to lose your own inhibitions and thusly choose your own philosophy and your own identity for the night. Are you Casanova? Are you the fool? Are you the asshole? The fighter? The slut? Or are you just here to forget?

The old man at the end of the bar raises his glass to "Cheers" you and you do the same. "Family Tradition" comes on the jukebox and the hour is waning. You finish your drink, and all you can wonder is whether you are going to have another or go home.

Chapter 32

I'll never forget my first apartment after college. I had lived in a studio apartment for four years until I finished school. However, now was the time to move up. Now was the time to get a one-bedroom apartment. I was really making my way in the world. Lucky for me, I found a deal on a two-bedroom, two-story condo about fifteen minutes from work. Not only would I have two bedrooms and two stories, but I'd have a small yard in the back as well for the same price as an apartment.

The move was simple enough and didn't take longer than a few hours. Really, all I had was my clothes, TV, and bed. My Dad helped me move in and made sure I had enough Jameson for the rest of the week.

That first night, I sat around, wondering what to do. Quinn lived about an hour away, and I wasn't seeing anyone at the time. I was bored beyond belief and wasn't sure how to spend my time. I decided to pour a double of Blanton's (expensive shit) and open my front door for a smoke break. Outside, the wind was kicking up a bit, and the clouds were beginning to overtake the sky. I loved it. I loved that feeling of an impending storm.

I sat on the ledge where the concrete meets the doorway. The complex is open and spacious; plenty of room everywhere to walk around and vast grass lawns as far back as the entrance.

I light a cigarette and hear the door in front of me opening. An old man with an already lit cigar comes out. He is ancient. Probably about eighty-five or ninety from what I can see. His mustache branches off to each side of his cheek like an appendage reaching out from his face. His beard almost reaches his stomach.

He slowly moves to the lounge chair he has in front of his flat. He sits down with a scotch glass in his right hand and the burning cigar in his left. He exhales.

"You just move in?"

I study him for a moment before answering.

"Yeah. First night."

He laughs before putting the cigar back in his mouth. He tells me he is from Algiers, but I don't pick up on an accent. I have no idea why he'd ever move out here.

"How do you like it?"

"It's better than the studios I'm used to," I say lowly

"Indeed. Roomier I'm sure." he takes a moment to study me before continuing, "Something troubling you?"

I look confused for a moment and then give a brief laugh under my breath.

"Nothing..."

"Then you're lying to yourself."

Well, he's getting awfully familiar awfully quick.

"No, really-"

"No....really." he cuts me off "What is it?"

I laugh once more.

"I guess I might be just a little lonely."

"Who isn't?"

"Yeah, well, you asked...so, what's your story?"

"No story. Just another member of the human race waiting for the end."

"Thanks for the optimism..." I drink from my glass

"Optimism is for the foolish. Pessimism is for the self-righteous. I am simply...here."

He takes another pull from his scotch glass and looks up toward the overcast sky. I say nothing.

"If I were to recount my entire life story, it would be a War, a marriage, and a whole lot of brown liquor."

"Sounds good to me."

Obviously, I'm not really captivated by this guy.

"Sure..." He says as he relaxes back in his makeshift chair

"What?"

"You got any goals?" He asks

"Do you have any kids?" I counter

"Nope. I can't conceive if you catch my drift."

"You said you were married?"

"I was. She left after she found out I couldn't have children. She has three now."

This conservation is bordering on despondency of the highest caliber. At least I have someone to drink with.

"I'm sorry..." I say half-heartedly

"Don't be. The sooner you realize the absurdity of it, the happier you'll be. Do you have a girlfriend?"

"No, I don't."

"Anyone you 'love'?"

Are you happy?

"I don't think so. I guess I'm just here for work and if someone comes along then great. I'm sure someone will come along once I become more assimilated on this side of town. I don't know..."

"You're looking for that? Just someone to 'come along'?"

Once again, this guy is getting way too intimate for our first meet and greet. Still, I find it impossible to stop answering him.

"Like I said, I don't know..."

"And your job, is it important?"

I laugh.

"Yeah, I mean, I think so."

"It isn't. Have you ever sacrificed everything for a cause? I mean given your absolute all to something you wanted?"

I rub the stubble on my chin and close my eyes for a moment. This guy is definitely drunk, senile, dying or....something. He's talking out of his ass for Christ's sake. I'm compelled to be honest with him all the same.

"Can't say that I have..."

There is a slow pause for a moment. I turn to him.

"Look, don't take this the wrong way, but it sounds like you did a half-ass job of reading some contemporary dissertation or textbook on existentialism and are regurgitating it back to impress me...."

He looks at me and winks before answering.

"I appreciate your candor. You know, when I grew up, I saw the world around me. I saw everyone in my early 20s, and they were running to get a job at a factory or an office. They were running to get any beautiful piece of ass they could. They were vying for a chance to beat their neighbors on the annual Christmas front yard pageantry. And do you know what I did?"

I didn't answer.

"I laughed. I laughed at everything they were doing. I lost friends to my laughter. I lost girlfriends to my chuckles. I lost jobs to my guffawing....and I haven't stopped laughing...."

I sat, trying to imagine myself laughing at my boss.

"Now, in our world today, it is funnier than ever. People sit and...what is it called? 'Binge-Watch'? Is that it? They sit and Binge-Watch in front of the television. The entertainment industry lulls the population into a subtle frenzy over mediocrity that they cannot get enough of. And they 'Binge-Watch' eternally. It is their religion... their savior. They need to 'Binge-Watch'. They need it to worship as their God. They don't want to face a world that is both infinitely beautiful and infinitely pointless and tragic. They need.... distraction."

"There are plenty of people still trying to live a somewhat virtuous life..." I remark

"And yet, in a world where having a legacy means everything, more and more people run to the screen. Girls are desperately turning to porn and boys are rushing to become YouTube stars," he breathes deeply before continuing "You of all people should know that this generation is isolated and only communicates on social media."

I stare at him with genuine surprise. That is the most sense the bastard has made all fucking night. I guess crazy people still have their A-Ha moments.

"I'll give you a look into the future." he continues, "I was working as a clerk for a company not long ago. I told my boss on my first day 'How should we start? You could tell me what you want, and I'll be your scribe.' My boss stares at me scratching his head before responding 'Scribe?' 'Yeah. Tell me what you want to be written, and I'll write it more eloquently.' 'Eloq-' 'What do you

- 188 -

want to be written on this paper?!' 'I....said...?' I rubbed my eyes and looked to the floor before pantomiming a pencil writing on paper. The dull man nodded before saying 'I....want...things...' and chuckling a little to himself. I laughed with dejection before jokingly yelling, "Boy, if you don't tell me what to write, I will raze this office to the ground!" He blinked slightly before asking, "How do you raise something to the ground?" With a stern shake of my head, I walked out of the office and never worked again."

I couldn't help but laugh at the old man's story.

"Wanna know what life is?" he asks again

"Enlighten me..."

"Life is you, standing in the middle of a thunderstorm that is subsequently hit by a dust storm. You just stare up at the sky and look as the rain beats on your face. You try and avoid each drop of rain, but you cannot. Finally, when you've had enough, you go in search of shelter, but the dust doesn't allow you to see even two feet in front of you. You only have two options: Fight the storm or die."

He examines me once more before finally saying:

"All I know is that a tortoise's life is the most tragic of all..."

"Mhmm" I mutter

"Care for some bread and jam?"

"What?!"

"Bread," he repeats calmly, "Care for some?"

"I don't think so...no offense, but I never take shit from strangers. Always that possibility that someone could poison you."

I'm still trying to figure out if this man is a maniac or a genius.

"Do. Don't. It doesn't really matter, does it?"

I roll my eyes so hard they almost get stuck in the back of my head. He walks into the house to grab some bread. I sit there pondering his message. For the most part, I think it is folly. Nothing he said is relatable to me. I am not about to abandon my upbringing and live like a bum. It's all bullshit, really. To think, I would abandon all of my hard work. I would be homeless. My friends wouldn't talk to me ever again. I couldn't do that. Utter madness.

All of a sudden, a cat walks up to me as I finish my second cigarette. It is entirely black with hair that is matted but longer than any cat's I have seen before. It has bald spots all over it that are covered in scars. It is incredibly hideous as far as cats go. I can't help but see a kind of beauty in her though. She has kind eyes. She rubs my leg unprovoked and stares at me with a "Meow".

"You found the stray." The old man says

"Stray?"

"She has been wondering this complex for about a year. She eats out of the garbage can, and the other cats attack her every night, hence the bald spots. She had a litter of kittens, but most of them died. The two that survived I called Peanut Butter and Jelly on account of their color. I found two homes for them."

She looks into my hazel eyes, and I look into her dark green ones.

"No one has ever taken her in?"

"Nope. I don't like cats, so I don't care about her."

My heart breaks. I have some leftover chicken, so I grab a plate and put it inside my living room, and she follows. She eats like a pig for the next thirty minutes. I give her water, and with another affectionate meow, I know she is grateful. I watch from outside through my open door as she finishes all the water as well. She becomes exceptionally doting and lies down on my couch to sleep.

"If you feed her, she'll never leave."

I look at her briefly on the couch while she sleeps as the rotting smell she brought in with her lingers for a moment.

"Good. I'm keeping her."

The old man takes a moment to laugh and nods at me with admiration.

"So, what will you call her?"

I take a moment to think. I laugh to myself before looking back at him and lighting another cigarette.

"Sour Dough"

"Sour Dough?! That's no name for a cat…"

"Does it really matter…"

He pauses for a moment while the realization of his name for her kittens' sets in. He looks at me with a genuine grin that I don't think he has had in years. His laugh is ancient and goodhearted. His stony blue eyes meet mine before he gives me a "cheers" and heads back inside.

I step outside my condo for a moment. I take a sip of my beer and light a cigarette as I sit down. The old man is not out tonight. His lights are on, but he's not sitting in his usual spot. I take a moment to take in the night. I stare up at the night sky and breath in the smoke from the filtered cigarette. I decide to play music on my mp3 player inside. Tool's "Sober" plays in the background while I ponder whether or not I'll be alone much longer.

When I was 13, I told myself I could die happy after I saw Slipknot live. When I was 18, I told myself I could die happy after I had slept with Claire; the girl with the biggest tits in our English 101 class. When I was 22, I told myself I could die happy after I taught my first year of English. When I was 24, I told myself I could die happy, but I was only fooling myself....

I hear a sound buzzing from across the way. I assume it's the summer June bugs dancing the night away. I look back inside to see Sour Dough. I am hoping she can hear it and react just to entertain me for a moment. She stays sitting on the ottoman for the time. I am looking at the lawn and waiting for another insect to materialize. Nothing.

I hear the sound again after I take another breath. I try to pinpoint the music of the insect's wings while sitting there. I look left and right. I look all around me. I hear it again. I finally look upwards and see a bee floating around my porch light. A bee at this time of the night. I see him battering himself trying to get into the ball of illumination. He cannot, for the life of him, understand why he can't get inside of it, so he continues to bash into the glass cylinder that holds that entrancing, majestic bulb of eminence. Under the cylinder is a grip of gnats and flies that have floated in there and died. He doesn't see them, but they were right in front of his buzzing face. He just kept trying to get into that little piece of heaven. I watched this bee for ten minutes as he tried to get in there. I finally extinguished my second cigarette and walked back inside. He didn't care about the dead insects before him or the impossibility of reaching his little paradise. He only cared about reaching the light. Before I locked the door, I turned my porch light off. His pain extinguished with the dissipating light.

I pitied this insect. I pitied him because I could relate to his plight and to his search.

Another day and another disappointment. Nothing terrible happened necessarily, but I just can't help but feel fed up with life at the moment. Every day is the same. Wake up, feed the cat, drive to work, hope for a call that a random bomb destroyed work, arrive at work, walk through the door, become absolutely brain-dead to a vegetable state until work is over, drive home, eat some food, workout, drink some beer and watch TV until I need to sleep. I don't get promiscuous texts from girls anymore. I don't get any house party invites from my buddies. There is no flavor in life. Instead, I decide to walk outside for a drink and a smoke.

The old man is outside with his scotch glass and a cigar. A low rumbling thunder imbued with lighting approaches with dark clouds. The old man is playing "Loud and Heavy" by Cody Jinks. He is smiling at me as though he is complacent in life. His beard flows a bit with the wind's current, and he strokes it over and over again. I wait for him to say his piece, as I am clearly not interested in saying anything.

"How are you tonight?"

How does he make it? How has he been single for over fifty years?

"Eh, I'm okay…"

"I believe that as much as I believe the Zodiac Killer was one man."

There he goes, speaking cryptically again.

"I'm just tired, I guess."

He looks at me and then smokes his cigar and drinks his scotch.

"Let me ask you something. If I were to tell you that I could put you into a chamber and when you awoke you would have a peaceful life. Your life would be free from conflict, and you would live in bliss until you died around 85 or 90, would you do it?"

"Would I-"

"You wouldn't know you were in the artificial chamber. You would be as you were now only happy all the time and in every place. You would be none the wiser. You would leave death, sorrow, pain, indifference, boredom, and hatred behind. Would you do it?"

"And I wouldn't know?"

"That's right..."

Tempting. I would have everything I ever wanted. I could wake up whenever I wanted. No money troubles. No listless dread. No girl problems. Nothing.

And yet, I think for a moment. Is there beauty in the real world? In a world that puts us through so much misery, is there some sort of attachment that keeps us engaged? Some kind of good in the bad? When we see a bad situation, do we not wish that it would go away? And yet, we grow from that situation."

The old man is sitting there, smiling, offering me infinite, hypothetical bliss and nirvana. He awaits my answer.

"No...I don't think that I would..."

"Good. You are learning then. And what if I offered you another proposition? Let's say I could give you a pill that would make you the most attractive and handsome young man around, and the woman of your dreams would most likely fall for you. However, soon, down the road, you would go bald. Or, you could not take the pill and just take your chances trying to win her over with hard work. Which do you choose?"

I sip my drink and think for a moment. The ice from the glass is sweating on each side.

"Honestly, in my experience, it doesn't matter. I would drive myself insane trying to figure out the most prudent action. If I go bald, she may hate me superficially. If I try my chances, the girl may never be mine. Either way, I would be slamming my fist against a wall for making the wrong decision. It wouldn't matter which I would choose and the whole deal is evil."

The old man seems generally surprised by my answer.

"Very good. You see every decision made in life is a deal with the Devil. So few people move on from their decisions in life. They sit in constant regret over what could have been. Mayhem and chance are the only absolute truths to life. But that is what makes you and I exiles of the world. It is what will make us exiles in the afterlife and in eternity."

He walks back inside of his house, and I sit outside miserable, smoking a cigarette, drinking my whiskey, and wondering if I made the right choice.

It's well past midnight, and I get a call for that bottle on top of my fridge. Blanton's. Good stuff.

I look outside, and I see the old man sitting near his stoop. His white, long hair brushing up against the back of his seat. The stain on his two fingers yellowed from years of smoking. His mustache attempting to dodge the flames of his cigar and the J&B in his scotch glass. He is out there selling his soul for just one night.

I remember when bourbon used to bite me. I remember when I'd take a shot of Whiskey, and the sting would hit the back of my throat and make my head shake involuntarily. I remember taking a shot of anything and having to chase it with beer. Now, it is just like water. The essence of life.

I decide to visit with him; to maybe soak up a good conversation. It's lonely out here. My Dad lives thirty minutes away, Quinn is in California for the next six months on work, and all of my friends have moved away. I walk out and sit as I usually do on the ledge of my doorstep and light a cigarette.

"Evening," the old man says glancing over at me

"How's it going?" I respond

He takes a minute to drink from his glass and nods his head. His arms wrinkled and a bit saggy from old age.

"Just fine."

He doesn't say much more. I don't know whether he wants to talk or not. I decide to just push the conversation for whatever is on my mind.

"Do you ever get anxiety?" I ask

"I assume you are asking because you get anxiety?"

"Well, who doesn't?" I answer curtly

"If you really believed that then why did you ask me?"

I roll my eyes at my own stupidity.

"I don't know. I sometimes worry. I get anxious about something bad happening."

"Like death?"

I take a moment to think.

"No, actually, not that. I don't think I ever worry about the future. Stuff like messing up really bad. Like, something I've done in the past will haunt me soon. A video was taken years ago that will ruin my career. Or something I said that will come back to bite me in the ass. I, uhhh, I guess you could say I have a proclivity for self-destruction."

"Sounds like you only worry about the future."

"I'm just always thinking 'Man, if I could just do more good, maybe these things will die off and the world will take pity on me.'"

"I'm sure a lot of people think that way. It's only human to think that doing more good now will alleviate previous transgressions. That whole 'Good things happen to bad people, and vice versa' is bullshit. Things just happen."

"You're a nihilist, aren't you…"

The old man laughed harder than I've ever heard him laugh before. Each breath was a deeper roar than the last.

"I suppose on some level nihilists are on to something. They see a world where nothing matters and can live free in that mindset. However, I am not a nihilist. Hell, I'm not even an atheist. I believe in a higher power. I know there is one up there. I just don't believe he interferes in our lives at all. He is the way a true father should be. Sitting back and watching his children make mistakes while hoping they learn from them. The majority would think this is blasphemous. Atheists would say I'm a fool for believing in an imaginary being and theists would call me a sinner for not reciting one religion or another. All I know is that Death twitches all of our ears and tells us to live because he is coming."

I'm certain I've heard that before. I move the ice around in my glass while I ponder his response. I think I'll have a beer next.

"Do good. Do bad. The world will see you however THEY want to see you. You can't change what others do though." He adds

"Can't argue with that..."

He studies me with contemplative eyes as he takes another puff from his cigar and chases it with a drink.

"I used to think suicide was the answer."

"What changed?" I ask

"Life is inherently meaningless. Sure, the nihilists got that right. However, we can make meaning and purpose in this life. Maybe that is God's test. Not that we follow the Ten Commandments, but that we create our own Ten Commandments..."

"Have you created a purpose in this life? Have you passed the test?"

Our eyes meet, and for the first time, I see an emotion I hadn't seen on him; worry. Maybe sadness, maybe malaise, but it was disconcerting to me.

He finishes his drink in one gulp and ashes his cigar. The old man doesn't say another word. He carelessly walks inside without a 'Goodnight'. I take another moment on the porch before going inside and grabbing another whiskey.

Chapter 33

The most remarkable advice my Father ever gave me was, "You cannot change what people think about you". How true that is.

I decide to wander down the rabbit hole a little further. There are so many afterlives that I have never even heard of.

- Jannah
- Shamayim
- True Existence
- Happy Hunting Ground
- Hedu kä misi

The next door just says "Memories" on it. I know as little about this door as the others. Much like those other doors, it intrigues me. I walk through the door and immediately notice projections on the walls. Movie projections, like an old-time family video collection, hundreds of them, just being pasted on the walls. Screenings of marriages, days at the beach, children being born, and even stubbing your toe.

"Hello!" a man that looks an awful lot like Shannon's brother in a blue collared shirt says as he approaches me

"Hey. So…Memories?"

"Yes, as you can see from the projections on the walls, this is the afterlife of memories. Where you can relive all of your past memories!"

"Over and over again for all eternity?"

"That's what most people say their first time here. Actually, what we do is a little different. The first run-through is a projection of your conscious. You get to view, from your eyes or outside of your body, every moment that ever happened throughout your life."

"First run through?"

"Right! Next, you can start over. This time you can fast forward or rewind through memories. In addition to this, you will also be able to read what your mind was thinking at that time."

"Uh-huh…"

It doesn't sound too bad, actually.

"Next, you get to start over, and you can actually recreate each moment in your life! Essentially, you could have a different life on each run through."

He takes a moment to hand me a pamphlet with all of the information on it as if we were at outpatient rehab.

"Finally, after your third life reenactment, you can create whatever you'd like out of life. Essentially, you would be like a God of your own world. Freeze time, control matter, change what others think."

"Why not just give that power to people on their first run through?"

"Hah! Yes, indeed, another 'frequently asked question'. Well, giving someone that power immediately would destroy the balance and purpose of this afterlife. See, the whole point is reflection. You need to see where you were, what you'd change, and where you might be, before giving you the power to change your world completely."

But it isn't real…

"I'd bet most people, after so many years of redoing their life, would change almost everything." I pause for a minute while I contemplate this "Friends, loved ones, careers…you'd forget who you were…"

The man looks a bit perturbed now. Uh-oh, I've pissed off another one of Shannon's relatives in her seemingly endless bloodline.

"You know, most people take the time to read our brochure and make up their minds in the waiting room…"

"Thanks, but I think I'll pass. I'm sort of in the process of reviewing my memories and life at the moment, and it's torturing enough without knowing what the fuck I was thinking while doing them."

'Bad first impressions' thy name is Delaney.

Chapter 34

May is my second favorite month of the year. Summer is coming up, and work is about to end. Work that I love. Work that I hate. I always reflect on my few years as an educator. I remember the year I decided I was going to be a teacher. I was a junior in High School, and it was the best year of my life. I was on the football team, dating Katelyn Perry, and working a good job. My English teacher was a huge inspiration. English was always my best subject, but he helped me truly understand and love the magnificence of it. I remember reading Whitman and Thoreau; the greatest of American authors. However, these days, I find my palate has become coarse with the German philosophers of the same time. And, much like the authors of my youth, I was optimistic and romantic at the infancy of my teaching career. And yet, the occupation that I had chosen had left me jaded and skeptical years later. I lived to teach, even in my latter years, but I found myself relating more and more with those philosophical realists than my once beloved transcendentalists.

We hold a graduation party after graduation for just the teachers. As part of the social committee, I get a say in what bar we host the party at. We want someplace close (since last year we had it across town) but also inconspicuous enough to not have students walking in and out. We decide on Frank's Pub and Grub. It is right up the street, which raises some alarms, but it's enough of a dive-bar to keep the students at bay.

The last order of business before the school year ends is night duty. See, every year, on the eve of graduation, about half of the seniors try and mess with the football field. They jump the fence and tag the track, or knock all the chairs down, or climb the snack bar roof and drink beers all night. This honor is usually bestowed upon Phil Anderson who has taught History here for 20 years or so. However, Phil died last semester. He had jaundice of the liver from chronic alcoholism. Twenty years of teaching will do that to you. James and I jump on the opportunity right away. We can't think of a more fun way to end the year. This is my life now. Fun comes from chasing kids off of a field and confiscating their spray paint and beer.

Graduation eve has come, and the sun is just resting on the mountainside. A low, dark overcast blankets what sunlight remains across the Eastern Valley. James and I meet up by the golf carts left by security. We ensure all the gates are open so that we can make our rounds around campus. I brought a carafe of coffee for the long night, and James brought along some crackers and Diet Soda.

We watch all of the locals come on and off the field. Residents who come here every night to jog on the track and talk with their loved ones. It is 7 PM now but as soon as it's 10 PM the course is closed. James and I park our golf carts next to one another and talk for hours as the lights around the track slowly start to fade away.

"Helluva thing about Phil no?" James begins

"Yeah. Jaundice. I was just talking to him a lot this year. I would have never thought he'd be sick."

"You're here one minute and the next you just get taken away. I brought something in his honor."

James continues to take a flask from his pocket and pour its contents into both our coffee cups. I have no idea what is inside, but it seems appropriate. We "cheers" to his memory and watch as the darkness fills the world around us.

The night carries on, and before long it is 2 AM. We took our last drink from our coffee cup hours ago, so the caffeine effect (if any) is long gone. We finally hear some people talking by the Northern parking lot. I decide to go around the Western parking lot to sneak up on the unsuspecting culprits. It must be students. It just has to be. No way a jogger is out here at two in the morning. I drive down Box LN and up Rural AVE to the entrance of the parking lot. I see two kids rushing around at the sound of my golf cart. They rush behind a post to try and conceal themselves. Unimpressed, I race the golf cart at 5 MPH right up to the position and shout "Hey! Who is that?!"

I, of course, am not surprised to see two of my seniors standing there with their tails between their legs. Eric and Kayden are more than surprised to see my face.

"Oh...hi Mr. Delaney..." they spurt out in unison

"Did you boys forget your backpack?" I ask facetiously, "Or your vape, perhaps?"

"No, we just..."

"You just nothing. It is two in the morning, and you need to get home. We have graduation practice in the morning. If you don't go to practice, you don't go to graduation."

"Sorry..."

They run off, lucky to not be in trouble. I manage a laugh while thinking about the shit I did in High School.

Out the corner of my eye, I see James's cart driving through the field. I hear:

"Hey! Get out of here!"

Of course. The senior class set it up so at least one side would be preoccupied. They didn't count on two of us. I drive as fast as I can to the Northern Gate to help him chase them off the field. The rest of the night is James and I chasing senior after senior off the grounds. One time, we actually saw a truck pull up in the Western Lot. We turned our lights off because we were just having fun with them now. We drove quietly along the soccer field as seven boys entered the Western Gate. As soon as we were close enough, we turned the lights on fast and chased after them. You'd never seen students so scared. They ran for their lives with a pitiful golf cart at their heels. I shouted in a hyperbolic tone:

"You're in big trouble!!"

And chased them to the pickup truck waiting for them outside. One kid almost didn't make it. He hung in the balance as his corpulent body hung off the back of the pickup truck. As the pickup sped through the entrance of the parking lot and made it out of the street, his body teetered like a Libra scale on the bed of the truck before he managed his weight into the actual vehicle.

The last two hours were very uneventful. James took a nap in the snack bar while I prayed for time to speed up so we could practice the ceremony, and I could go home and sleep until graduation. I haven't slept in about 36 hours now.

7 AM and teachers are finally starting to pull their cars into the lots. James and I give the golf carts to security and walk into the front office to meet the rest of the social committee. I glance at a reflection of myself from the front door window and notice my bloodshot eyes. Other than that, I actually look terrific. I imagine that if someone took a

picture of me though, I would look like absolute shit. It doesn't matter. It is an illusion of reality that keeps us going. My confidence is now boosted, and I am recharged.

Everyone asks about the night before, and of course, we tell them all the gritty details. We chased a bunch of kids off. They were so surprised. Blah, blah, blah. Like I said, this is my life now. This is our life. Teachers are fawning over us to hear about last night, and we got to live it. We are celebrities for a brief moment in time. Our fifteen minutes of fame. Our immortality.

It's only after all of the teacher-paparazzi flood us that I find out the news. My favorite singer of all-time, Chris Cornell, has killed himself.

This isn't a story about a teacher. This is a story about Jack Delaney. With that in mind, I won't bore you with the graduation. I woke up, I did my due diligence, and I was off. The ceremony ended around 8 PM, and if you were to fly a camera or drone over the end of the ceremony, it would be a sight to see. You would see 130 teachers in black robes rushing off the field while 2 thousand parents rushed onto the field. It was like little black ants running away from the multitude of red ants. All of those little black ants headed to the same place; Frank's Pub and grub.

I tried my damnedest to get James to come, but he never comes to work events that he doesn't need to. Actually, most teachers don't. This is the one time of the year that we can get everyone (most everyone) together; a reunion of sorts where we aren't hindered by the intricacies of our personal lives. The one night of the year where colleagues can actually talk to one another without some arduous pontification on curriculum or classroom management. We have three extensive checks coming our way in the next month and no responsibilities until August. That is, aside from taking care of our families…and lesson planning for next year….and recertifying ourselves….and answering angry parent emails about their student failing. Yep! No worries at all.

I rush home and take a cab to the pub. I don't want to pick it up from work in the morning, and I know I'm getting fucked up tonight. The place is already filled with teachers that are shoulder to shoulder. The DJ is playing the soundtrack to all of the most famous 90s songs anyone has ever heard. And then, like a resurgence of memory's past, I had an epiphany. This is a fucking karaoke bar on Thursdays and Fridays. Great. The entire night's soundtrack will be nothing more than teachers singing "Sweet Caroline" and "Total Eclipse of the Heart" for the next six hours. I've heard worse…

I meet up with Dave at the edge of the bar, and he is drinking a Lagunitas, and I order a pint of Coors Light. A myriad of teachers greets me as they rush towards the bar to order their drinks. I finish my first pint in about five minutes. I order a second and down that one in about ten minutes. It's been a tough year.

Dave and I are talking while I order my third. He brings up Chris Cornell's death and how he thought it might have been Auto-Erotic Asphyxiation. I laugh and say:

"Yeah, maybe."

I know it wasn't that. I know that whatever demons he was facing were too horrible to confront.

"Are you going to sing karaoke tonight?"

It's a stupid question. James, Dave, and I are the most reclusive teachers you have ever met. We are goal-oriented. We hate being silly and we hate any frivolity. We are there to teach English and instruct students. We love our students. We have fun with them. We make them laugh. We do not reciprocate that with our colleagues though. And yet, here we are, amongst a hundred teachers that are singing, "I Want it That Way" while we sit and drink beer in the back.

I order a Lagunitas and a Coors Light with two shots of tequila on the side. Why not? I give the second shot to Dave, and I'm waiting to see what he is made of. He empties it like I do and we order another two beers. Dave switches to Coors Light. Smart man. Lighter beer can take you further.

We are finally two hours in, and it is eleven o'clock. We are ten beers and three shots deep, and Dave is urging me to go on stage. At this point, I don't really care. I walk up to the DJ, and he asks me what I want to sing. I stare at him for a moment with a blank, drunken stare as I sway back and forth. I didn't really think about it. Then it hits me.

"Like a Stone…" I slur

He laughs and says:

"Good choice. Very appropriate."

I walk to the bathroom to gather my thoughts. I look into the mirror, and I'm still impressed (or surprised) with how healthy I look. So why am I feeling so shitty? As I walk out I hear two Art teachers finishing their rendition of "How Do I Live" while the DJ says:

"Next up, NEXT UP! We have a special tribute from none other than Jack Dah-Lay-Kneeeeeeee!"

I walk, surprisingly sober, to the microphone. I take it and say deeply:

"This is for Chris Cornell. Rest in Peace."

At that moment, I couldn't help but think of Anna.

The bass from the track plays lightly until it picks up and I am on the mic. To everyone's surprise, I am singing exceptionally well. At least, I think I am. Teachers are funneling around the empty tables to watch as I sing the chorus. The song is flowing through me like blood in my veins. Each pulse from the speakers is a heartbeat. The lyrics to this song are lost on the more casual listeners. They hum only the chorus, but the entire song is an homage to something much more significant and much more real.

I'm not even thinking about singing at this point. I am too drunk. I can hear my own voice, and it isn't slurred. It isn't some self-gratifying drunk solo. I am doing the best karaoke the world has ever heard. The lyrics speak to me. My time on this earth has been molded around this song.

I just sing. Sing and sing until I cannot sing anymore. The entire bar erupts in applause. Once again, I am immortal. I am immortal in my own little world. There cannot be a soul who doesn't speak about this for ages to come. I can die happy.

I walk back to Dave, and we talk more about the song…or at least I think we do. Gemini is standing next to us and smiling quite a bit. I smile back. She walks over and starts talking up a storm. She has always been the quietest in the English Department, and now she is talking to Dave, and I like we never skipped a beat. She introduces us to her husband as Dave and I shake his hand. He is there for literally ten minutes before he goes home.

She enjoyed my solo and talks to Dave about the Freshman curriculum. She asks me how the Seniors have been, and I go back and forth with her on the difference between Freshman and Seniors and how there really isn't one other than the Freshman being more mature than the Seniors. I laugh. Dave is gone after this point. Gemini asks if I would like to talk outside. I go with her.

We talk for what seems like hours, but when you are drunk, hours are minutes. We have the same interest in books and authors. We laugh about the nonsense from the most recent transgressive literary movement but take a moment to reflect on its beauty. I tell her about all the weird dreams I had after reading *House of Leaves*. I tell her that I love that song "Like A Stone" but it has become a "Love Song" in the populous eye and it is one that everyone knows.

"So, do one that no one knows…"

I think for a moment before standing up and slurring:

"You're right!"

I rush back inside and tell the DJ I want to sing "Rusty Cage". In hindsight, it probably wasn't one of Soundgarden's deeper tracks. The DJ tells me I'm up next, and I grab the mic. I sing the song, and now the crowd can tell that I am drunk. The last song was smooth and pure, but this one is going the opposite. I am belting out tune after tune. I don't even care, I am giving my all on this one. It is my favorite song of his.

I finish and, amongst a crowd of perplexed teachers, Gemini asks if I would like a ride from her.

"Thanks but I live on the other side of town…"

"Where?"

"Burbank and the 30."

"I live at Table and the 30."

Just one street East of me. I tell her thanks, and we walk out to her car. She asks me if I like some band from Sweden that sings weird-ass songs. Luckily, I have an ex-girlfriend (the one from Anna's wedding) that loved this band. It is all she used to listen to. I must admit, I kind of like them too. I ask her to play their marquee song "Hi Skinny Soft Soft". She laughs and plays the song immediately.

I think she is talking to me the whole way…I don't remember. Like usual, I'm incredibly fucked up. Vaguely, I remember her pulling off to the side of the road and asking me questions. Christ, I hope I didn't forget where I live and make her drive out of her way. Either way, after a while, she gets to my house. I'm drunk.

"So, this is your place?"

"Yeah. Thanks for the ride." I say with my chin literally touching my chest trying to raise it and stay awake "And now I have a new friend in the English department!"

"I know!"

She seems happy. I ask off of instinct.

"You wanna come in and hang out?"

"No." She laughs a bit nervously, "I'm okay."

That was a stupid thing to ask. I immediately regret the question. Honestly, I didn't mean anything by it. It was just a question of cordiality since she had been so lovely and talkative all night.

"Cool. See you in the Fall."

After Gemini dropped me off, I made an attempt to walk straight into my house. I stumble and almost fall but grab onto the wall of the old man's place. His blinds are all messed up, and his lamp is knocked over. I'm too drunk for any small talk, so I just grab my keys and try and figure out which one fits in the keyhole. After my third attempt, I just stare up at the sky and yell, "Fuuuuuck ittttt!". I am completely burnt. I cannot even stare at a tree without it swirling and getting lost in my double vision. And yet, I am not done. I am revitalized. My batteries have been recharged. I am ready to take off. After five minutes of sitting on my stoop, I grab my keys and hit the road.

I drive out of my complex and arrive at the Circle K about a tenth of a mile from my house. I walk in and get a twelve-pack of beer and pack of turquoise American Spirits. *I can't possibly finish these all before I pass out.* Or, so I thought. *Sounds like a challenge to me.*

Looking at it now, I am so confused. I can't believe the things I did on this trip. Sure, it was summer, and I was single, and I hadn't a care in the world, but I had work in three months. A DUI would tarnish me. Spending the night in jail is easy. Losing the career you love is not.

I take off from the Circle K, and I just drive. I remember this all like it was yesterday. I drive down Main Street. I pick up a little speed, and the next thing I know, I am going 65 MPH. Dangerous, even for a sober driver. I never hesitate, though. Each and every second is just more weight on the gas pedal.

My first stop is Taco Bell. I drive through the drive-thru and ask for a crunch wrap supreme and a double-decker taco. At first, I thought I drove through the front of the drive-thru and up to the main window. I really drove, in reverse, from the exit to where they take your order and then backwards to the teller window. Sucking on a Coors Light and looking out of my passenger window, I talk to the guy at the window who thinks it is hysterical. He is alone, so I give him two beers, and he gives me whatever food is closest.

The next thing I remember is driving out of Taco Bell and going in the opposite direction. I definitely remember this. I continue straight ahead to make a left-hand turn, but there is a median in my way. I literally hop onto the median. Most people would stop at this point. Most people would say:

"Okay, I'm drunk. I can't go any further. I have reached the limit. Let the cops take me."

But I don't care. I am driving straight through it. There could be a cop next to me, and I wouldn't know or care. At this moment, a sane, sober person would have a panic attack, but I'm neither of those things.

I spin the wheels to an invisible crowd that I have manifested in my drunken stupor. They are cheering me on before I continue mounting the rest of the median. If a cop came through at that point, he would hardly care about my lights being out; he would just pull me over.

I get over the median, and to my surprise, there are no lights behind me. This is Oblivion. This is non-existence. This is the state of inebriation where nothing matters and what happens from here on out is nothing more than an informal stage in life. If I had a fuck to give its name would be "Anna".

The speeds I'm reaching would merit a late-night call to the National Guard. Skip the road spikes, they'd just shoot me down at this point. I am driving down Main Street at 85 MPH listening to Metallica and Pantera to get me to these speeds. Each guitar lick is another mile an hour added on to the sturm and drang of the night. Six beers are now missing from my twelve-pack. "Five Minutes Alone" is playing and pushing me further to the end. I look back, and I cannot fathom why I would be driving like this. This is for no one. It isn't even for myself. I just drive.

I am speeding through light after light. Where are the police? Please pull me over.

No one pulls me over. I decide to light a cigarette. I pull off to a parking lot and let the smoke sear my lungs while the nicotine courses through my veins. As always, alcohol has made me forget who I am. It has made me apathetic to my surroundings and all I care about. Life, in this moment, is meaningless.

Just as I start my engine, I hear a knock on my passenger side window. It has to be the police. I look straight ahead and, for once, felt remorse and regret my actions and the life I am about to lose when I talk to this cop. Yet, as I turn my head, I notice a homeless person outside the window waving. I roll down the window.

"Help me out, brother?" the man asked as a wave of B.O. and alcohol hit my face "I need to get three blocks up, and I'm too drunk to walk. The cops might pull me over."

I smile and exhale smoke.

"Get in."

"Can I bum one of those?"

Leaving the parking lot, I toss the homeless man three cigarettes, light another one for myself and rev my engine until the RPM meter is about to break. *Someone hear me, please. Someone save*

me. I am asking for it. I have a long summer ahead
of me, but I don't even care. I just speed away down
Main street back to my condo. I can recall almost
every time I drank and drove, and just how cautious
I was even when I got my DUI. I swore I would
never drink and drive again, and yet here I am,
flying down the main roads, begging to be caught.

My speed finally tops out at 90 MPH as the
homeless man goes from subtly manic to flat out
frantic. He grabs the 'OH SHIT!' bar above the
window and holds on for dear life as I speed
through red lights and pass cars that I almost
narrowly hit. His words weren't exactly words but
rather grunts of adrenaline. Through the excitement,
the homeless man could only point a finger to
indicate his stop. In a split second, I turned my
wheel harshly and slammed on the brakes, arriving
at his final destination.

"Jesus!" he looked back incredulously
"We're alive?!"

I exhaled my cigarette and laughed lightly
before looking at him and saying:

"Unfortunately…"

I arrive at my house and park crooked in my
parking space. I jostle the keys in my hand once
more in an attempt to find the right one, but I am
distracted by the red and white lights engulfing the
corridor where my front door is.

Have the police followed me home?
Did someone call in my license plate?
I'm screwed…

Then I remembered that cops have red and
blue lights, not red and white. I saunter around the
corner to my front door and see paramedics walking
in and out of the old man's house. The stretcher
brings him out with a black bag beneath him. Just

from the look of him, I can tell he is cold. Paramedics are taking notes and calling it. He's dead.

"What happened?" I say trying to sound sober as I walk closer to my door

"No cause of death yet. Did you know him?"

"Yeah. He is…was my neighbor."

"Do you know any next of kin?"

"He didn't have any…"

"When did you see him last?"

"I don't know…a few nights ago. He only came out at night."

The paramedic nodded his head while he continued to write in his notebook. I took one last look at the old man before they zippered him up. His face was almost completely grey and his eyes were staring off into the sky. They had the courtesy to close them before pulling the zipper all the way up over his head. And that's how I'll remember him. Grey, lifeless and closed off to the rest of the world.

Summer had officially begun, and Quinn was coming up that day to go to a concert. He pleaded with me to go, but I just didn't really feel like going to a Country concert. I explained to him that I'd love to go out afterward and he should stay at my place that night. He laughed and agreed to come over for a few beers before I take him to the concert.

Around 2 PM Quinn arrived with a 12 pack of beer and his clothes for the night. I put the beer in the fridge and gave one to him as I opened mine.

"Who is this?" Quinn motioned as he pointed to my cat

"Sour Dough" I laughed
"What kind of a name is Sour Dough?!"
I looked at him and smiled a bit, and all I could muster was.
"Long story."
Quinn laughed as the three of us headed outside for a smoke. He lit up a cigarette and told me that Anna would be there tonight. I nodded my head and said, "Cool…"
Truth be told, I hadn't seen Anna since her wedding. Of course, I could never forget her face.
Quinn scratched Sour Dough's head for a minute while he sipped his beer and puffed on his cigarette. I took out my phone and took a candid picture. I looked at it and scrolled through my contacts list. I was amazed to still see Anna's number in there. I hadn't seen her in over a year. I hadn't texted or called her in over four or five. I pushed down on her name and hit "send". It wasn't long before she replied with a picture of her and her friend that said "Hello". I didn't respond.
"So, I need to take a shower and change. You're cool to take me down there?"
"Yeah, for sure. I'll come back and shower and then head over when you text me that it's done. We'll head out to the bars afterward."
Quinn cracked open his third beer.
"Cool. I'm gonna go shower then."
Quinn walked upstairs and got to it. He still had his beer with him in the shower. I remember because there was an empty beer can on the sink the next day.
When he was ready, we drove down the I-10 to the pavilion. The guy playing the concert must've been pretty famous because it took an hour to drive ten miles on the freeway. They were all headed to

the same place. Quinn and I talked and caught up before his phone rang.

"Hello. Oh hey. Yeah, we are headed there now. Probably like…ten minutes. Yeah, he is. No, he isn't. Hold on."

I look over at Quinn a bit puzzled.

"Here…"

I don't ask any questions. I put the phone to my ear.

"Yeah?"

"Why aren't you coming to the concert?"

"Uhhhh, I don't know, I don't really like country music."

"Neither do I…"

"Who is this?"

I recognized Anna's voice almost immediately but I want to fuck with her.

"Who do you think?"

"I wouldn't ask if I had any clue…"

"It's Anna."

"Ohhh, yeah. You going out afterward?"

"Of course!"

"Sweet…well, I'll see you after."

I hand the phone back to Quinn.

"Okay dude. See you in a bit."

Quinn hangs up the phone, and we are just arriving. I drop him off and tell him to text me. He gives me a thumbs-up before running off to meet up with Anna. I head back onto the freeway and go home. I take a shower and have a few beers while I watch television. It's 9 o'clock. I have two more beers. It's ten o'clock. I open another beer. My phone vibrates, and I look at the text.

"Concert is done in ten."

I grab my keys and rush out the door. It's a sin to waste beer, but I need to get them. My plan was to pick them up, drive to the bars, and then leave my truck there and get a cab home.

Back at the pavilion, Anna, her friend, and Quinn are waiting on the sidewalk away from the pressure of the crowd. I honk the horn, and they rush into the truck as I speed off.

"How was the concert?"

"Dude, he fucking killed it!" Quinn responds, a bit drunker than I am

"It was great. I can't believe you missed it!"

"Yeah, what're you gonna do?" I shrug

"Jack, this is Leslie."

I turn my head to the back of the truck for a minute and see the pretty blonde girl waving back at me.

"Don't get any ideas. She is getting married next year. Too bad..." Quinn laughs

"Don't worry...I'm not," I say as I briefly look into the rear-view mirror and Anna and I lock eyes only for a moment

It was only later that I realized her friend Leslie might have taken that as a slight. Oh well. So it goes...

We pull up to "East Gate". It is the metropolis of bars and restaurants on this side of town. It went up about five years ago when the new football stadium was put into place. It has a bar to match every genre. A Mexican Margarita bar. An Irish Pub. A Country Bar. A College Bar. A Nightclub. A Sports Bar. A Trendy Bar with a thousand different craft beers and men twisting their mustaches. However, the one we are seeking out is one of the only remaining heavy metal bars in town. It isn't like a Heavy Metal club though. No. It has almost a country bar feel, but they only play 80s,

90s, and 2000s heavy metal. As fate would have it, it is called "Hell's Half Acre".

We walk in, already buzzed, and start ordering at the bar. Anna and Leslie go to the bathroom and are in there for about ten minutes. Quinn and I come to the conclusion that Leslie is most likely throwing up. Still, after five more minutes, both of them walk out and are ready to go. We start off with a Jäger Bomb for all of us. Then we order four pints and head out to the back porch.

This moment is what I remember most vividly. This night is the most graphic in my mind that summer.

We drink for an hour and shoot the shit. "Hot for Teacher" comes on and I start playing the air guitar to the amusement of my company. Then Quinn tells a story about some bar fight we got into from five years ago that I only vaguely remember. I apprise a story about the time Quinn, and I got arrested for throwing dry ice bombs at his crush's house in high school. What a friendship.

Four beers in and I feel warm. Quinn drunkenly chimes in.

"I miss Sandra." He starts, "I think of her all the time. She is the one that got away..."

I half laugh half scoff.

"The one that got away..." I drunkenly mumble, "I know that feeling..."

Anna looks deeply into my eyes.

"And who would that be?" she asks

Anna and I are locked inside a staring contest as I choose not to respond. We do this for about an hour while all of us talk, and I've never felt more intimate with anyone in my life. I don't even care about what we are talking about. I don't think Anna does either.

Thirty minutes later and I am headed to the bar for the next round. Okay, now I remember this very well. I remember it because I wasn't even that drunk. Yeah, everyone who is drunk says "I wasn't that drunk" but come on people; you know me. I've had eight beers and a shot in three hours. At the bar, I ask the bartender for four more beers. In an instant, someone is tapping on my shoulder.

Great. Who could this be?

The bouncer is staring me straight in the face and telling me I've had too much. Too much?! This prick is on a power trip! I've been kicked out of bars for "too much" before but right now? I can't believe it. Quinn rushes to my side and tries to convince the doorman otherwise. I laugh cause I know it isn't going to happen. Quinn pleads his case like one of those NBA players trying to convince the ref he didn't foul anyone. It isn't going to happen. I shrug and walk out the front door. While I wait for Quinn and the girls to finish their drinks and meet me out front, I figure I'd put it in the doorman's face. I stand 15 yards away from him, and I start doing my own field sobriety test. I touch both hands to my nose one at a time, and I walk in a straight line. I begin doing cartwheels and even a backflip off of the fountain and laugh my ass off. He knows I wasn't drunk. He just doesn't like the cut of my jib.

After ten minutes, I meet Quinn and the girls outside. We hop on over to the Irish Pub and drink for another hour or so. Quinn and I are still ready to drink, but the girls have had a skinful and are prepared to go, so we head out. Anna immediately grabs my arm and hooks it with her elbow. I look at her and she to me, and we smile. I keep walking to the parking lot where I wait to hail a cab. Anna talks to me for a moment, but I don't exactly know what she says. I only notice that the sky is beginning to gather clouds. They are almost ominous in nature.

I think about kissing Anna for a moment, but decide against it. Maybe I am drunker than I thought. Anna's hair billowed about in the summer breeze.

"What is it?" Anna asks

"Nothing." I smile

Twenty-five minutes later, we are at Anna's house, and it is beautiful. Gio must do well because they are practically living on a ranch with other neighbors. Whatever. At least I love my job.

Inside, Anna offers us all beers, which we accept. We are all feeling a little drunk and decide to go outside. I am not as talkative with Anna. We walk to the backside of her fence and see horses on the other side. All of us try and coerce them towards us until, finally, a Quarter horse makes its way to our side of the ranch. We have nothing to give him; nothing at all. We just put out our hands and hope that he'll lick us. He snubs Quinn, then Leslie, then Anna, but finally, he comes to my hand. He doesn't touch it. He just stares at me. He rests his head on my hand, and I scratch the other side of his face. I feel at peace for a moment

"He never does that!" Anna exclaims

"I guess I have a way with animals..."

I scratch it for a few seconds more before he is called back to his string. Anna just smiles at me and doesn't say a word. We go over to her table in the back yard and sit down.

"Gio is asleep. I'll get the pretzels." Anna whispers

We bullshit for another thirty minutes or so before Quinn finally says that we need to go. I agree and head out the front door while he calls a cab. Anna and I head outside. She hooks my arm again like she pities me. I don't know what to think.

"Did you have a good time?" she says still smiling

"Yeah. It was good seeing you."

"You too. I've missed this."

I am drunk, and I make my move. I lean in to give her a kiss. She moves her head. She is smiling again, and it makes me feel like an idiot. It makes me feel like I am that one guy that tries to kiss you when I shouldn't. Just some drunk asshole. I thought I did the right thing coming onto Anna. She doesn't want me. This is payback. This is her retribution and restitution. She scorned me like I scorned her so long ago.

"Sorry..." I manage

"It's okay. I see tonight the same as I see a lot of things..."

"A lot of things?"

"What could've been. What is still there. What it could be."

I am too drunk to put the pieces together.

"Right..." I say

Finally, the wind blows up in the distance and pushes her hair into my face. She is beautiful. She has always been absolutely bewitching. She stares at me and smiles, and I know it is coming.

"Are you happy?"

How do I answer this age-old question? Am I? I don't know...

"Yeah. I guess. I don't know."

Just then, Quinn and Leslie come outside, and the cab is arriving. Please, why can't this moment last an eternity? Why can't I talk to her just a little longer? And then I realize, this is what she wants. Is she tormenting me? Is she trying to get me to go crazy here?

"I'll see ya sis. Text me tomorrow."

"I will!"

Anna and I share one last glance before the car pulls away and Quinn and I go back home. The rest of the night is Quinn and I smoking and drinking beers until 5:30 AM before we go to bed. It still wasn't enough to make me forget.

It's only been a week since our last encounter. Every time I check my phone I am hoping to see a message from her. I'm sure you are all familiar with that feeling; that feeling of "What's next?" that feeling of "Will this pan out?". A year ago I wasn't even thinking about Anna, and now I am entombed in a sepulcher of perpetual passion. A year ago, I thought it was all over. A year ago I was wondering where my life with my current girlfriend would go. Yet here I am, trapped in a state of anxiety about whether or not I'll hear from her again.

I get a text message. It's from my mom. I get a text message. It's from Quinn. I get a text message. It's from work. I get a text message. It's from Anna. Yes, Anna.

"Hey! Do you know where I can get certified for this?"

I assume she's asking since I work for the state.

"Yeah. I need to get mine renewed anyway. I can pick you up, and we'll go together."

I am so fucking cool.

"Okay! I'll let you know when I am going."

That didn't take long. Honestly, it has to be that she wants to see me. I mean, how hard is it to

Google "Certification". Once again, I await a text message from her. I used to be so laissez-faire about this kind of stuff. I never cared. If it happens, it happens. I don't know what came over me.

A week went by. I went to my cousin's wedding. Two weeks go by. I went to the bar with Quinn. Finally, after three weeks, she sends me a text and says that she doesn't need it for a while. Forget it. I can take myself. It is not time-sensitive. Her certification is not time-sensitive, but life is. I only respond:

"No prob. Keep in touch."

"You too…"

That's it then. I want to punch myself. I, instead, settle for a drink. One drink becomes two and, well, drinking begets more drinking, begets more…you get the point.

She is just a girl. Maybe this is my punishment for all the times I fucked some girl over. My penance for all the times I said: "*Sorry to lead you on. Sorry, it was just a one-time thing. Sorry, just…sorry.*" This is all my comeuppance for that one time I said: "*You're my best friend's sister. You are too young.*"

I can't even remember how much drinking I did over those following three weeks. I had a routine:

- Wake Up
- Drink a gallon of water
- Eat a little food
- Go Workout
- Drink your protein shake
- Drink an entire bottle of bourbon

For Christ's Sake, she is married! You are an idiot to think she wants anything to do with you. You are fantasizing about something that is almost seven years old. It's over. Get that through your

head and move on. What would the old man say?
He would be so disappointed in me right now. I
could just see it now:
"Let it go...Slide..."

Eventually, I do. She never leaves my mind but I manage to go on with my daily routine. I usually like to take a week off from drinking after a bender just to let myself know I am still in control, but I hardly see the point anymore. Do I love Anna or am I just lonely? Living by myself in my condo with no company except Sour Dough. Have I really become what I always hated? Have I really become that whiny, depressed little bitch? Slowly, but surely, I shake myself out of my maudlin stupor.

Life is going to pull your pants down and fuck you no matter how hard you fight it. You just have to pray for enough lube to alleviate that experience. In November, everything had changed in my life. The air temperature dropped, the clouds had settled in the sky, and for the first time in ten years, I was happy. Happy with acceptance.

Midway through the month, I had made plans to go on a fishing trip with one of my friends. Everything was perfect; I would get paid on Thursday, get beer and whiskey, and do nothing but relax and cast my fishing line on my three-day weekend. However, the friend I had initially planned on going with had backed out at the last second. Determined to still have a good Veterans Day weekend, I called Quinn to see if he wanted to go out donnybrooking. I wasn't expecting much since it was short notice, but when he obliged, I was elated.

Tuesday night of that week, I sat grading papers from my students' most recent prompt. Argumentative writing was the lesson, and every single one lacked objectivity. There were no counterclaims. There were no rebuttals. There was nothing but biased bullshit regurgitated from their Fathers. I hate the liberally biased papers because they are poorly written with a certain level of smug, self-assurance that would send even your local college professors running. I hate the conservatively biased essays because they are (mostly) well-written but serve only the purpose of pissing off the opposing side. I'm genuinely brought to tears when the ten percent of students who listened to me on how to write these papers actually pull through.

In the haze of scotch and poor grammar, I receive a call at around 9:36 PM. I didn't recognize the number, but it was too late for a bill collector to call, so I answered. It was my assistant principal. She said she wanted to tell me before anyone else found out the next day. This was it. I knew the time would come when they would eventually let me go.

"One of your sophomores killed himself...."

I took a moment to process the information. This was the fourth student I had had in four years that killed himself. The first, Marvin, had brought a gun to school and shot himself in the head in the breezeway. The second, Allan, had killed himself after his mother was murdered by her ex-boyfriend. The third, and most difficult for me, was Matt. I had had Matt for two years. He hanged himself after he lost all of his track scholarships from showing up to a football game drunk. The last one was Rory. I have no idea why he would do it. The only thing that mattered was the shock I was in. The same clash with the other students who had offed themselves. The only similarity they shared was that you would have never suspected them. As a matter of fact, in the most recent case, I had reported two other students as "red flags" in his class. I never suspected him.

It's never easy. I was a wreck on Wednesday. Everyone was asking me how I was doing. Teachers I had never even spoken to had stopped by during my prep hour to ask if I needed anything and if I was going to be okay. I would thank them and tell them I was fine, all the while staring at the seat that Rory used to occupy. The exhaustion that comes from the shock of losing a student is absolutely, mentally taxing. The mental gymnastics your brain does to distract you from becoming pensive leaves you torn down and crestfallen for hours.

I got home that afternoon and flung myself onto the couch. Staring at the ceiling, I had time to reflect. I had time to think about my unexamined life. My head felt two sizes too small for my brain, and I could barely keep my eyes open. Usually, I would have gone to the gym, came home, read a book, or watched a movie, showered, and gone to bed. I just couldn't bring myself to do any of it.

My phone vibrates, and I muster the ambition to check it. It's a text from Quinn.

"Hey! I'll be down tomorrow afternoon dude! I figured we could bar hop. I also told Anna to meet us for a few drinks. I haven't seen her for a little bit. She said she would meet us around 5."

It wasn't much, but it definitely put me in a better mood. Anna. My ecstasy. My dopamine. The only drink I'll ever need the rest of my life. For the remainder of the night, I thought of Anna and only Anna. True happiness is the cure for sobriety.

The workday passed like a cool, fall breeze, and I left without a word to anyone else. In my haste, I had forgotten several papers that I was initially going to grade over the weekend. No doubt, Rory's would be amongst them. With that thought, I paused. Frankly, my recent apoplexy had come to a halt. Just the thought of the poor kid turned my mood sour. I stopped and tried to think of what I should be feeling at that moment. I couldn't gather the appropriate response, and simply kept walking, head down, to my truck.

At my house, I wasted no time getting ready to go out. What do I need?

- Cologne
- Clean shirt
- Hat
- Scratch that, no hat
- Cigarettes

Quinn shows up about an hour late, but I don't mind. We have a few beers before we smoke another cigarette and head out to the local Brewery. Quinn gets a call from Anna first.

"Hey" Quinn announces

He pauses while he talks to Anna on the other side.

"I don't know." Quinn says "Here" as he hands me the phone

Play it cool....

"What's up Anna."

"Hey! Do you guys know where the brewery is at?"

"Yep. We'll see you there in a bit."

I hand the phone back to Quinn, and we shoot out the door. I just remember checking my hair and how I looked about ten times in the vanity mirror on the ride. Narcissism and vanity are not on my long list of transgressions, but I could not be stopped. We arrive at the open-aired Brewery and INXS's *Need You Tonight* is playing for the entire bar to hear. I lock eyes with Anna immediately. Her stare sends me into an immediate state of euphoria. The following symptoms include, but are not limited to: Dizziness, Heart Palpitations, the desire to dance, the incredibly rare thought of seeing myself with only one person the rest of my life. I hate clichés, but they are clichés for a reason.

Anna was already having a beer by the time we got there. She smiled as we approached, and I gave her a side hug and squeezed her as tightly as I could. We sit down at a patio table and all order another round of beer. I try my hardest to only look at Anna momentarily, but I find myself looking into her eyes more and more. Before long, Quinn excuses himself to smoke and leaves Anna and I to fend for ourselves; just what I was hoping for. I can't even tell you what we talked about. I was so lost in her that my mind was on auto-pilot. Quinn came back in an instant and sat down. Bullocks... I thought he would be gone longer than thirty seconds...

"That was fast." Anna said, "Did you not smoke? You were only gone like one minute."

"Um no." Quinn checks his phone, "I was gone for seven actually."

Anna and I share a furtive and confused glance. Had it really been seven minutes? It felt so fast.

We paid our bar tab and headed out to the next bar. Quinn suggested that Anna invite Gio after he gets off work. A pox on you Quinn... Of course, I was selfish. Anna was married. I feel the same feelings I've had for a while. However, they are only met by reason.

We walk through the gate at the pub down the street, and I make sure that I am sitting next to Anna this time. Chris Isaak's *Wicked Game* plays on the overhead speaker, and I figure it must be an 80's weekend. We are all a little looser at this point, and the conversation picks up. Quinn, Anna and I all laugh over stories of our past, and I can tell that Anna keeps staring at me out the corner of my eye. After we break the seal, Quinn, Anna and I play a game to see who can take the shortest time in the bathroom.

Before long, Gio shows up and sits right across from me. He has always been quiet. In fact, he is a foil to my character. He talks for a little bit about how school is going and orders some food and a beer. I had only wished that it could be just the three of us that night. Anna slides me her Blue Moon and asks if I could help her finish it. A back and forth ensues as I give her shit for not being able to finish her beer. She comes back with having to drive and how only a "big strong man" could help her with her beer.

About 30 minutes after Gio's arrival, I go in and pay the check. I figured (or knew) this was probably going to be the last time I would see Anna for a while; my final romantic gesture for another six months. My last-ditch effort to impress Anna. A measly $83.56 for her love that I would gladly spill blood for.

Gio heads to his car, and Anna comes over to Quinn and I to covertly smoke a cigarette away from Gio's gaze. As if I couldn't love her anymore. We shoot the shit, and Quinn asks how the living situation is going with Gio back in school.

"It's okay." Anna says lowly, "I'm kind of giving him a grace period of doing what he wants while he is in school. We'll see..."

I notice once more from my peripheral vision that Anna glances at me. It isn't my business but is she hinting at something? No.

"Well, he's lucky to have you" Quinn goes on

I don't say a word.

Anna heads out, and Quinn and I go back to my place. Only about halfway to our destination and *Freak on a Leash* by Korn comes on the radio. Naturally, Quinn and I are immediately taken back to our youth. The days of old, where drinking warm, old champagne and throwing up on my mother's carpet was commonplace.

Quinn and I milled about the house for a bit, drinking beer and smoking cigarettes on the back porch. We started getting drunk and playing with Sour Dough, and I took pictures and videos and sent them to Anna. She responded each time with either a photo of her or an image of hookah smoke being blown off her back porch. I laugh insanely at one of Quinn's jokes. I'm just happy I got to see Anna.

"Did you snort coke or something?" Quinn responds

"Something like that..." I look away and laugh

"Can I... can I have some?"

A few hours later, we are at the first bar, and it is decently packed for a Thursday night. An enormous Country Bar with live music and a dance floor. We get shots and beers and begin to walk around. The rest of the night was the same as any other. I'm just happy to have Quinn in my life.

About three months after Veterans Day, I got a text from Anna. She told me that her and Gio were on the rocks. I told her I was sorry and that if she needed to talk, I was there for her. Finally, about 30 minutes later, I send a regular selfie with the caption "The most frightening filter of them all" to cheer up Anna. Anna sends one back with her face and says, "Never! This one is…" I cannot tell you what got into me, but I decided to just text back "Yeah right. You are beautiful…" The same old clichés came into effect as we both went back and forth with "Yes you are" and "No I am not….you are". Finally, she drops the question, "Do you really feel that way?" Judgment Day. The Rapture. What will the result be? Armageddon or Heaven? I respond, "Anna, I have always thought that. I have never stopped thinking about you." The riskiest text I have ever sent. I get a text back that says, "I feel the same way…"

She responds yet again, "I have never stopped feeling that for you…" I feel dopamine and endorphins running through my brain. It's no longer about finding someone. It's only about Anna. Adrenaline is pulsing through every single one of my veins.

She asked me to meet her at a bar called Draw 10 on the other side of town tomorrow. I told her I'd be there.

The ride to Draw 10 was a juxtaposition of ecstasy and distress. I immediately questioned whether or not I was making the right move. It was 12:45 now, and I was just arriving at Draw 10. The air had a brisk chill that sent shivers up my spine. I loved it. I loved the breeze. It inevitably reminded me of Anna. I parked my truck on the side of the unfamiliar bar and made my way inside, adrenaline pulsing through my veins wondering whether or not Anna would already be there or not.

Inside, the bar was clean. It came off as a dive/biker bar from the outside, but the bar clearly went through some renovations over the last year or so. I walked toward the South end of the bar. However, almost every other seat was taken. I waltzed over to the North end of the bar where nobody was at and sat down. 12:55. I didn't usually order a beer this early unless it was a special occasion or Spring Break but when the bartender asked I acquiesced. I ordered the large pint.

With half my pint gone, I checked my phone, and it was 1:00 PM on the dot and *We Belong* by Pat Benetar played over the speakers… apropos of nothing. I put my phone up and looked to my side only to see Anna looking at me. She smiled, and I stood up to hug her. Our embrace was the envy of the Angels in the Heaven above and the Demons down under the sea. She smiled and sat down right beside me, almost immediately touching her knee to mine.

"So?" Anna starts

"So what?" I ask while taking a sip of my beer

"What are we going to do?"

And in that moment, there was an amazing, foreign feeling that I had never encountered before. It was the realization that someone feels for you the same way you feel for them. Humans strive their entire lives to find this feeling, and only a lucky few can capture this moment. It is unbelievable. Even with the two girlfriends I had in the past, I always worked to make it to that "I Love You" stage that was never real, where we both think we love each other, and yet, here we were. It wasn't just an infatuation. It was ten years worth of unrequited love finally coming to a culmination here at a shanty on the east side of town.

"I don't know," I respond, "What do you think?"

"I'm married," she begins, "Things with Gio have been down for almost a year. It's February now and I just don't know if things will get better."

"Are you happy?" I ask

The irony is not lost on either of us.

"No. I don't think that I am."

"Is that why you came here? Just because you were unhappy in your marriage?"

Anna takes a long, hard gulp from her tall Blue Moon.

"No. I've had these feelings for so long. I can't believe we finally had that conversation last night. I don't know what to do. It's been ten years I've been with Gio! And yet, I've never stopped thinking of you…"

"What a fortunate tragedy we have put ourselves into…"

She cannot help but laugh. She is beautiful. How could I be so lucky to share this intimate conversation with such an angel? What did I do to deserve this?

Anna checks her phone, and it is precisely 1:20 PM.

"I have to be back home at 2:20."

"Then we have no time to waste!" I say sarcastically

Her smile sends me into a frenzy.

We talk for what seems like an eternity. She opens up about her feelings towards me and how each and every night after the Country Concert, she would take long runs and walks to get her mind off of me. I explain how each day this summer, I would go on a bender to relieve the malady of her memory, and it never worked, so I would just keep drinking. She said she had a bottle of wine each night. I check my phone, and it is precisely 1:40.

"Each time we check our phone, it has been exactly 20 minutes," Anna says

"When I checked my phone, just before I saw you, it was exactly 1:00."

We continued on about how long it would take after Gio for us to seriously think about dating. What she will have to do with Gio. Her life is about to be turned upside down.

"Is this what you want?" I ask, "I want nothing more than to be with you, Anna. I always have. But there are two parties here…"

"It is," Anna says melancholically

At that moment, I could only think about how much I hated my Father for leaving my mother for another woman. And yet, here I was, the complicit party in a possible divorce. Human beings will eventually accept any act over time and even embrace it, no matter how immoral.

"Look, Anna, you know how I feel. I don't want you to do anything you don't want-" she interrupts me abruptly

"I do. I have the same feelings and what I have now is not what I want."

She puts her hands on my knee, and for a moment, we get lost in each other's eyes. I am not speaking metaphorically. We both locked eyes and felt our souls coursing through the pupils of one another. We both snap out of it and instinctively check our phones. It is 2:00 exactly. We pay our tab and try to walk out of the bar together before a voice slurs behind me.

"J-Jackie!" the voice slurs as I turn

It's just some old guy. Maybe in his fifties. He does look vaguely familiar, though.

"It's me!" the man hiccups, "Steve O'Shea!"

"Oh, shit…Mr. O'Shea. Hi…"

My response gives him pause, but I cannot help but seem shocked. Mr. O'Shea was the Father of an old friend of mine from grade school. His son and I were in Boy Scouts together, and he used to be our troop leader. He was married, clean-cut, and the definition of a stern, reputable, salt of the earth type man. However, now, I had seen him and not recognized him, running around stumbling and trying to chase after girls half his age all night. How could you lose respect for a man you used to fear and revere for so long ago?

"Jack!" he comes in close smelling of stale beer and whatever snacks they left out for the barflies "Jack…I need you to do me a favor."

I nod my head in agreement but am almost horrified by the scene. I attempt to slowly push him off of me as he is now resting his cheek on my shoulder.

"I need you-" he starts slowly before an odd noise emits from his mouth

He is sobbing. He is breathlessly sobbing into my shirt. His cries send me into a state of despondency. However, it was nothing compared to what he asked next.

"I need you to talk to my son for me. I need you to tell him that dad loves him. Will you-" He stops to blow his nose into a bar napkin "Will you do that for me? Tell him his dad misses and loves him very much-"

- 237 -

I hadn't seen his son in 15 years. Mr. O'Shea walked outside on the porch, still teared up with whatever beer is left in his mug, to smoke a cigarette. I look at Anna in disbelief, and she takes my hand to lead me outside the front entrance.

It's mid-afternoon, and the sun is high in the sky. I almost never say goodbye to Anna during the day. As a matter of fact, almost every encounter with Anna throughout my life has happened at night. It is February though, and the wind still picks her hair up and blows it right in my face as I embrace her for a hug once more. She begins to speak.

"I am happy..." Anna announces

"So am I..." I smile and embrace her

I drive home and contemplate the future. This is a different feeling than I have ever had with a girl; and yet, it is going to be the hardest relationship I've had with a girl if this works out. If this is serious, she still has to go through a divorce. I remember telling myself after my parents got a divorce that I would never tarnish or pervert the sanctity of marriage. As a matter of fact, it is the sole reason I have never gotten into more than two serious relationships over my life. I didn't reflect on it until recently, but I figure the biggest reason I never entered into a serious relationship and just hooked up with girls was because I feared it. I saw my Dad leave and everything my mother went through. Even meaningless relationships in High School were pushed aside unless I was 100% invested. I never was. Even when I committed to a girl, I was apprehensive. And yet, here I am, with a girl I have loved since I first saw her. I feel no apprehension.

I got home that afternoon with a picture text from Anna showing me that she got home okay. We talked for the rest of the day via text message. I don't remember the last time I was so happy. Was this real? I had initially thought that I was actually dead, and this was all a figment of my soulful imagination. I would take it either way.

Later that night, Anna and I talked on the phone. I called her around 7 PM, and we spoke on the phone until 3 AM. She stayed downstairs on the couch while we chatted. We talked about the future, about Quinn and what he would think, about what would need to happen if this were really to go through with this. We played 21 questions. Simple questions at first:

- What is your favorite restaurant?
- Your ideal vacation spot?
- What do you like about me?

I know what you're thinking. "Jack, like every other squeeze in your life, you are taking advantage of a vulnerable girl." Usually, I would agree. I would stand beside you and chide myself, but this was different. Everything flowed so naturally. We had only expressed our feelings a day prior, and now we were talking about the kids we may have and what it would be like at our wedding and the rest of our life. Typically, if a girl had made these impositions, I'd be long gone. Not with Anna. I felt everything with her.

After eight hours of talking, Anna sounded distressed on the other line.

"Hang on…" she said

There was some indiscernible chatter on the other end of the line. I waited.

"I'll talk to you later…"

She hung up.

On Saturday, the next morning, I awaited a response from Anna. Every tone from my phone was a possible indication of communication with her. I finally laid in my bed to bring the pressure down. Would she even text me? Would she even follow through on this? And finally... a text.

"I can't do this. I have a marriage. I have these feelings for you, but it just isn't right. I'm sorry..."

I knew this was coming. Some piece of me always knew that she felt the same way, but I also understand her situation. I was prepared for this.

"Don't be sorry, Anna. I don't want you to feel like shit. It's probably for the best....and that crushes me, I mean really crushes me, but I've gone this long without you..."

"No matter what someone is getting hurt. It is a lose-lose situation for me. I'm sorry I put you through this."

"Don't be sorry. Stay up, kid. We'll always have the country concert. Love always..."

"Yeah, we will. Bye Jack..."

Goodbye Anna. My one last chance at happiness.

The next few months felt like a dream. One Saturday in April, Dad invited me over to watch the boxing match. I actually felt somewhat fine. Sure, someone I had pined over the last ten years or so had just fallen through my fingers, but, like I said, 'I've gone this long without you...' I needed to sober up with a drink. I needed to snap out of it. I can be such a pussy sometimes. "My one last chance at happiness?" Who the fuck says that?! Get it together Jack!

I get to Dad's and try to drown the memory of the last two months out with a combination of beer and Friday Night Fights. Dad begins to pick up the conversation by asking how things are going for me, but I quickly switch it over to him; anything to distract me right now. He goes on about work for a bit while he generously pours whiskey into my glass after giving me another beer. My plan is working out so far; get drunk and forget where I am.

Sunday is a constant reminder that I am still in this world. I am still a living, breathing human being that must deal with the maladies of life. I decide to head to the gym to attempt to work out the horrid weekend. I am surprisingly chipper. My mind can do the gymnastics necessary to void any memory of Anna. When I finally get home, I have a protein shake and a beer. Well, you've been with me long enough in this story, you know that one beer turns to ten (or more) and I sit on the couch and try and enjoy some mind-numbing television.

I drink, and I drink. I watch Michael Scott make blunder after blunder. And yet, even with the humor of The Office playing for me, I can't help but think of Anna at that moment. It was only after Anna told me that it was over and she was staying with Gio that I understood why people go into a depression. It physically hurt to not be able to speak to her; not just mentally anymore. I sit there and feel my face scrunch up. I hold it back. I hate this feeling. Finally, I lose it. I pause the show, and I start balling my eyes out.

"Oh, Anna..." I squeal, tears now entirely flowing down my face as I tighten my eyes "Oh....Anna...."

Each word is a pathetic cry out for help. I'm a fucking child. I can't even stop myself. I gather my shit and head upstairs to fall asleep. Are there at least two drinks left? Is there enough to put me into non-remembrance? Will it be enough? I could forget her. I could push her away. But, I could never leave her.

The next day, after work, I find myself at the gym once more. I am on my third workout before I check my phone. It is from Anna.

"I know I said I was done, but I really need to talk to you. If you don't hate me, can you call me when you can? If not, that's okay...."

I'd like to tell you I finished my workout. I'd like to tell you that I let Anna sit on that message for another hour. But I like Anna, not you. I walk out of the gym at once. I leave all of my belongings behind and call her immediately. She tells me that she left Gio. She told him it was over and she is now sitting in the parking lot of a Walgreens. I talk to her from 7PM until 12:30 that morning.

I won't bore you with the remaining conversation. Anna and I spent the next several months in an entirely blissful state. From April on, we were inseparable. At first, our meetings were utterly innocuous. Go to the bar for a drink and have a long hug afterward. It wasn't until a week later that we actually kissed. Then, we did foreplay. Until one night, we had finally gone all the way. Are you just about done with this rollercoaster of bullshit between Anna and I? I told you that you would hate me.

What I felt with Anna could not be described. An actual connection. A rapture beyond reason. It was as if we were living the same lives in that very moment; a relationship that melted us.

I'll never forget the moment she told me she loved me. I said it back immediately. However, I had a dream that very night. I dreamt that I was on the Eastern side of the Berlin Wall, and Anna was on the Western side. We could see one another from over the wall of our rooms. It was only brick and mortar that kept us away from one another. I placed my hand on the window while she stared lovingly at me. I mouthed the words "I love you," but before she could do the same, I woke up.

Life was manageable. I couldn't remember the last time I savored life. Being with Anna was benediction. We spent most of our time together. She was a modest woman. She had only been with one man her entire life. And yet, she still had a good time. She drank with me every night, and most of the time, it was Anna who initiated this. Anna was a Victorian Era woman with a lush's soul. A virgin with the devil's spirit. She is the perfect woman.

"I love you" she'd say

"I love you too" I'd respond with a smile

Her eyes, sincere, soft, and kind, stared at me and then through me.

We talked at length about our futures together, about growing old together. It was only in those moments that I truly neglected the old man's philosophies. The pondering questions that left nothing but a void in my soul all those nights while sitting on our porch. And yet, life is always ready to hit the alarm button. You can press snooze only so many times before you must wake up.

I always thought back to my seniors and teaching *Macbeth* Act 5, Scene 5. I would make sure to milk it for all it's worth. "Out, out, brief candle!" A beginning to an end. "Life's but a walking shadow, a poor player, that struts and frets his hour upon the stage, and then is heard no more. It is a tale told by an idiot, full of sound and fury, signifying....nothing."

"I want you to think about this line." I'd always say

I'd go on my lecture, asking them about the true meaning of life and the absurdities it brings with it. A human experience wrought with deception, malice, constant striving, urgency, and despair.

It was a Tuesday when it happened. Tuesdays are the worst. It is a day that everyone dreads. Tuesday is nothing. At least people hate Mondays.

Anna called me at work during my prep hour. She was already hysterical when I answered the phone.

"Anna? What's wrong?!"

"Well, I was thinking about what you were saying this morning, and even though I was confident I wasn't, I went to CVS and got a pregnancy test..."

A lump in my throat forms instantaneously. A cold sweat fills the area of my brows. Nothing will ever be the same.

"And...?"

A moment of pause, yet I already know the answer.

"And I'm pregnant..."

I falter. I reach for the words to say, but I am choked up.

"Jack? Are you there?!"

"Y-yeah, yeah I'm, I'm here. What do you need? What do we do?"

"I don't know" She sobs and trails off "I took the day off work I can't do this!"

"Okay, okay. I'll be there right after work Bell! Let me know if you need anything at all."

"Okay… hurry. I love you."

"I love you too."

I end the call. I am ecstatic, I think. I am relieved that I can reproduce. I am confused. I am…too mind fucked to know what to feel and what to think. Instead, I slowly take to shaking. I never thought I would get this news. All of these years of unprotected sex and I never slipped one past the goalie. Anna sounded anything but ecstatic though. I suppose I can't blame her. I am not necessarily ecstatic either.

I rush over to Anna's house and bring a pizza since I'm sure she hasn't eaten all day. As I walk in, I am not greeted by the standard, heartfelt, and emotional hug and "Hello Baby!" that I'm used to now. I put the pizza down in the kitchen and immediately rush over to Anna, who is on the couch. She is crying, and I am embracing her. I tell her that everything is going to be okay and that I need her to talk to me. After half an hour of calming her down and consoling her, Anna composes herself just enough to look me in the eyes. Those same eyes that hypnotize my very being are drowned in tears.

"I can't do it." Anna gasps

I nod my head in understanding.

"I know." I drop my head slowly "I know it is going to be hard-"

"No, Jack…." She pauses, "I cannot do this. I cannot do this so soon. I cannot do this with everything that is going on. I haven't even told anyone that we are together. What will people think?"

I pause and just stare at her. I understand, but I have to come to terms with it.

"It's all I have ever wanted with you Jack." She begins "But I cannot-"

Uncontrollable sobs shake her once more as she clutches to my shirt and smears eyeliner all over it. In my speechless state, I understand that this is a prudent choice. I am, in every way, against abortion. It isn't a political belief I harbor. It is, in fact, something I believe people should have the right to do. It isn't a religious/moral/ethical belief that I stand on this principle. No. It is because, if I personally ever was faced with the decision, I know that I have made a choice to conceive or not be careful and I must stick with it. But I will never tell Anna that. I will never argue with her over this decision, and I will love her unconditionally through the process. When you love someone, no matter how much it counters or subverts your beliefs and opinions, you stick with them. Their choice has now become yours. No matter what, come Hell or high water, you will tattoo that choice on your chest for all to see and claim it as your own.

However, as I found out soon after the $500 procedure that we split, it wouldn't last long. Neither of us could look at one another the same way. Nights were filled with infinite sorrow and interminable episodes of crying. Maybe, it was me. Perhaps I didn't try hard enough. Maybe... I had let her down. And finally, in one of those final nights, I thought about a quote I had misinterpreted back in college.

"Directly after copulation, the Devil's laughter is heard."

I grabbed Anna in that final night at her place.

Tuesdays are cruel. Tuesdays are brutal. Tuesdays are harsh. No one likes Tuesday.

I pulled her close to me in what I knew would be our last visit. I slowly began dancing with her in the living room. The living room was devoid of all light, and we could barely make out each other's silhouettes in the abyss. She managed a tearful laugh.

"We have no music to dance with." She sobbed lightly

"We don't need music..." I answered

We danced for what seemed like an eternity in an impassionate room surrounded by an impassive world.

On my walk out of the apartment that night, I noticed one of Anna's neighbors moving a decorative art piece into their place. It simply read:

"What comes with the wind will go with the rain."

Much to both our dismay and with an incredibly tear-filled goodbye that I will neither go into detail on nor think of again, Anna and I separated.

Chapter 35

All I can give you is my soul… lest the devil take
that too.

Chapter 36

Three years had passed. Three years and I hadn't heard from Anna. Quinn briefly told me a while back that she got back with Gio for a while. They didn't last long after that. I had gotten past it eventually. I cut off all ties. I quit Instagram, Facebook, and any other social media I was connected to. I even replaced my smartphone with a flip phone I had kept since I was in high school. I only had two numbers on it; Quinn's and my Father's. Sour Dough and I moved out of my condo a month after Anna and I's split. The last thing I did before driving off was pouring the rest of the J&B the old man had given me on his stoop.

I moved into a one-bedroom apartment not far from Quinn and hundreds of miles away from Anna. My drinking picked up to its wonted state. After work, I usually had half a bottle of whiskey or vodka; not enough to blackout, but enough to get me not caring. On weekend afternoons, I would sit in front of my TV and watch old reruns of Seinfeld or Roseanne while finishing two bottles of cheap, fortified wine. Then, every night, Quinn and I would go and get blackout drunk at the local dive bar up the street. Sometimes we drove. Sometimes we walked. Either way, we always reached a state of inebriation that would put down a horse. Every day that I leave for work, I look at the edge of my room and see a poem I drunkenly made for Anna one night when we were in each other's arms. The sloppy, waggish handwriting read:

> *"and I will never let us be grateful,*
> *as I have solved the labour of my*
> *breath*
> *the sun was burning mid barren*

hills,
and I will never let it die"

The alcohol isn't the cause of the demons in my head; it is the solution.

One night, at the local pub, an elderly man who frequented the place was slouching drunk near me. Barely able to lift his hands, he drunkenly picked up his head as much as he could and looked at me.

"What did you give up for Lent?" he questioned

Was it March already? And with my eyes nearly glued to the floor, I moved them slowly up to meet the man's visage.

"My faith..." I muttered

I never saw him again.

I had always gotten over girls quickly. I would only need Quinn, time, a new girl, and alcohol to get past a fling here and there. I saw a few girls since Anna, but none of them matched the curse she had left on me. I can only describe my love for her as an impractical force of nature that has left me with little to do but fraternize with demons the remainder of my life. I am past the point of caring. I have been told my whole life that to be happy you must:

- Get Educated
- Get a Degree
- Have a Career
- Get Married
- Have Children

I am 3/5 of the way there, but the meaning is getting blurry and ceasing to matter. Is it so wrong to just pine after another individual for the rest of your life? Do I need to settle to be happy? Or will that only push me further into apathy and scorn?

Can't I just regret a decision I made over ten years ago and chase that dream for the rest of my life? I won't accept a settlement on behalf of my shortcomings.

At the beginning of November, Quinn called me and said that Anna is having a birthday party for her kid that she and Gio had about two years ago before they finally got divorced. I guess they went for the 'Have a kid to save the marriage' route. I don't take this as an opportunity. If Anna wanted to be with me, she would have years ago. But Quinn... Quinn is my best friend. I tell him I'll be there and I'll drive. Anna lives in California now. I'm certain she's happy there. She always wanted to live in a kingdom by the sea. She lives off the coast of Venice Beach and is having a party for Frankie there. Frankie. His real name is Francis, but they just call him Frankie.

Quinn and I get on Interstate 8 to get to California. I don't really know what to say, but Quinn starts pouring his guts out right away.

"Well, what now dude?"

I laugh for a moment as I look over to him.

"What, what?" I ask

"I mean, is there anything more than this?"

"More than what? What are you talking about?"

I'm just as well assuming that Quinn is drunk.

"Like, is there more than what we have already done? Or have we just reached our peak?" He lights a cigarette as he finishes saying this

"Good question..."

I guess...

"I drive a truck, Jackie. I go from town to town for six months at a time, and I come back for two months at a time. Even if I got a regular job at a desk, would it make a difference?"

"You're trying to make a difference in this world?"

"Seriously. How many people live like this? Are we just fodder for the world? I have no kids, no girlfriend, no real life. My only enjoyment in life is going out with you...."

"Jesus Quinn!" I yell getting upset at his inordinate philosophical rambling "Are you trying to be deep or something? Maybe you just need a girlfriend."

And just like that, without thinking, I have touted what I never wanted to. I have given the advice of so many that I have hated. I have been conditioned to excrement what everyone before me has:

Be normal

"Yeah. Maybe I should..."

Quinn seems subtly perturbed by my response.

"I don't have the answers Quinn. I wish I did. Forget what I just said. What do you want to do with your life?"

"I guess I haven't really thought that one through yet..."

"No, honestly, if you could be anything, right now, what would it be?"

"An artist."

I almost piss my pants from laughing.

"An artist?! Jesus Quinn, most people would say 'A fireman' or 'An Astronaut' but..."

I interrupt myself again. I have just done what everyone else does: judge others on their desires. I have consumed the purpose of grandeur that everyone deludes themselves into wanting to be, and I have mocked the legitimate purpose that one feels. In short, I'm an asshole.

"Well, I can dream…"

"No. Don't listen to me. You should go for it."

"I'm not an artist Jack. I couldn't be. I'd need to go to school, and I'd need to take time off work. It isn't going to happen. All I do in my spare time is draw. I draw shit that I've never seen before. I draw my dreams. I draw my nightmares. I draw a life I wish I could have had. I can tell myself all day I'm an artist. I can look in the mirror and tell myself I'll be an artist, but no matter what, I am a truck driver. Dreams are meant to be forgotten."

He's right though. I can't remember the last dream I had. Even the best dream I had. I can't remember it for anything. Time is an enigma. It takes away our dreams and replaces them with nightmares. What we thought was attractive or promiscuous a year ago doesn't hold the same clout now. Does anything stand the test of time?

"Funny you should say that about a girlfriend though." He says while sniffling, "I kind of almost had one again."

"Go on!" I exclaim, "Speak on it."

"Actually… I don't know."

"Don't know what? If she was into you?"

"Nah." Quinn says, ashing his cigarette and lighting a new one, "I wasn't planning on telling anyone this."

I raise an eyebrow and give him a look of indignity due to his lack of trust.

"We had this mandatory suicide awareness seminar for everyone in the company with a CDL. I guess more truck drivers were offing themselves every month. Anyway, the seminar was on the ninth floor of some office building on a Friday, and I couldn't wait to get it over with and just go the fuck home. Some woman starts the fucking thing by telling us if we have to leave-"

Quinn chokes up for a second. He coughs in a way that is meant to conceal his emotions.

"Quinn-"

"I'm fine. I'm fine!"

He pushes my hand away before grabbing his flask and drinking from it. He composes himself.

"She says… 'If you need to leave for the bathroom, give me a thumbs up, so I don't follow you out and make certain you are okay. I have to do this legally'. The next thing I knew a woman came through the door and introduced herself as Kat. She was beautiful man. A little big in the hips and I was sure she was in her like mid-30s, but I didn't care. She went on with her 3-hour lecture but made eye contact with me the whole time. I made a move on her as soon as she walked out of the door. It didn't feel like love, but honestly, I never really knew what love or happiness felt like anyway. We met at my place later that night and fucked the night away. She held onto me the whole night. I felt terrific but trapped. I don't know how to act right man."

"And then….?"

Quinn stared at me for what felt like an eternity.

"She got pregnant." He wiped what was obviously a tear from his right eye, "I told her I couldn't be a Father. Wrong time. Wrong person. I am not a Dad. I cou- couldn't be with her."

I don't respond. I just place my hand on Quinn's arm and squeeze.

"She decided to keep the baby, and I was actually coming around to the idea of being a Father. The idea of being with her and having a kid actually gave me some purpose that I hadn't felt before. Something other than just working, buying, shopping, drinking, and fucking. I guess, like three months later, she was lecturing at some seminar in the same room we were in. She put on some movie with actors telling the audience how losing someone is not the end, and that love and life find a way or some bullshit. She walked toward the door after giving her partner a thumbs up. She jumped off the ninth floor and died on impact. I was planning on telling her. I really wa-"

Quinn can't even complete his sentence before he loses it. He starts banging the side of my truck violently and accidentally burns himself on his cigarette. He doesn't even flinch though. The pain drives him further into a frenzy before he sobs and finally retches out of the window. We pull over at the next off-ramp and don't say another word. We sit on my tailgate and drink from his flask while watching the clouds consume the sun. We stayed at a seedy motel that night instead of at Anna's. We shared a handle of Jameson and talked the rest of the night away.

The next day, we arrive at the beach about an hour after the birthday party has already begun. Quinn and I walk towards the shore. In the distance, a canopy has arisen, and children are running around it. Waves crash amongst the coast, and the bite of the cold fall day is everywhere. Most people are wearing a hoodie or a jacket, but Quinn and I are wearing our t-shirts. We look around for Anna before finally finding her by the ramada.

She is beautiful. She looks the same as the first day I saw her. That perfectly cute face and her green eyes throw a spear through my heart. Having a child hasn't even ruined her figure. It wouldn't matter if it did though. I will always love her.
I am almost apprehensive about seeing her. I cannot fathom even talking to her at this point. And yet, she runs up to us anyway. Nowhere to go now. I cannot duck out of this one. Her hair is in a braid, and it runs down the shoulder of her white hooded sweatshirt.

"Hey! Glad you guys could make it." Anna says

"I wouldn't miss my favorite nephew's birthday! I don't see him enough."

"Hey Jackie," Anna says with a smile

She lights up a cigarette right there in front of us. You would've never been able to tell that she had a baby. Some women just have that gift. They have a child, and they are back to themselves in a day's time.

"Hey Anna. How is Frankie?"

"Doing well." She says quickly before changing the subject, "How was the drive up?"

"Nothing too bad. We had one another to keep us company." Quinn says looking at the ground and handing me a cigarette

"What have you been up to Jack?"

"Same old same old. You moved out here about two years ago, yeah? Do you like it?"

"I love the sea. It's been peaceful enough. I have a good job out here."

The overcast clouds are the worst I've ever seen. The wind blows in intervals. It blows hard and strong but only for short periods.

"Oh, and here comes the birthday boy," Quinn says as he readies himself to grab Frankie

Frankie doesn't run to Quinn, though. He runs straight to Anna and grabs her by the sweater and tugs. Anna looks down and smiles. I can only see his thick brown hair from behind. His face is buried in Anna's jeans.

"Go and say hi to your guests Frankie," Anna says waving him on with only the slightest quiver in her voice

He walks towards Quinn and me before stopping short. He stares at me for a moment before I drop down to one knee. The eyes are unmistakable. The face is the same. All of his characteristics match. I can't believe it. He looks just like….me. I begin to turn pale. The heir apparent to my life of tragedy. I look up at Anna with distress. She looks down on me with contempt. I don't even think. I just turn my whole body to the side and drop before throwing up on all fours. Vomit everywhere. Frankie is terrified.

"Jesus! How much have you had to drink?!" Quinn remarks

I throw up once and manage to compose myself long enough to look back at Anna for one second more. How could she not tell me? Why?

Things without all remedy should be without regard; what's done, is done….

Her braided hair is blowing in the wind. The smell of the sea is coursing through the air and diving deep into my nostrils. She looks at me, and it seems as though she is about to cry. She almost does, but she holds it back briefly before saying:

"Are you happy?"

Two hundred and fifty dollars in a money clip flailed in front of me like a willow tree in the wind....

Chapter 37

And that's that. You know the highlights of my life. No, I'm not the hero. I'm the villain. At least, that's how I feel. Anna is the Hero. She is strong, and I am weak. My name is Jack, "The Antagonist" Delaney. But, I'm assuming you already knew that.

You can spend eternity wishing you would have changed things, but what's done is done. No memory chamber or infinite bliss can change that. What's real has already happened. Anna. I miss you.

I'm sitting here in the waiting room of the afterlives and feeling more dead inside than I do out. I planned on proposing to Anna before I died. I was going to drive up to California and ask her to marry me the day after the car accident. I have no idea whether she was going to say yes or not. **THAT** is the real unknown. But things happen. Nothing is in your control.

If it seems like my tone has gone from juvenile and egocentric before diving into a misanthropic and self-deprecating tale of self-worth, then I laud you for being engaged this long. Reminiscing is the last thing I want to do. It only reminds me of how horrible things have been. So, why not go to Heaven now? Why not leave it all behind and just live in infinite bliss? I'm past that. Or, at least, I'm too numb for that. The prospect of death is frightening, but life is what is currently gripping me with terror. I don't know that I want to be proactive, or lazy, or evil, or benevolent, or anything. I don't know what to do. I now know why there are so many people in the waiting room. Humans aren't as dumb as I thought.

I make my way to the waiting room and see my Old Man. He is in a corner by himself with no one around. This entire waiting room is packed, but Dad found the only section with no one around. I walk over to him and grab him by the shoulder. He looks up at me, soberly and with a smile.

"Little Bijou"

"Other people are supposed to call me that. Not you…"

"Hah…I know. How are you?"

"I'm okay."

I take a seat and look at him dead in the eyes. I wasn't planning on telling him, but it just comes out.

"I have a son."

He looks at me and smiles. His smile is not happy. It isn't regretful. It is a cross between sorrow and delight.

"I was married before your mother." He says

And just like that, my world of comfort and false narratives that I have been fed my whole life come crashing down. The Delaney Curse doesn't hold a candle to this one. I have learned everything there is to the "unknown", the afterlife, but I didn't think I would hear that. How many other secrets are kept from me? How many things from my friends and family? I swallow my thoughts and realize it is time to stop asking questions. I have asked enough questions. Questions are meaningless at this point.

Without a word, I just confidently nod my head.

"When I used to work in the beer industry, I was close to the edge. I was nearly physically dependent on the sauce. Do you know why I moderated myself? How I kept it in control all of these years?" he asks

I don't say anything. I just stare at him.

"You were born…" he says

I remember one thing my mother told me that always stood out. She used to laugh and say 'If anyone else in this world drank the way your Father drank, they'd be an alcoholic'. I always just thought it was funny. Yet now, I think back on all the years I drank, and I realize, the only reason I never went over the 'edge' is because of my Father. The only reason I didn't lose complete control over my drinking was because of Him. I couldn't bear to have the stain of His son's rehab and addiction plague Him. Not because it would be pricey but because it would bring shame to the family legacy. The first Delaney to go to rehab because he has a "problem". The first Delaney to need help.

"You know what my favorite song is?" He asked

"House of the Rising Sun?"

He always loved that song. Every single time I heard it, I thought of Him. He laughed and shook His head.

"Cat's in the Cradle?" I nervously laugh

He manages a smile that turns into a grimace. Almost as if to express *"I deserve that."*

"Bad joke. Stairway to Heaven?" I ask again

He laughs for a moment.

"Sorry," I manage a responsive laugh, "I wasn't trying to be ironic."

I think of my Father every time I hear that song. I always remember VH1 doing a Led Zeppelin 30-year tribute and Heart doing a live cover of that song in front of the remaining members of Led Zeppelin. Jon Bonham's son is playing the drums, and Robert Plant is slowly becoming more and more emotional as the song plays. He almost begins to cry at certain parts during the song. He is staring off into nowhere as if he knows something that everyone else doesn't.

"Do you know what I always wanted to be?"

"No," I say awaiting his answer with sincerity

"I always wanted to be a songwriter. I wanted to write the next Led Zeppelin song. I wanted to be the next person to help B.B. King write a single. I think I got it from my Father. Did you know that? Did you know that your Grandpa wanted to write music too?"

I shake my head.

"He did. He wrote quite a few songs. His wife at the time sent them to me after he passed. I'll never forget that moment. I was thirty years old and staring at my Father's music written out onto this paper. Almost as if, the person who wrote them was never truly real. At that moment, it crushed me and frightened me to know that he was dead, and his music was never heard by another. I didn't know what to do. Should I pick up the torch and run with it? Or do I continue on the safe path?"

Finally, a perspective into my Father's real-life before I was born.

"He always kept them with him. They were brilliant. They were hits. He could have developed them, but the War came, and he was called to duty. He came back and dropped his dream. He married my mother. Then he married three other stepmothers after that. He never pursued his dream. I didn't know until after his death that he wanted this. I had been writing songs since I was in high-school. If we had just talked, I might have been a huge success. He might have been a huge success.

But I didn't. And now, here we are. I'm dead, and so is my son, and I am responsible."

"You aren't respon-"

"I am…I just want to tell you when it all started before I go. When I started writing…"

"Go?!"

"Just please… listen…"

"Okay."

I don't argue anymore.

"I was sixteen years old, and your Uncle Michael and I were driving to Havasu. We were going for the weekend because we heard our Dad's friend was away on business and wouldn't be checking on his houseboat so we thought we'd hijack it for the weekend. We had a few cases of beer and a carton of cigarettes. Well, just as we were passing Needles to make our way to the London Bridge, your Uncle Mike put an Eight Track on the stereo. The electric keyboard started playing, and the next thing I know the guitar is whaling. Not whaling in the way that it screams but slow and methodically. I'll never forget it. I asked your uncle who it is and he says 'Blind Faith! That's Clapton on the guitar!' Blind Faith. They were instantly my favorite band as we listened over and over to Winwood sing. He just couldn't find his way home…"

I remember Dad playing that once before.

"That's my favorite song. It changed me. I wanted to touch people the same way that band had touched me. The way their lyrics reached out from the speakers and slapped me in the face. I wanted to create the lyrics and the chords that they did."

"Why didn't you?"

I promised I wouldn't ask any more questions.

"Life happened. I needed a job, and I joined the beer industry, and I never got my head above water enough after that to do it. Year after year, I buried myself in more responsibilities. I gave up on it. Time happened Jackie... time."

I look into His eyes. We meet once more as Father and son. He sees me and looks at me as though it were the first time. The first time He held me after I came from the womb. He had lain Himself bare. No secrets. No illusions. Only Himself. My Father, the world's greatest songwriter that never wrote a song. The world's greatest dreamer.

I take a moment. I think of Quinn. I wonder what he's thinking right now? I think of Anna. I think of us and how things would have been over the years. Would she have loved me? Would I have loved her? Every time I look into her eyes, I melt but would that have lasted? Would we have still gone to the fair after a year and laughed? Would we have held a semblance of what we felt as kids five, ten, twenty, fifty years later? I know the answer is yes, but that could just be my optimistic attitude in the face of annihilation.

When I look up, my Father is gone.

Chapter 38

This final memory was my moment of self-discovery. It was during the coldest night our town had ever seen one February years ago. Quinn and I had tied one on and decided to head to Quinn's favorite dive bar that was known for harboring the local senior citizen winos. The plan was to meet a bunch of the guys there, and Anna would tag along for the night. Quinn was a regular there since it was right next to his apartment and I'm sure being the only patron under 50 boosted his self-esteem a little.

By the time we arrived, Colin, Michael, Nick, and Thomas were waiting outside. Thomas was a *'Monday Mick'*. He liked to play at being Irish to fit in with us just a little more. I had always considered Thomas one of my closest friends, but he wasn't exactly like us. He could hold his own drinking and was as funny as all hell, but he never confronted anyone. He never got too "wild", and he would usually chide us for doing just that. All around, a great guy, just not a member of the tribe.

The air was freezing. I remember it almost burning my nostril hairs it was so frigid. And like some ill-fated omen that our town had never truly known, mother nature brought snow down from above. Lucky for us, we're only wearing t-shirts, jeans, and a beanie. The snow fell flake by flake as we moved into the sullen establishment.

My memory fades, even now, as I can't even remember his name. I had known him for most of my adult life and yet I can't, for the life of me, remember his name now. I've been here too long in limbo and can't even remember his name or why I was so bellicose towards him, but as soon as I walked through the door, I saw an old adversary's face and swung without thinking. The bar fell silent as on-lookers with saggy skin and surly eyes gasped and covered their mouths with liver-spotted hands. He shot back up almost right away and broke my nose with his first punch, as I didn't have time to cover up. Grappling and swinging, we landed blow for blow and broke a table on our way down. Punches missed, and jabs landed as each connection to my face felt like a dull, vitiated dagger to my senses. After a great struggle and before knocking someone's oxygen tank over, I grabbed him by the back of his shirt and threw him out the door as he stumbled to get up. By this time, his friends, my friends, and what interested patrons remained, followed us out into the snow-covered parking lot. The hoariness of the street blinded me momentarily.

My shirt, which was ripped to shit, only slowed me down, so I tore the rest of it off. He did the same. I stared briefly at him and sized him up once more. His eyes, filled with vitriol and hostility, almost left me feeling exposed for a moment. He had a missing tooth now, blood from his ears, and a piece of his skull now showing from the fall. Maybe it was just snow, but the blood seeping from his forehead seemed to simply wash over that blanched centimeter on his forehead. I just as well assumed I looked no different from him. In all of the sturm and drang of the fight, I began to notice that this moment was too perfect. Drunk and intrepid with the adrenaline cascading through my veins, I could only hear one thing being shouted from the crowd:

"Come on, you fucking pussies! I wanna see some God Damn BLOOD!"

He made one final dash at me, clumsily, before I threw one punch upward to his chin that sent him down on one, wobbling knee. I caught his right arm on the fall down. I yelled with a visceral, almost haughty, voice once more:

"Is this your FUCKING liver?!"

As blood spat in his face from my mouth. I punched and punched him right in the organ I had held so dear for so long before delivering the final blow; a knee soaring directly into his temple.

I turned back, filled to the brim with querulous rage and testosterone. I yelled to no one in particular:

"Any mother fucker wants it next! Anyone! Join your FUCKING friend!"

I had become, in that instant, an ineffable, bilious shade of my former self. The man that drank himself half-silly before getting into a donnybrook at the local retirement watering hole was to become a future teacher and a lad with hopes of a promising future. I want to be moral. I want to be right and just; everything in me screams to be so. But, by the curse of my choices, I have a derangement possessing me that will never be anything more than dissolute. I can only be bare in this world. I can only lack convention. The pinnacle of wisdom that I can attain is only lost on my appetite for intemperance in vice. Even looking back on this memory now, with all the truths of this life and the other laid bare, I cannot retroactively invent excuses for my actions. My life has been one long look into the future. An ignis fatuus that has been focused on what might happen, instead of what is happening.

And in that instant, with my shirt off, in the snow, blood coming out of each orifice, I had my realization. I had my moment of clarity. I stared at Michael, beer in hand, with his shirt off, howling up at the stillborn moon in revelry. I saw Colin, shirt off as well, mouthing "Fucking Right!" in what almost felt like slow motion. Quinn, shirt ripped half off, was grabbing me around the waist and lifting me up in drunken joy. I even saw Anna with a glass of whiskey, screaming and hailing the victory I had won. It was only Thomas, in the middle of all that bedlam, that had his shirt on still. Only Thomas looked down before going back into the bar.

As the on-lookers left the scene and raced away from the cold, I looked upon my friends, still hurrahing at the fight, while the name-less man laid bloody and unconscious on the ground with his shirt torn to shreds. And then I realized, we were all the same; all of us, even my foe. We were thrill-seekers. We were drunks. We were brawlers, lecherers, and gamblers. All of us were just like our Fathers, and all of us never had our Fathers. We were products of a single mom household. Feeling unwanted, we had become byproducts of a life filled with unconditional love and being our own Father. Only Thomas, who I love dearly, grew up in the nuclear family. Only Thomas could not relate to the thrill, the anxiety, the deception; the absence of a God figure to admire, to love, and to know.

Chapter 39

I wait for, what could possibly be, an eternity in the waiting room. Sober for the first time in 15 years and all I can think is whether I should wait or not. Should I wait for Anna and Frankie? Should I greet them? That is what most of these people are doing. Should I?

I can do it. I could wait in an ocean of time for them while my mind rots. It makes no difference to me. I would and should do it. The lost time is enough to make me want to plant myself in this seat and go nowhere. We can go to Heaven together. I don't care about its otiose nature. I will wait.

And yet, a thought crosses my mind. The little man is going to grow up without me. Anna will find a new husband soon, or maybe she will raise him on her own. He will never know me. When he is 80, he will not care who I am. He made it through life without me; he can damn sure make it through the afterlife without me. They don't need me. I'm being selfish. I stand up and decide to find my Dad.

I walk through the hallway and ask soul after soul:

"Have you seen my Dad?"

"Do you know where Jack Delaney is?"

I am five years old again searching for my Father in a mall. For whatever reason, I can hear Frank Sinatra's "My Way" playing from one of the rooms. Someone finally points me to Him. It is the man from AA. He says Dad has gone through that door. He is solemn as he points. I run down the hallway immediately yet it stretches and stretches and stretches to its original infinite doorways. Stretches until all I am doing is running in place. I'm treading water. After a minute or two, I drop to my knees and put my face in my hands just before the door regresses its way back to me. I walk through immediately. It isn't long before I notice the defeated Satan and his secretary. They look at me before looking back at my Dad. My Old Man is standing there in the door ready to take the plunge.

"Dad! Jesus Christ! What are you doing?!"

My Father turns around, somberly.

"Jackie..."

"Dad! So you didn't become a songwriter! Who cares?! Let's get out of here together and find peace! We can go to Heaven or the Spirit World! I don't really fucking care!"

"Jackie, I'm trying to find peace. I was the reason you got into that accident."

"Dad, no! It was the other driver's fault remember! It wasn't because I was driving!"

"We wouldn't have been there if I didn't ask for a ride...or even, if I had stopped you from driving while you were drunk. I knew we were both fucked up. I shouldn't have gone. I shouldn't have let you go."

"Dad! We are here now! You don't need to do this. The afterlife isn't so bad! We all have a choice."

"Jackie... I have plenty to account for. You find peace in this afterlife. I cannot come with you. I love you, son."

I reach for my Dad's sleeve, but it is too late. He is falling into an endless pit of fire. His atonement for sins I forgave him for.

I look to Satan, and he only has a solemn head turned down. I only now realize that the Devil is temptation. It isn't Lucifer that makes us do things. It is ourselves. Satan isn't evil incarnate... humans are.

Chapter 40

I slip away. I fade away. I slowly roll back while I comprehend what has happened. I look up, and Satan isn't smiling. He is just standing there with a grave stare that drifts into nowhere. I feel the same pain that he feels. He didn't want this job. From the look on his face, I'm certain he hates it when each person purges themselves into the fire. This is not what he envisioned when he led a rebellion against God. Like all of us, he is a damned product of the choices he made. He is at a lack of words each time people throw themselves to this eternal punishment. As I stare at him in disbelief, he finally says:

"People hate Judas for what he did… but without him, there would never be a chance for salvation."

With his words, I keep walking backward until I reach the hallway. I need a drink. I need a seat.

I take a seat in the waiting room once again. I start to feel a feeling I am all too familiar with and that I now, finally, embrace; I am alone. I am amongst a million people, and I am alone. I don't know what to think. I haven't even chosen my afterlife, and I am in Hell. Do I doom myself to a life of frivolity in Heaven? Do I rewind time? Should I find peace with the Buddhists? I have no other route. I have to choose. I can't stay here anymore. There are so many that I haven't even seen yet, but, at that moment, I know. I know where I am going. It is only right. It is the only peace I can find.

I stand and stare for a moment. Stare into an abyss of people in white cloaks and a hallway with white cloth before walking down that same hallway.

Shannon looks at me once more. There is a look of gloom drawn across her face. She already knows where I am headed. And from behind her, the English Bulldog from my dreams pops out. Shannon leans down to remove his leash and collar. With a bewildered stare, I slowly walk towards her and the dog. He slowly meets me as I get within ten feet of Shannon. I bend down to pat his head, and he lazily licks my hand. We stare into one another's eyes for what seems like an eternity. I finally manage my final and only words to the animal:

"*Goodbye, old friend...*"

I walk past Heaven and the hordes of people running through the door. I walk past Hell and its vacant reminder of my Father. I walk past the spirit world and its ghosts floating aimlessly. I walk past the endless afterlives with their delusions of grandeur and specious reasoning for supremacy. I finally arrive at the end of the hallway.

Oblivion awaits as I walk through the black door. This is the only way. It's funny; as a mortal, I would have never chosen this door. All of mankind would have walked through Heaven or wherever, but never here. They would have thought I was mad doing this, and yet, in this moment, it's all that makes sense. I push a little further, and I am all the way through the door. Immediately, the first thing I hear is "Hello, My Name is Human" being played from above. It was the first song I heard on the radio the morning I found out one of my students had killed himself. It always had a special place in my soul. It is fitting, and I am confident it is being played for me.

The first thing I see is the men in gray robes looking at me. They are smiling. Not with joy, but with honest sincerity. The look in their eyes tells me that they knew I was going to pick this all along. Yet, they give me no reassurance that I am making the right decision. They just nod their heads as I move slowly towards them. One of them finally says:

"Choice is not merely a fact... it is an essence, Jack."

I stand there for a moment. I rub my face. I feel so much pain. Pain from the mortal world. Pain from my Father. Pain from everything. I just stand there.

The man who spoke to me before waves his hand in the direction of reception. His open palm is pointed upwards toward the desk, and I follow. Another gray-robed man is there, and he pours me a shot of some brown liquor. He then hands me an already lit cigarette. I laugh for a moment and then look at the glass. It is full and murky. I look back up at him.

"I am a mole..." I laugh softly

He laughs softly back.

"We all are, Jack," he begins "If I may, I'd like to leave you with a quote from one of our acolytes."

I nod my head, but even now, I can feel that my eyes are drifting towards Oblivion's gate.

"There is only one inborn error, and that is the notion that we exist to be happy. So long as we persist in this inborn error, the world will seem to us full of contradictions. For, at every step, in great things and small, we are bound to experience that the world and life are certainly not arranged for the purpose of being happy."

Jack...

I hear a voice whispering faintly. I turn my head towards the hallway's slowly closing door to listen.

Are you happy?

Momentarily, I stare back down the hallway. I stare deeply until my eyes begin to blur. I blink and turn my head back towards the man just as the door shuts.

His words make sense, but I can't help but be facetious.

"Thank you for those light-hearted words..."

"There's that famous Delaney brass..." the robed man says, expressionless

My last mortal emotion that helped me get through life; sarcasm.

I swallow the shot in one gulp. I taste nothing but feel it all the same. I say nothing more to them and move toward the door.

I open the door slowly and take a look at the darkness. If I could relate it to you in any way possible, it would be like staring off the top of Mount Everest at Midnight with no moon in the sky; no peace amongst the soul. I can feel that there is nothing beneath or above me. I take a moment to finish the cigarette he lit. I flick the burning filter into the darkness. I look back at the room only for a moment before turning my head and taking the plunge.

I descended endlessly as the song fades from the now disappearing light of the room and yet still goes on in my head.

"Anna...I love you."

And then... darkness...

CPSIA information can be obtained
at www.ICGtesting.com
Printed in the USA
LVHW092355180321
681904LV00008B/384